THE BEATLES

DOWN UNDER
The 1964 Australian & New Zealand Tour

by
Glenn A. Baker

THE BEATLES

DOWN UNDER
The 1964 Australian & New Zealand Tour

by
Glenn A. Baker

Published by

The Magnum Imprint
Magnum House
High Street
Lane End
Buckinghamshire, HP14 3JG
UNITED KINGDOM

ISBN 0 9527961 1 2

The official Australian Tour photograph, taken in Brisbane. Beatles press officer Derek Taylor is at right of front row, compere Alan Field is left. Road manager Lloyd Ravenscroft is behind Ringo, co-promoter Dick Lean behind John, and co-promoter Kenn Brodziak behind Paul. Roadie Mal Evans is second from left in third row, Sounds Incorporated are behind him. Local supports Johnny Devlin (third from right), Johnny Chester (fourth from left) and the Phantoms are in the back row.

Printed in the United Kingdom by Chord Print, Surbiton, Surrey.

THE BEATLES

DOWN UNDER
The 1964 Australian & New Zealand Tour

by
Glenn A. Baker

CONTENTS

Though this book was conceived and commenced some two years before his tragic death, it is dedicated with love to John Winston Lennon.

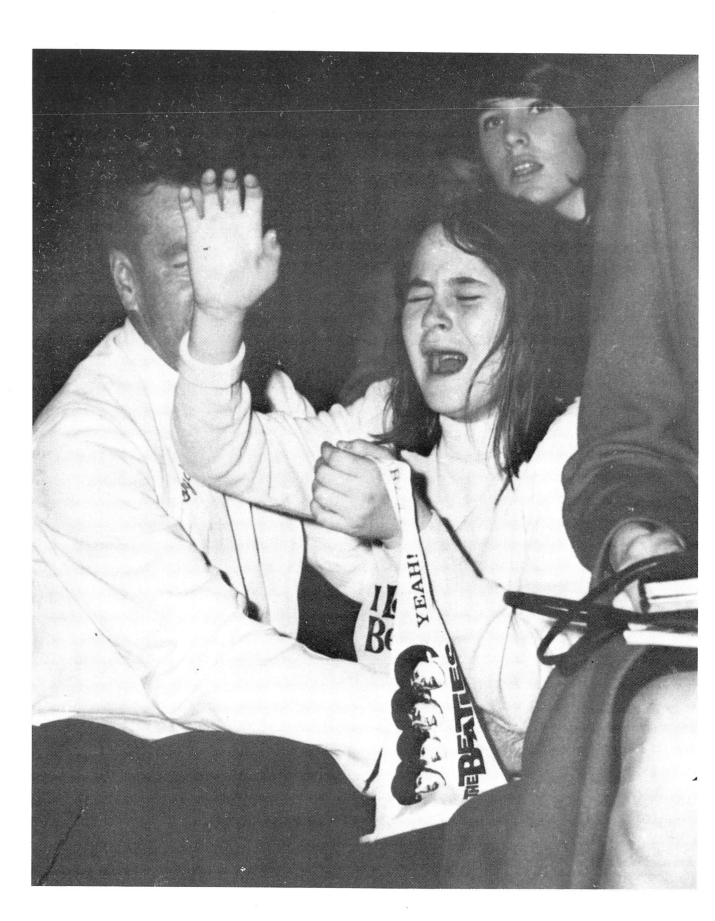

No single instance of Beatlemania throughout the globe ever came close to the intensity and sheer magnitude of the social upheaval which accompanied the 1964 Australian Beatles' tour. No street crowds in New York, London or Liverpool ever eclipsed the antipodean hordes which, at times, comprised more than half the entire population of a city.

One strict aspect of Beatle protocol was that the group always appraised cities (and the reaction extended therein) equally, so as to never threaten civic pride or leave themselves vulnerable to charges of favouritism. But this rule was rent asunder in Adelaide and then Melbourne as John Lennon declared, repeatedly and incredulously, "This is the greatest reaction we have ever received anywhere in the world!"

Yet, for all its extraordinary features, the visit is invariably dismissed in Beatles reference books with a single throwaway line — *June 1964: Far East Tour* — which is followed by copious detail of the *Hard Day's Night* film premiere in London. The only aspect generally known about the jaunt, outside of Australasia, is that stand-in drummer Jimmy Nicol deputised for Ringo on some dates. The three and a half weeks remain until now an unaccounted gap in Beatle history.

But while the visit has escaped the attention of most Beatle fans, a staggering portion of the Australian public recall it fondly and emotionally as a flash of frantic excitement during a dull and ominous period of a new uncertain decade.

As the world teetered back from the armageddon which the Cuban missile crisis had threatened, and most of the civilised world was applauding the passage of the U.S. Civil Rights Bill, South East Asia was simmering in the juices of armed conflict. America was just beginning its long and catastrophic involvement in the internal affairs of Viet Nam, while Indonesia had invaded Malaysian Borneo as part of Sukarno's aspirations for "a united Irian, from Sorong to Samarai."

Indonesia's militancy was being carefully monitored in Australia. Old Diggers were convinced that an invasion was imminent and antipodean youth were being gravely warned that there would be no time for foolish crazes and music sensations during wartime.

But the ears of the post-war baby boom mass were closed to such rantings and open only to the incredibly envigorating sounds from England that poured out of the portable radios which were part of the new consumerism sweeping the western world.

Australia reacted to the visit by the Beatles with such fervour because, young and old, it was crying out for a tangible manifestation of the new freedoms which were emerging in England and America; freedoms it didn't quite understand. The Beatles were a sign from above, a skewer to lance the boil of stifling conservatism.

If John Lennon was amused by American fans in burmuda shorts, horn-rimmed glasses and pink zinc noses, he probably convulsed over greasy, pointed-shoe'd, kiss-curled, Aussie larrikins. Bodgies and widgies who suddenly became spiffy mods.

The Beatles, their presence and their lingering influence, became a catalyst for the suppressed frustrations of kids who had begun to realise that unquestioning obedience to everyone older was no longer a sacred law. To a sixteen-year-old in 1964, standing outside a hotel in a public street screaming at the top of one's voice was a breathtakingly daring act, an adrenalin-drenched escape from the combined muzzle of school, parents and community standards.

This book is as much about the Australian public in June 1964 as it is about the Beatles. For all the charisma the four emitted, the real stars of the tour were the hundreds of thousands of ordinary people who screamed in public and viewed in private who were caught up by accident or intent in the joyful madness that swept the land more than seventeen years ago.

A rare shot of the five Beatles: at the Melbourne press conference.

"Catch him Paul!" shrieked the sad mother through the gray gale, as she hurled the little spastic at the Beatles.

The child was wan, 6 or maybe 7 and very weak. He was drenched and also terrified. McCartney, unsteady in the dawn downpour on the open milktruck rickety-rattling around the apron at Sydney airport, caught the child and clutched him close. "May God bless you," howled the mother and Paul cried back in panic: "He's lovely! Great! You take him now!"

The mother, her hair streaming in rat's-tails across her face, chased the truck till the driver saw her and slowed. She grasped the wet child-bundle, kissed it desperately and wept. "He's better! Oh, he's better!"

Somewhere beyond the bouncing pebbled rain, mingled with the screaming wind came a wild thousand-throated wail of welcome. All in black, drainpipe-trousered, cloaked and soaked like spidery pop messiahs with umbrellas, The Beatles had come to Australia in rain as relentless as Noah's 40 days.

It was clear that many of the 11 million people in Australia viewed The Beatles in a messianic light. They were invited to lay their hands on cripples, to pose on balconies before almost the entire populations of many large cities, to watch ethnic dance displays and to attend mayoral receptions like visiting heads of state.

Derek Taylor
Beatles Press Officer 1964
Reprinted from Los Angeles
Times, May 1967

"Yea Australia, just satirycon, just think of satirycon with four musicians going through it . . . Wherever we went there was always a whole thing going on. Derek and Neil's rooms were always full of fuck knows what. We had to do something and what do you do when the pills wear off?

"They didn't call them groupies, they called it something else. If we couldn't get groupies we'd have whores and whatever else was going."

John Lennon to
Jann Wenner, Rolling Stone
January 21, 1971

1: PRELIMINARIES

Kenn Brodziak's presentation of the Fab Four from Liverpool, still cited as the greatest entertainment coup Australia has ever witnessed, was not the result of great vision or adept negotiation. It was, in fact, a classic piece of accidental good luck.

Brodziak imported his first international entertainment act into Australia in 1954 when a young jazz buff convinced him of the viability of touring drummer Gene Krupa. The modest success of the venture commenced an illustrious career spanning more than a quarter century for the forty-one-year-old former playwrite of Polish-Jewish extraction.

A voracious and extremely able promoter, Brodziak went on to present such acts as Marlene Dietrich, Sophie Tucker, the Vienna Boys' Choir, the Black and White Minstrels, Peter Paul and Mary, Carol Channing, and in June 1964, the Beatles.

On February 21, 1963, EMI Records issued their first Beatles single in Australia. *Please Please Me* was swiftly moving towards the number two spot in England (as their second hit) but in the colonies it was treated with a fair amount of indifference. So it was not surprising that when Kenn Brodziak arrived in London in July (just as *From Me To You* was entering the Australian charts) he had very little awareness of the group that was fast becoming Britain's premier chart act.

What few mutterings he had heard had eminated from Dick Lean, the managing director of Stadiums Limited, who had in turn been alerted by his right hand man Bruce Stewart. Manager of hot instrumental outfit the Phantoms and presenter of Sunday afternoon rock and roll concerts (for Lean) at Melbourne's Festival Hall, Stewart had picked up on the Beatles earlier than the painfully conservative Australian media and entertainment industry. (EMI had imported a few hundred jackets for the first *Please Please Me* album release, after deeming it uneconomical to have printing plates made up for a group who just happened to have a number one hit in England.)

"I heard *Please Please Me* just once on the radio," Stewart recalls, "and I sent my old man out to buy it for me. But only a handful had been pressed and he couldn't find a copy anywhere. I just loved the song so at Festival Hall the next Sunday I asked the audience what English act they'd like to see. I got pretty strong reaction for Gerry and the Pacemakers, Brian Poole and the Tremeloes and Billy J. Kramer and the Dakotas, but when I mentioned the Beatles they just went crazy. So I told Dick about it. He said, 'You know that no English act has made money here for years,' and I replied, 'Trust me.' "

Meanwhile, Brodziak was in the London office of booking agent Cyril Berlin, who was offering him six young beat groups. "I didn't really want them so I thought I'd just take a chance on one. I looked at a scrap of paper that Cyril had written the names on and decided that I liked the sound of the Beatles best. It was as simple as that." On July 5, 1963, Kenn Brodziak secured the Liverpool act for £1000 per week (accommodation not initially included) on a verbal contract that was not bound in ink until the following December.

Those six months saw the establishment and global recognition of Beatlemania. The press began to use the term when thousands of screaming fans jammed London streets as the Beatles' performance at the Palladium was being televised to fifteen million viewers in October. Later in the month the group themselves began to realize the scope of their popularity, as thousands of fans awaited their return from a brief Swedish tour at Heathrow Airport. The cap was put on it all on November 4 when they appeared at the Prince of Wales Theatre before Princess Margaret, Lord Snowdon and the Queen Mother in a Royal Variety Performance.

By this point, hungry American promoters were offering up to $50,000 for a single show and back in Australia fingernails were being chewed dangerously low. Real fears that the verbal contract would be laid aside were allayed when scrupulously honourable Brian Epstein sent a note to Cyril Berlin which included the immortal words, "You'll think me a very naughty boy but I want £1500 per week for Australia." At ten times that it would still have been an outrageous steal. Epstein capped the deal with a telegram to Brodziak proclaiming, "I made an agreement and I will stick to it. The Beatles will come to Australia."

Around this time, Surfers Paradise entrepreneur Lou Devon claimed that he had been offered a Beatles tour by a Liverpool agent back in

Rehearsing with Jimmy Nicol at EMI Studios during the evening of June 3.

The Phantoms

March 1963, four months before Brodziak arrived in London. The offer apparently came in a letter containing a box brownie snap of the group on a Mersey ferry. But even though the asking price was only £120 a show (plus airfares and travelling expenses) Devon was unable to find a single Gold Coast venue willing to book the unknown quartet. Had he taken the group, he would have had an eighteen month option on a second tour.

Once the contract had been formally signed on December 2, 1963 and June dates decided upon, Brodziak and Lean sat down to draw up procedures. Their relationship was strong and proven — Lean controlled the venues, Brodziak always snared the best acts available. Because Cyril Berlin was the exclusive agent of local promoter Jack Neary, time-honoured protocol directed that he receive five per cent of profits. This came from the share of Aztec Services (Brodziak) who then got forty-five per cent. The remaining half went to Stadiums Limited (Lean). The cosmetic company Nicholas-Marigny signed on as a sponsor, as did BMC who agreed to provide a fleet of Morris 1100 and Austin Princess cars for the tour party.

Fourteen playing dates were set: three each in Melbourne and Sydney, two in Brisbane, Auckland and Wellington and one in Christchurch and Dunedin. At this stage Adelaide and Perth were ruled out for economic reasons but Adelaide was later added, largely due to the efforts of Adelaide DJ Bob Francis. The New Zealand leg automatically went to compatriot Sir Robert Kerridge, the Brodziak of the shaky isles. Lloyd Ravenscroft, who had worked at ATN 7 with Jack Neary as a talent manager and had taken all manner of acts on the road (except rock), including Winifred Atwell, the Scots Guards Band and the Luton Girls' Choir, was invited to be tour manager.

"We worked out the details in what was pretty much one giant shouting match," recalls Lean wryly. "Kenn took on the responsibility of the staging while I accepted all the security arrangements. We approached Ansett ANA for a transport deal and they offered a ten per cent discount. The next day TAA countered with twenty per cent but the next day Ansett came back to us and said we could have it all for nothing."

At the same time, the fairly new Southern Cross Hotel, having troubles because its rates were thought to be too high, offered a free floor, provided that it could be announced that £500 a day was paid for it, something the pair were hardly going to argue about.

Setting of ticket prices became a contentious issue. Brodziak revealed that he was under strong pressure from some associates to charge £5 (about $10) but he held out for a ceiling of £1 17s 6d ($3.75) graduating down to 15s 6d. Even this was hardly cheap when the average adult male wage was around £15 weekly.

Lean handled the booking of supports. Johnny Chester was a Melbourne rock hero of wide appeal who had already supported Connie Francis, Bobby Rydell, Roy Orbison and the Everly Bros., and was compering the TV show *Teen Time*, with a tally of nine hits under his belt. He willingly accepted the paltry £125 a week fee, hoping to capture an interstate market, although he baulked at not being able to use his own group, the Chessmen.

Canny Bruce Stewart, realising that the solo supports would need a common economical backing unit, had been pushing crack instrumental unit the Phantoms, which he just happened to manage. They were added.

From England came word that Epstein was sending out his newest beat discovery with the Beatles — the unknown instrumental outfit Sounds Incorporated. Alan Field, an adult comedian from the working-man's clubs of northern England, who had worked with the Fab Four on a dozen or so occasions, was named as compere.

In 1964 even a top-line rock tour was expected to be staged like a cabaret night, with a full and varied bill of entertainment. Accordingly feminine content was sought in the form of red-headed Sydney thrush Del Juliana, who was offered a spot on the tour in February. In March she received a telegram withdrawing the offer but in April it was extended again. Upset by the confusion, she took her grievance to a press keen for any Beatle titbit. She was quoted as complaining, "The fee is ridiculous and I have to provide my own accommodation. I would lose money on the tour so I have said no, after a talk with mum. Naturally I am bitter but there is a principle involved. I'm not even going to see the Beatles."

The bill was finally completed with New Zealand rocker Johnny Devlin who, as A&R man for RCA Records, rang the promoters in an attempt to place would-be teen idol Paul Wayne on the shows. Johnny had crossed the Tasman in 1959, at the peak of astronomical popularity in his homeland (including the country's first domestic gold single), and established himself strongly in Sydney with a string of seven hits within two years, including two top tens. At the end of 1963, after two years off the charts, he had scored a freak top five smash with the clever *Stomp the Tumbarumba*. With current success in Sydney (to balance Chester's Melbourne standing) and God-like status in New Zealand he was the perfect addition to a support roster which, seen in retrospect, underlined the degree to which overseas music trends had left Australia behind. It would not really be until the Beatles had departed that scores of shaggy quartets would emerge down under.

Men's fashion figure Peter Jackson designed a Beatle jacket for national television personality Graham Kennedy.

Regular news despatches from England reported that the up-coming tour would be very much a family affair, with Ringo's and George's parents, John's aunt and Paul's dad coming along for the ride. As the weeks went on the Roster shrank. James McCartney decided that a thirty-hour flight was just a bit too much and opted to go to America in August instead. Mr. and Mrs. Graves-Starkey demurred because "Dad's not very keen on flying," and then the Harrisons, freshly returned from three weeks at Montego Bay in Jamaica, decided that they were spending far too much of their son's money, although Harold Harrison had first announced, "I think it will be good for George that we are going along. We will probably be able to take a load off his shoulders by dealing with fans out there."

As June approached, only John's aunt Mimi (Mrs. Mary Smith) was left in the running and she had no chance of being scratched. "You can't budge him you know," she exasperated."He won't listen to arguments if he thinks he's right. He just rang me one day and said 'You're coming with us, go and get your wardrobe stocked and your bags packed.' What was there for me to say but Ta!" John's terms of travel were not entirely to Mimi's liking though. He insisted that she change planes in Hong Kong and fly direct to Wellington, New Zealand, where her cousins lived. But she could be just as stubborn as her nephew as was evidenced when she told a London newspaper, "I would love to spend a few hours in Hong Kong. I mean it's silly flying there and not seeing any of it. Because I'm getting on and don't know anyone in Sydney, John thinks I'll run into trouble there too. So I rang John's manager today and told him he'd better get me a night in Hong Kong and a few days in Sydney — or else. But knowing what John's like, it probably won't do any good." In the end John relented and compromised with a plan to send Mimi on to Wellington as he went on to Adelaide.

By the beginning of 1964 the Beatles had racked up five UK smash hits in a little over a year, three of which — *From Me To You, She Loves You* and *I Want To Hold Your Hand* — made number one. The American charts had not yet admitted them but their presence was certainly being felt in Australia where they had scored four top tens, two of which — *I Want to Hold Your Hand* and *I Saw Her Standing There / Love Me Do* — shot straight to the summit position.

Melbourne Beatlemaniacs Jenny Begbie (left) and Wendy Carter exhibit their Fab Four artifacts to the press.

This was to be the year that the Fab Four took their potent aura to the world. Apart from their regular Hamburg engagements between 1960 and 1962, they had not played outside Britain, save for five Swedish shows in October 1963, the return from which saw the first airport riots. They had saturated England during 1963, criss-crossing the country with Helen Shapiro in February, Chris Montez and Tommy Roe in March, Roy Orbison and Gerry and the Pacemakers in May, and under their own banner for the remainder of the year. Altogether, the group played around 200 British dates throughout the year, 150 as headliners.

International touring had commenced seriously in January 1964 when the Beatles kicked off a three week French stint in Versailles. Initial reviews were poor, with Trini Lopez commanding more attention at the Paris O'Lympia. For a fleeting moment it had seemed that

The Beatles in Paris with top-billers Trini Lopez and Sylvie Vartan.

Beatlemania was a peculiarly British fixation of transient nature. The clamour of international booking enquiries had actually diminished slightly.

The Beatles had returned to London and a rowdy airport welcome on February 5, the same day that publicity agent Brian Sommerville set out for New York. The four had arrived two days later to a tumultuous reception from 10,000 fans at Kennedy International Airport, generated in part by the national number one placing of *I Want to Hold Your Hand* and the strong support from "boss" DJ "Murray the K." It would be later revealed that Capitol Records had sunk $50,000 into igniting Beatlemania in America and every radio announcer in the country was smothered with a range of promotional items. Copybook American overkill, it worked magnificently.

During their two weeks on the American east coast, the Fab Four had appeared twice on the Ed Sullivan Show (and taped a third spot), drawing the largest audience in television history. They had played at the Washington Coliseum and New York's Carnegie Hall and holidayed in style at Miami. During their stay they met Tuesday Weld, Stella Stevens, Tommy Roe, Don Rickles, Muhammed Ali, Hank Ballard and the Ronettes. Al Aronwitz introduced them to Bob Dylan who introduced them to marijuana, a neat adjunct to the pills they had learned to pop in Hamburg. The Australian fan club wired congratulations on the conquering of the US, promising that an even bigger reception awaited them down under.

Performing at Carnegie Hall, New York, on February 12, 1964. The seating of fans on the stage was a once-only occurrence.

Home just nine days, the hard-working quartet had commenced the filming of *A Hard Day's Night* at London's Twickenham Studios on March 2. At this point, seven positions on the Australian top forty were occupied by Beatle discs. *She Loves You* alone stayed on the charts for forty-two weeks.

As filming had continued through March, with concert scenes shot at the Scala Theatre on the 26th, John was awarded the Foyle's Literary Prize for *In His Own Write;* the *Meet the Beatles* LP moved past the three-and-a-half million sales point in America; the *Saturday Evening Post* placed the group on their front cover; the Variety Club of Great Britain honoured them with "Outstanding Entertainer" awards; five of the US top singles were by the Beatles; the April 4 issue of *Record Mirror* announced a June tour of the Far East and Australia; the film soundtrack album was commenced at Abbey Road studios on April 16; Madame Tussaud's Waxworks placed moptop effigys on display; a slew of (quickly hushed) paternity suits against Paul arose in Liverpool; George met Patti Boyd on the film set; appearances were made on the *Top of the Pops, Ready Steady Go* and *Morecambe and Wise* TV shows; John and Cynthia and George and Patti chartered a plane for a private Easter weekend in Ireland; and concerts were staged at the Liverpool Empire Theatre during location filming in the city.

A Hard Day's Night was wrapped up by director Dick Lester on April 24. Two days later the group topped the bill at the *New Musical Express* pollwinners concert at Wembley Empire Pool and, the following day, began filming their first TV special — Jack Good's classic *Around the Beatles.*

During the final week of April, they were guests of the Rt. Hon. Sir Eric Harrison, Australian High Commissioner, at a press reception inside Australia House. As fans milled outside in the Strand in pouring rain, the Beatles sampled Tasmanian apples and received kangaroo lapel pins from girls borrowed from the typing pool.

Sampling Tasmanian apples at Australia House in London.

Other stars, such as Dick Van Dyke, Wilfred Brambell and actress Jessie Matthews, were elbowed aside by 700 guests all seeking autographs. Paul was heard to despair, "Will it be like this in Australia then? Blimey!"

The four finally pushed their way through the throng to a private office where Ringo plucked an apple from a giant map of Australia made entirely of apples and declared to the startled Ambassador, "It's bonza mate." Each was presented with a hamper containing two magnums of Australian champagne and tins of pears, peaches and apricots. John quipped, "Where's the Aussie beer we've heard so much about then?"

As the arduous proceedings wore on, Sir Eric, who had left a Downing Street reception by Prime Minister Douglas-Home to preside at the function, became visably taxed and angry. He willingly told reporters, "There has never been a reception quite like this in Australia House and I hope there will never be another one. I guess I am what you would call a square but those photographers were just too much. They climbed all over the chairs and then when we went inside an enclosed office they were thrusting their cameras through the windows and rapping on the glass. I threatened to draw the blinds unless they could comport themselves."

The Beatles with Australian High Commissioner to London, the Rt. Hon. Sir Eric Harrison. He was somewhat less than impressed with Beatlemania.

This was not their first contact with a notable Australian. They had come across Rolf 'Tie Me Kangaroo Down Sport' Harris early in 1963 when the BBC had assigned him to interview them in George Martin's EMI office. "Everyone seemed to be a bit frightened of them because they could be very sharp and cutting with stupid interviewers. George Martin suggested that I ask them some unexpected questions, so I opened with 'Ringo, what do you think of spaghetti?' He broke up laughing and the ice was broken, we all became good friends."

Rolf was chosen to compere the two week 1963 Christmas show season at the Finsbury Park Astoria (later to become the Rainbow Theatre), on a bill with Cilla Black, the Fourmost, and Billy J. Kramer and the Dakotas. "They asked me a lot about Australia then," Rolf recalls. "We talked quite deeply about my interest in Aboriginals and I explained a lot of Australian terms to them. Paul was the most interested, he asked the most questions."

The relationship between the Australian board wobbler and the Fab Four became strained by the end of the Christmas season, due to an incident where John and Paul used an offstage mic to cut into Rolf's act. He stormed into their dressing room after he left the stage and told them to be "a bit bloody professional." They were, he points out, "understandably very full of themselves and not used to being spoken to harshly by anybody. I got more respect from that point but less friendship." This did not stop Rolf from recording a song called *Ringo for President* during 1964, however.

Rolf Harris (seen behind George) compered the Beatles' 1963 Christmas concert season at Finsbury Park Astoria. The bill also included the Fourmost, Billy J. Kramer and the Dakotas, and Cilla Black.

At the same time that the father of fifteen-year-old Larry Robinson was appealing against his son's suspension from a Delaware high school in America for sporting a Beatles hair-cut, Australia's conservative education system was having kittens all of its own. The first malcontent to make large headlines was Miss P. Evans, the headmistress of Sydney's Ravenswood Methodist School for Girls.

This staunch disciplinarian called a special assembly and instructed the girls with Beatle-style hairdos to have their hair recut and restyled immediately. She also declared a ban on the carrying of all Beatles photographs and gave one girl an ultimatum to either resign as secretary of a local fan club chapter or "sever her connection with the school."

After extensive press coverage which quoted parents' support for their daughters' Beatle interest, Miss Evans spoke to the press, stating, "We don't want Ravenswood to be involved with those screaming teenage mobs. I want to safeguard these children from something they do not understand."

She said she had been told, by another teacher, about a girl who screamed uncontrollably at a "beat" concert and, as far as she was concerned, "the teenagers who get themselves into such situations are usually members of these fan clubs. It is a very frightening and humiliating experience. As headmistress it is my duty to scotch these teenage crazes early. The girls have a mass of good music within the school." Noting that the membership for the Beatles Fan Club was 7s, Miss Evans told the girls it would be far wiser to donate the amount to the to the School Charities Fund.

Not quite so concerned however was the enlightened Miss Betty Archdale, principal of Abbotsleigh School for Girls at Wahroonga. She allowed her borders to pin hundreds of Beatle photographs to their dormitory walls and even delayed dinner one evening to allow the students to watch a Beatles performance on television. "I watched it myself," she said, "I see no harm in the Beatles or the craze they have started."

Unfortunately, Miss Archdale's views were not commonly held. At North Sydney's Monte Sant' Angelo College, principal Mother Baptista also ordered a ban on moptop hairstyles after deciding: "They look ugly and untidy and are quite unsuitable for uniformed young ladies." At Hornsby High School, on the much-perturbed North Shore, prefects were instructed to enforce a ban on the singing of Beatles songs in, around or on the way to and from school.

Not all of those horrified by Beatlemania were educationists. Alderman J.J. Gander in the Sydney suburb of Marrickville blamed the Beatles for an upsurge in vandalism. He pointed out that since the group had become popular "hundreds of pounds worth of damage had been caused to local schools and recreational areas." In the same week, Australian opera star John Shaw told the press: "The Beatles drive me around the bend. I can't stand them. Ugh! It is most infuriating and annoying when people like that can become so successful with so little training. They get up on stage and not a note of music comes out of them."

For two butchers in the Sydney suburb of Dulwich Hill, all the ruckus became inspiration for a profitable stunt. Jim Ryan (34) and Brian Crossfield (24) donned Beatle wigs and hummed *I Want to Hold Your Hand* behind the counter, generating a crush of curious customers and an increase of some £400 in the daily take. The *Daily Mirror* sent reporter Charles Stokes out into the streets in a Beatle suit and wig to gauge reactions. Adults generally "glared or stared in disapproval or sad resignation," while teenagers gathered around eagerly to ask for autographs.

When Gerry and the Pacemakers, Dusty Springfield, Brian Poole and the Tremeloes, and Gene Pitney flew into Sydney in early April for a Merseysound package tour (with Johnny O'Keefe and the Echoes), the *Sun* ran off street posters screaming "Beatles Rivals Here," with the middle word in smaller type size. The *Mirror* countered with ridicule, claiming that only "twenty dreamy-eyed girls and a half dozen disc jockeys" had been present at what their rivals described as "one of the noisiest receptions ever for visiting show business celebrities." A month earlier the *Sun* had kicked off a series of laudatory editorials, which would proliferate with nauseous rapidity three months later, gushing: "It seems that adult Australians are beginning to over-rate the danger of Beatlemania and under-rate the commonsense and balance of this country's teenagers. Now it's the Beatles, next year it will be someone and something else. It's just another way in which boys and girls sing about being boys and girls and the endlessly recurring miracle in which they find each other."

The print media was almost a latecomer, compared to the swift and ambitious actions of Australian radio. Back in March, Bill Stephenson, General Manager of leading Sydney popular music station 2SM, had sat down with Brodziak and Lean in Melbourne to map out cross-promotion plans. With financial backing from the makers of Surf washing powder, Stephenson despatched station manager Kevin O'Donohue to London to wave a virtual blank cheque before Brian Epstein. Within thirty-six hours and with a modest expenditure of £5000, O'Donohue had secured a contract which gave his station broadcast rights for one show and virtual "ownership" of the Beatles for the duration of their antipodean travels. Epstein agreed to allow a single station personality to accompany each inch of the caravan and record interviews each day, which would be expressed back to 2SM and then syndicated onto the "Beatle Network" which included Melbourne's 3UZ, Brisbane's 4BK and a score of regional outlets. (A rival "Beatle Network" was set up by 2UW in Sydney, with the participation of 3AK, 4BH, 5KA and 6PR.)

The interviewer who got the nod was the strongly established Bob Rogers, a thirty-nine-year-old who had been among the first radio personalities to give serious airplay to rock and roll in the Fifties. Though married with three children, he projected a sufficiently young image to pull off the demanding assignment. But radio station 2SM also had an ulterior motive. Rogers' contract was about to expire and he had been having talks with 2UE about an adult-oriented morning shift. With the enticement of the Beatles assignment, Bob agreed to stay with 2SM for another two years.

From the moment it seemed reasonably certain that they had the tour tied up, 2SM hurled itself into a dizzying level of all-out Mersey madness. First off the mark was the loony Mad Mel, an eighteen-year-old Californian jock who wore outsized mock glasses, comic strip clothes and honked a decidedly rude hooter on air. Mel suggested to his listeners that they do something very Australian for the boys, something like the knitting of a giant woollen scarf.

"Within a few days it was coming in by the sackload," he boasts, "six inches wide and in lengths ranging from a few inches to seven feet— from as far away as the Pacific Islands and Tasmania. There were so many sackfuls that it spilled into the basement, which upset the news teams who couldn't park their cars properly. To get it out of the way I had thirty to fifty schoolgirls come in after school to sew it together. That really clogged the news department! One day a Qantas pilot dropped in thirty-four pieces from Fiji." The end product was blinding. It had every colour imaginable and some of the kids had even knitted faces, names, guitars and maps of Australia into the pattern. The length claim of 8128 feet is probably Mel hype but there was believed to be a total of 11,765 pieces in the finished item. To accompany it, Mel prepared a fourteen inch by thirty-two feet concertina card with the names of every person who contributed a section.

Sydney schoolgirls Linda Flax, 12, of Annandale, Leone Lucas, 18, of Seaforth, Tracy Gillings, 15, of Castlereagh, and Kate Hopkinson, 14, of Castlereagh, manned the sewing machines set up in the foyer of 2SM for the joining together of Mad Mel's mighty scarf.

Mike Walsh, the 2SM "Good Guy" who followed Rogers and preceeded Mad Mel in the evenings, pulled off the cleverest stunt of all. "There was an incredible battle among disc jockeys to get hold of personalised Beatle ID voice tracks out of England, from whatever contacts you could muster. I realised I didn't have a chance of getting hold of a real one so I found this Liverpool kid, took him into the studio and had him imitate Ringo's voice. It worked perfectly and I ran the tapes for months, upsetting every other jock in town who were wondering how the hell I had got to Ringo."

Walsh, much to the Beatles later dismay, was very much responsible for the tons of jelly babies that were being hoarded in readiness for the concerts. As compere of the Gerry and the Pacemakers Mersey-sound show at the Stadium in April, he had informed the kids of the jelly baby showers occurring overseas and encouraged them to bring along lots in June.

However, radio's defection from the sounds of Aussie beaches to the murky Mersey had not been exactly streamlined. Well before the concert details had been firmed and most of Australia had succumbed completely to Beatlemania, the conversion process had encountered some amusing obstacles. The first taped interviews for Australia came from Roger Henning, a native based in London who, at the time of the tour, recounted, "I first met the Beatles against my will very early in 1963. EMI's export manager had let me use his office to record interviews and his offsider Barry Kingston begged and begged me to hear *Please Please Me* which the Beatles had performed on a Radio Luxemburg programme. I liked it, I did the interview, and that night a tape was on its way by plane to 3DB in Melbourne. There was no reply.

"I saw the Beatles again a few weeks later and recorded another interview which I sent back with other interviews of Cliff Richard and Gerry and the Pacemakers. Back came a letter from the station saying 'Thanks for the Cliff tape but don't waste your time on unknown artists.'

"I became good friends with the four of them but they could never remember my name, so they always bellowed at me 'G'day, red terror kangaroo from down under.' As their popularity grew out of hand, it was harder to get near them with a tape recorder but I got backstage on May 9 at the Royal Albert Hall where they were performing on a show compered by Rolf Harris. They dared me to switch my tape recorder on and when I did they grinned broadly and started to sing a murderous version of *Waltzing Matilda*. I also persuaded them to send a cheerio to 3DB DJ Barry Ferber who was one of the first people on Australian radio to play their records."

During the filming of *A Hard Day's Night,* Henning grabbed a brief interview on the train from Liverpool to London. Asked how much he knew about Australia, George answered, "It's warm and sunny and they keep all the convicts out there at Botany Bay . . . Sir."

Another Australian to make their acquaintance was Ernie Sigley, who as a Radio Luxemburg announcer from 1960 to 1963 gave Beatle discs some of their earliest exposure. He actually beat Rogers to London, cleverly missing the Beatles by arriving the very day that they flew out to Tahiti and the Virgin Islands. He returned home empty-handed.

During May the Beatles and their assorted wives and girlfriends vacationed in exotic locales, angering certain portions of the press with their flagrant display of premarital cohabitation. While Ringo and Maureen and Paul and Jane lolled about St. Thomas Island in the Virgin chain, John and Cynthia and George and Patti headed for the South Seas. After being hounded out of Hawaii by relentless reporters, they flew into Papeete in Tahiti. Asked, "Why are you leaving Hawaii so soon?" John snapped, "Why didn't you leave us alone. How would you like a microphone always stuck in your face while you are on holiday?" To a shouted question of "How long will you be in Tahiti?" George tossed back, "An hour." News of the relative proximity of two actual moptops was carried by the Australian press, with thinly veiled suggestions that the pair would be calling into Australia on their way home. The *Sydney Morning Herald* went so far as to publish details of flights that they *might* be on, sending a few dozen diehard fans out to Mascot Airport on a vain mission.

Meanwhile the madness was mounting. Sydney Symphony Orchestra conductor-to-be Dean Dixon announced that he planned to ask the Beatles to appear in a joint performance during their tour; while up in Queensland a Townsville doctor (also chairman of the Anglican Schools Commission) told a parents' meeting in Mount Isa, "There is nothing wrong with screaming, stamping the feet and writing.

Adults should encourage the modern crazes." At the Gold Coast High School a lunchtime debate on Beatlemania had to be postponed a day when almost the entire school of 600 tried to squeeze into one classroom.

Back in Sydney, former Australasian dance champion Charlie Ring gave a demonstration of his latest creation, the Beatlemania Stomp, calling it "a combination of the electrifying rhythm of the stomp and the provocative percussion and sonic excitement of the Beatles' music." In the corporate sphere, leading costume jewellery designer Christine Lyne and her patent attorney discovered that the trademark for the word "Beatles" had not been taken up in Australia and proceeded to lodge their own claim, sending a warning letter to another company manufacturing trinket items for good measure.

All such commercial exploitation came to an abrupt halt three weeks before the tour, when Malcolm Evans, Vice President of Seltaeb Inc. flew into Sydney to brief law firm Stephen, Jaques and Stephen on the protection of Beatle marketing rights. (Not Mal Evans the roadie, but a twenty-five-year-old former junior executive of Rediffusion Television who caused as much confusion as George Harrison of the Liverpool Echo.) He proudly told up-market newspapers that his company expected to earn £150,000 from merchandising rights as a result of the tour and its after effect.

So by the time the concerts were formally announced in March, Beatle interest was at a fever pitch in the general community. The most expensive seats (37s) were opened for sale on Monday April 13 in eastern cities. In Brisbane, queues began forming on Saturday afternoon with 200 camping in the street on Sunday night. Sydney was a trifle sedate, with the first girls not arriving until Sunday afternoon. Jean Allen of Padstow and Kathy Wolger and Pat Canfielde of East Hills actually started the line in error.

"We heard on the radio that a queue was already forming," explained Jean, "but we didn't find until we arrived at Palings that it was happening in Melbourne and not Sydney."

As radio stations reported the arrival of the three girls, others rushed into the city to take a place in the line. Most were well equipped with blankets, thermos flasks, packs of sandwiches and the inevitable transistor radios. The police mounted regular patrols of the line and were on hand to control the situation when firemen arrived to answer a hoax call in Ash Street, near Palings record store.

When the four Sydney ticket outlets (David Jones, Palings, Nicholsons and Kippax) opened their doors at 8.30 a.m. trading was certainly brisk. At David Jones' department store, six sales assistants had to put their backs into the doors as they were being opened, to prevent the collapse of a twenty-deep crowd. Once the front runners were inside, their mad dash to the ticket counter caused displays and tables of goods to be bowled over. Mrs. V. Scott, the twenty-year veteran head of the booking section gasped, "I have survived plenty of ticket rushes in my time but never anything like this. We just couldn't cope. I'll be glad when it's over."

The long wait outside Palings Record Store in Ash Street, Sydney.

The first day saw 7000 tickets sold, eclipsing a record held by Johnnie Ray in 1954. This situation was repeated in Brisbane and Melbourne. Harry Miller, Sydney manager of Stadiums Limited, offered, "I can't remember anything like this since the Burns-Patrick fight of 1954." Sales of 27s tickets opened on May 9 but there was no repeat of the April clamour.

The *Sun* and radio station 2GB joined together to buy 1200 ring-side seats, offering them as prizes in a competition which required a twenty-five word entry on "Why I Must Have Beatle Tickets." One Redfern housewife scored a pair with the wise comment: "I must have Beatle tickets as I think it will be extremely difficult to get into the stadium without them."

Two of the tickets went to Nancy Summers, tutor at Sydney University and *Daily Mirror* "Woman of the Year." She claimed that she had been queueing in a pharmacy and had filled in a coupon for the sake of something to do. Informed of her win she offered, "I'll exchange the two tickets for just a corner of a seat at Arthur Ruben-stein's concert!" She may have had some takers, as sold-out ringside tickets were commanding £8, according to classified ads placed boldly by scalpers.

Lorraine Saldern, 16, of Lewisham, Sydney, overjoyed at her purchase of a prime location Beatles ticket.

Slightly less enthusiasm from Melbourne ticket buyers — perhaps because their seats were't quite so close to the stage.

A ticket queuer's best friend: a transistor radio forever pumping out Beatles songs.

Australians should have considered themselves fortunate indeed to be able to buy tickets. Just a few weeks previously, an Israeli government spokesman for an inter-ministerial committee which ruled on the granting of performance permits, announced: "We have found no reason why Israeli youth should be exposed to an attack of mass hysteria." His committee ruled that a proposed concert by the Beatles would be "unsuitable for those teenage audiences most likely to be interested in it."

All through May and early June, Australian officialdom twisted itself into an idiotic red panic. Four of Sydney's leading hotels, the Menzies, Chevron, Hotel Australia and Town House, all refused to accommodate the group after senior and regular patrons had raised objections; even though the Chevron had initially requested the booking. Brodziak announced that he would be placing each Beatle in a separate hotel until Bert Dunn, owner of the Sheraton Motel Hotel in Macleay Street, Potts Point (directly opposite the Chevron) said that not only would he be pleased to have them stay, they could even perform in his lobby if they wished. This offer has been singularly responsible for almost twenty years of constant free publicity for a small hotel.

When Chevron manager Frank Christie heard of the booking he laughed at the irony. "We originally refused the Beatles because we feared the jams outside and inside the hotel," he said. "Now we get the crush without the money and publicity. Anyway, my kids are happy. They will be able to see the group from their front window."

Next, Fireman's Union Secretary Mr. J.W. Lambert claimed that "crowds of hysterical teenagers could turn Sydney Stadium into a death trap" and asked the Chief Secretary to move the concerts to another location. Harry Miller responded angrily, claiming that there was enough equipment in the old barn to fight the Great Fire of London and that with wide exits, clear passageways and a cut in capacity from 12,000 to 10,800, no venue could possibly be safer. Miller suggested that the gentleman was suffering from an overdose of Beatlemania. "Mr. Lambert is getting more excited than the teenagers," he said.

But that was just minor nitpicking compared to the asinine carry-on happening at even higher levels. The police and Department of Civil Aviation got together to announce that all Beatle fans would be banned from Sydney and Adelaide airports. After an uproar from all corners of the community they backpeddled slightly and unveiled 'Operation Beatles,' an insidious little plan which incorporated high-powered water hoses, the calling up of police reserves and flying squads of back-up units able to reach the airport within minutes. Workmen were deployed in the construction of a three-foot, six-inch steel barricade outside the international terminal building (120 feet from the aircraft point) and a sombre warning was issued that the Beatles' plane would be diverted to Richmond RAAF base if fans "got out of control." Dry practice runs for the defencing forces were scheduled for the week prior to B-Day.

New South Wales police superintendant George Barnes let it be known that the expected 6.35 a.m. arrival time would clash with the starting time of factories in the Mascot airport area. "Our main job will be to see that crowds don't interfere with people getting to their jobs. I suppose we shouldn't admit it but this Beatle business will be the biggest thing to hit Sydney since the 1954 Royal tour. But we don't want to make it appear that these four young men are getting any special treatment. After all, they're not anybody really important, are they?"

The morbid fears gave insurance companies their best business in years. First Johnny Devlin announced that he was covering himself for £25,000 against personal injury, which was good publicity. Then the Sheraton Hotel admitted that it had upped its cover, and finally the Dorchester Private Hotel, next door, decided to remove four valuable lamp standards from the footpath after encountering difficulties in insuring them against riot damage.

The only portion of the community not embroiled in futile fear was the fans and, in particular, those who had given their allegiance (and 7s) to the official club in Sydney. Commenced very early in 1963 by sixteen-year-old Angela Letchford of Little Bay, who worked as a domestic for the (boat empire) Halverson family in Turramurra, it had two thousand members in the weeks proceeding arrival, with a hudnred letters a day pouring in. Radio station 2UW eventually came to the rescue by giving the club a free office in their city building. Angela ran the club, approved by Beatle headquarters in England, with her friends

Lynn Andrews (secretary), Lyndsay Miller (joint secretary), Marie Holmes (treasurer) and brother Terry (vice president). Miller was a real Liverpudlian, who breathlessly revealed to the press that Paul's brother Mike McGear once cut her hair.

Fan club staff and members attempting to handle the volume of mail initiated by the imminent arrival of the Beatles. Left to right: Lynn Andrews, Angela Letchford, Marie Holmes, Mary Ramsay, Lyndsay Miller.

Women's Weekly journalist Kerry Yates received an unexpected Beatle fringe haircut at the Beatle Stomp at Beatle Village, May 1964.

Sydney Beatle Fan Club Officials, from left: Lynn Andrews, 16, of Matraville, Terry Letchford, 16, of Little Bay, Angela Letchford, 17, of Little Bay, and Marie Holmes, 17, of Matraville.

The club had its first open meeting in late March at Beatle Village in Kings Cross. Clone group the D-Men from Liverpool (Sydney) played clumsy beat/stomp music for around two hundred members, of which only eighty were boys. *Women's Weekly* junior reporter Kerry Yates was sent along to cover the event and had to submit to a fringe haircut before being allowed entry and honorary membership.

The D-Men from Liverpool (Sydney) played at the first public gathering of the Sydney Beatles Fan Club, staged at Beatle Village.

All four Beatles had returned to England in time to play two shows at the Prince of Wales Theatre on May 31, as part of Brian Epstein's "Pops Alive!" concert series. They also taped a TV interview for Australia with ATN 7 camera operator Mayo Hunter and met up with Bob Rogers at Abbey Road Studios, while doctoring some *A Hard Day's Night* tracks. They had fully intended to cram in a full recording session during the first days of June but all plans were thrown into disarray when Ringo collapsed at a *Saturday Evening Post* photo session on the morning of Wednesday June 3 and was rushed to University College Hospital suffering from acute tonsilitis and pharyngitis.

There is every likelihood that such a catastrophe had been anticipated because there was an almost indecent haste in the proceedings that followed. With less than twenty-four hours till a planned departure for Denmark, and the realisation that the Far East tour *had* to be got out of the way before the next American venture, Brian Epstein instructed producer George Martin to find a replacement, but fast.

Jimmy Nicol, twenty-four year-old Cockney drummer with the Shub Dubs, who had recently played on an EMI session with Georgie Fame, sprung to Martin's mind first. "I was having a bit of a lie down after lunch when the phone rang," Nicol later recounted. "It was EMI asking if I could come down to the studio to rehearse with the Beatles. Two hours after I got there I was told to pack my bags for Denmark."

"The difficulty," said Epstein, referring to Nicol's ragged fringe

cut, "was finding someone who looked like a Beatle and not an outcast." For Martin, the difficulty lay with George Harrison. "John and Paul readily agreed that it was a sensible thing to do," he recently revealed, "but George was a little more difficult, in fact he was downright truculent. He said, 'If Ringo's not going then neither am I, you can find two replacements.' Brian and I had quite a difficult job persuading him that it was in the best interests of the group as a whole to go and put up with Jimmy. In the end he went off and the group was a success, even without Ringo. But we never expected Jimmy to get as far as Australia."

The group rehearsed into the night with Nicol, with a photographer sent by to capture the new lineup for the European press. Australian jazz musician and journalist Dick Hughes had conned his way into the studio to watch the rehearsals (which he insists were taped by Martin) and during a break Paul told him, "This fellow is fine but we just can't afford to be without Ringo at a real recording session because the kids would always know that that record was the one without him."

Hughes found that there was but a minor smattering of knowledge of Australia among the whole group. George said he thought it was "a sort of desert continent with one city at the top and another at the bottom," while John admitted that his impressions were based on long-forgotten school history studies.

Their relative ignorance had been well exhibited at a press conference held on the day of their "Pops Alive!" concert at the Prince of Wales Theatre. "I'm looking forward to the trip very much," Paul had said. "We've been told all about those dingoes, wallabies and people running around playing didgeridoos. You see we've known Rolf Harris for about three years now. If we meet plenty of Aussies like him we'll be happy." John added, "We're dying to get down there, but what a pity it's winter. But it's not cold is it? We like a good welcome and those Aussies will probably be pretty fit after all that surfing and stuff. I don't know very much about Australia, my geography teacher didn't enlighten me much — the nit."

When Ringo was told it was winter down under, he retorted, "No birds on beaches or anything? The trip's off, I'm not going!" George consoled: "You can take pictures of that bridge Ringo, you won't have time for much more," and added, "tell that lot down under that John's Aunt Mimi will be coming with us. They're deporting her from England for stealing a loaf of bread."

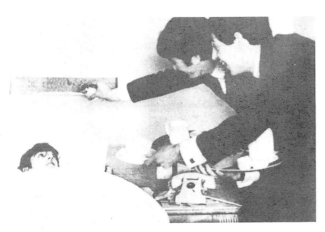

John and Paul visiting Ringo at University College Hospital on the eve of their departure to Copenhagen.

British European Airlines corporate logo was deftly adapted to capitalise on the celebrity cargo being transported to Copenhagen.

Nicol's familiarity with the repertoire was not too much of a problem, as every beat band in England was well versed in Beatle songs. With precious little time to pack for their six weeks away, the group dashed to London airport on the morning of June 4 to board a BEA flight (before the other passengers) to Copenhagen. After checking in at the Royal Hotel, under seige from 6000 crazed kids (most of whom were at the airport), more furious rehearsals were undertaken in the Tivoli Gardens, lasting most of the afternoon and disturbed by a visit from the British Ambassador. That night the ten song set (there were usually eleven but Ringo's obligatory *I Wanna Be Your Man* was left out) went off without a hitch before 4500 with Jimmy's solid bass beat holding it together. After the show he declared, "It was all great fun and I had no trouble following them." George added, "Playing without Ringo is like driving a car on three wheels but Jimmy has grasped our rhythm very quickly." However this did not deter them from shooting off a telegram to Ringo which read, "Didn't think we could miss you so much. Get well soon." At this point, Brian Epstein was in New York with Billy J. Kramer and the Dakotas and the lad was left to cope with his 103° temperature alone. The hospital switchboard complained that it was being swamped with concerned calls from American girls.

Toward the end of the Hillegram, Holland, second concert, fans joined the Beatles on stage for a wild dancing and shouting finale.

Jimmy borrowed a Beatle suit for a television interview at the Treslong Studios of VARA Broadcasting Company in Hillegram.

On June 5 the Beatles flew into Schiphol Airport near Amsterdam and continued rehearsals at Tresling Studio in Hillegram, twenty-six miles out of the city. After a concert that evening they headed for Amsterdam's Walletjes red light district and, according to some reports, spent the night in a brothel. Photographs are reputed to exist of John on his hands and knees, unable to walk, in the doorway of a house of ill repute.

The next day they were paraded through normally sedate Amsterdam before 30,000 people. A trip in a glass-topped boat along the seventy canal network resulted in scenes of hysteria and frenzied irrational behaviour that had not previously been witnessed. Bob Rogers was on hand by the side of the Ansall Canal and conveyed every detail of the two hour upheaval by phone to the "National Beatle Network."

More than thirty determined Dutch fans leapt into the water and swam towards the regal craft, which had been used by Queen Juliana during her 1962 Silver Wedding festivities. John and Paul hauled aboard the sodden young girls, physically protecting them from water police who were savagely weilding rubber truncheons. Jimmy huddled in a corner as a barrage of chewing gum, firecrackers, tiny dolls and all manner of refuse fell upon the laughing, approving Beatles. Two thousand police, recalled from leave, failed to restore any degree of calm and traffic on canal bridges was paralysed. That night at the Blokker Cabbage Auction Hall, thirty-six miles out of Amsterdam (by police motorcycle escort), 150 steel helmeted riot police and 250 civil guards battled two shifts of three thousand rioting concert fans — six of whom climbed the hall walls and swung onto the stage from steel girders. The screaming pitch reportedly shattered windows in a nearby building.

Jimmy Nicol observes George's assimilation of local customs in Holland.

A thunderstruck Jimmy takes his place in the Royal Yacht for a tour of Amsterdam's canals.

George and John cruising the Ansall Canal.

On the morning of Sunday June 7, the Beatles flew into London, dropped off Cynthia and collected John's Aunt Mimi. A 10.15 a.m. BOAC Boeing 707 flight to Hong Kong was held on the ground one hour to allow the group to make the connection. Press officer Derek Taylor, roadies Mal Evans and Neil Aspinall, compere Alan Field, Sounds Incorporated and eighteen guitars comprised the tour party. Also on board was a battery of reporters, including Bob Rogers, Dick Hughes, cameraman Mayo Hunter from Australia and the infamous George Harrison from the Liverpool *Echo*.

Touching down in Beirut that evening, the contingent observed in amazement as Lebanese police turned fire fighting foam on hundreds of screaming, battling teenagers who had invaded the tarmac. The ugly scenes developed when the Beatles, exhausted from their European jaunt, ruled out a terminal building appearance. Infuriated fans hurled themselves against a wall of police guarding the plane ramps, with an agile two breaking through to climb up a catering wagon and actually enter the aircraft.

The mood in the air was light and combustible. A rowdy pillow fight instigated by John and Paul against the accompanying scribes was filmed by Mayo Hunter and expressed on to Sydney, where the Seven network rushed it to air.

The second refuelling stop was at the Pakistani capital of Karachi on the Arabian Sea, at about 2 a.m. on Monday morning. Paul chanced an embarkment to buy souvenirs, only to be sent running back to the sanctuary of the aircraft by a mob of shrieking locals who materialised in the terminal "from out of nowhere." At 6 a.m. it was a cup of tea in the terminal building at Calcutta. Hughes recalls that John was dismayed by the heat and humidity and asked if it would be like that in Australia. Specifics of the antipodean winter were then conveyed. Hughes' only other vivid recollection of the flight, for what it's worth, was that "Paul was a ferocious and unabashed nose picker."

Scenes similar to Beirut occurred in Bangkok later in the morning. Almost a thousand fans, mostly in school uniforms, over-ran the airport, chanting "Beatles Come Out." Although they had planned to stay on board, the group descended the ramp to sign autographs and be kissed, while Jimmy went into the terminal to buy a 'camel seat,' whatever that may have been. Paul continually assured the tarmac horde, "We hope to come back to Thailand."

On the tarmac at Hong Kong's Tai Tak Airport.

By comparison, their official destination was somewhat of an anti-climax. The reception at Kai Tak Airport in Hong Kong was quiet and subdued, with no police clashes and only spasmodic bursts of screaming. Esconded on the fifteenth floor of the President Hotel in Kowloon, they finally encountered some Beatlemania, as a handful of fans ran screaming through the lobby and upstairs corridors. The English language Hong Kong *Tiger Standard* newspaper ran an editorial criticising police for "monopolizing" the Beatles and keeping them from their fans. The group had by-passed customs and immigration formalities and were kept completely under cover from the moment of their touchdown.

Jimmy took full advantage of his lack of familiarity and busied himself with shopping, sightseeing and swimming. For the other three it was the standard hotel room isolation. Local traders were invited to parade their wares before the captive musicians, with price tags well in excess of what faceless tourists would have encountered on the street.

Paul was the most eager shopper. He beat down a wily merchant from $HK 160 to $100 on a wristwatch, which he wore in addition to his existing timepiece for the duration of the tour, set at Greenwich Mean Time. He and Neil Aspinall also each ordered a couple of twenty-four hour suits.

Bob Rogers was greeted with a rude shock in Hong Kong, a development which threatened to shatter his monopoly on the capturing of Beatle utterances. As he explains it, "David Joseph, my former manager, had become boss of 3AK and he had flown up to meet the tour with DJ Malcolm Searle. They began to make it very stiff because every so often they scooped me and then I was in terrible trouble back home. You see all the living and subsequently all the stories occurred between midnight and dawn and although there were lots of little pills floating around, I wouldn't touch them. That put me at a disadvantage with many of the other interviewers."

That Monday evening, heavily fatigued and wanting nothing more than a solid night's sleep, the in-house celebrities were fully expected to be in attendance at the Miss Hong Kong Pageant being staged in the hotel. So tearful was the reaction to their refusal that John (of all people!) consented to drag his weary carcass into the convention hall for a brief appearance. He shook the contestants' hands and stirred up some whoops (not easy in inscrutable Asia) with some smooth lines about the beauty of Hong Kong femininity.

Their two concerts at the Princess Theatre on Tuesday night were only half full, which may have had something to do with the ticket prices. At £7 they represented the average weekly income for a Hong Kong worker. The Beatles themselves were highly critical of the pricing. Those who could afford the event kept up a steady chant of "Bitlz . . . Bitlz . . . Bitlz" throughout.

The Chinese language morning newspapers censured the event, carrying stern warnings that such nonsense as screaming at western entertainers was more appropriate for Occidental youth than the traditionally reserved Chinese. The right-wing *Sing Pao* newspaper said, "The incessant shrieking of fans was mental torture to those in the audience who came to appreciate music," while the Communist *Wen Wei Pao* criticised the "fantastic noises." Far kinder was the daily *Tin Tin Yat Po*, which seemed delighted that "youth and its rhapsody had shaken Hong Kong." One reporter dubbed them Kong Yan, Cantonese for "frenzied ones."

After resting for most of Wednesday, the group flew out that afternoon, farewelled by some 500 fans, most of them British. Back at the hotel, squealing fans invaded the departed suites, rolling on beds, kissing sheets, foraging for cigarette butts, gnawing wizened apple cores and pocketing discarded socks. "I was just in time to stop them stealing the pillow cases and sheets," said a hotel maid.

In Australia, all newspapers and most radio stations were carrying regular bulletins on the state of Ringo's health and the likelihood of him making it to Adelaide in time for the opening concerts. Sydney teen DJ David Ford became strangely affronted by the presence in the troupe of Jimmy Nicol. In a newspaper column he thundered, "I see no need for them to bring Nicol. In Sydney just about every young instrumental group which has cashed in on the Beatle plague craze has a drummer complete with Beatle wig. So why not give one of these mimic artists a chance?"

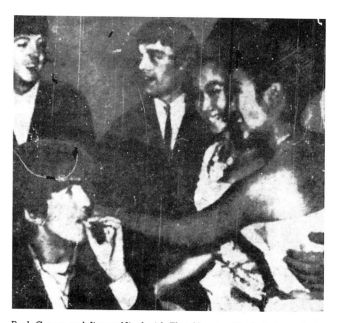

Paul, George and Jimmy Nicol with Thai film stars Unchuli Anantakul (left) and Busara Narumit at Hong Kong's President Hotel.

Fans await the Beatles at rainswept Darwin Airport, not knowing if the plane will land for a refuel or fly direct to Sydney.

Clockwise from left:

Australian comedian/singer Rolf Harris promoting his "Ringo for President" single in his own inimitable fashion.

Paul McCartney climbs out onto the deck of Queen Juliana's yacht to view the siege by Amsterdam fans, who seemed to know no fear.

BOAC hostess Anne Creech from Liverpool was assigned to the Beatles' flight from London to the Far East to help the Fab Four "feel at home."

Brian Epstein signing Sounds Incorporated to his Nems Empire, which also boasted Billy J. Kramer & the Dakotas, Paddy Klaus & Gibson, Cilla Black and the Fourmost.

Departing from Copenhagen and Amsterdam with replacement drummer Jimmy Nicol of Georgie Fame's band and the Shub Dubs.

2: SYDNEY
THE FIRST TIME

Well before the Beatles had left Hong Kong, the police chief had forwarded a confidential report to the Sydney CIB. Miffed by the knockback of an offer of a boat trip around their beloved island, the report was surly and petulant, reading in part: "The Beatles themselves are an amiable if cringing group who hole up in their rooms and whimper like children while their supporters besiege the hotel demanding to see them. You must maintain the most stringent vigilance against small girl infiltrators in pink, blue and white party dresses, aged from ten to twenty-four; they are more ruthless than our Tong killers.

"In our experience you can rely upon the Beatles to co-operate with you in the preservation of law and order — so long as they lose no box office takings by public-spirited collaboration with the police. Apart from their performances they lay dazed in their suites."

This report arrived just a few days after the New York City Police Department had declared: "The Beatles will give Australian police their toughest time ever. Everywhere they go there will be chaos and confusion. We're glad they're going to Sydney instead of coming back here."

In Sydney, the agents of such confusion were gazing warily toward the heavens and seriously evaluating the extent of their loyalty as the skies blackened ominously. The truly loyal had begun to gather at Kingsford Smith Airport on Wednesday morning. The first to arrive were Kay Strickland, 17, of Lakemba and Vicki Griffin, 16, of Belmore. Both had waited eighteen hours for concert tickets back in April and claimed 1100 Beatle photographs between them.

As the BOAC flight set out over the South China Sea, Australia's northern gateway was being wracked with an unexpected spasm of Beatlemania. Early on Wednesday morning Civil Aviation Authorities, concerned at a turbulent weather pattern over the eastern seaboard, gave indication that all flights from Hong Kong might have to refuel in Darwin to ensure the safety of a diversion to Brisbane if cross winds at Sydney prevented a landing.

Alerted by opportunist radio broadcasts, Darwin youth began arriving at the airport before noon and by 10.00 p.m. some 200 had assembled, most having come from a conveniently arranged session at the local cinema. Official confirmation of the diversion was announced at 11.00 p.m.

By 2.20 a.m. on Thursday morning 400 fans were on hand and all refused to believe Qantas announcements that one of their landing jets did not carry the Fab Four. They were convinced only when a BOAC plane dropped onto the tarmac at 2.35 a.m., complete with official confirmation of the celebrity content. The Beatles were the last to alight and as they moved down the gangway a sixteen-year-old girl vaulted the barriers and easily outpaced a portly constable 200 yards to the closed door of the Civil Aviation car into which they had been bundled. She was hastily packed off to a quarantine unit where, the next day, according to press reports, she was shot full of smallpox and typhoid serums, although no one was quite sure why.

After completion of customs and immigration formalities, the bright and eager Beatles were thrust among a hastily assembled Northern Territory media. The very first question on Australian soil came from reporter John Edwards, who uttered to Paul, "Welcome to Australia, which one am I talking to?"

Within the scant few minutes allowed on the ground, Paul indicated that he had not expected to find a soul in wait at the primitive outpost and that he was most keen to come face to face with a variety of marsupials. "I wouldn't like to have a kangaroo dropped in my lap," he explained, "but it would be great to have a good look at one. I have heard the usual things about Australia but I've always doubted that bit about them standing on their heads. I see that you lot are on your feet and you look pretty steady to me, as if you've done it before."

Surveying the press representatives, John barked, "You men must be from the nose-papers. Well don't blow the story up too big!" Asked if he had any preconceived notions about Australia he said, "No cobber mate cobber. I've got a clear mind because no place is what you expect it to be beforehand. We'd like to see some of your night life though." After briefly waving to fans from the balcony of an upstairs lounge, the four returned to the aircraft.

Meanwhile, Sydney fans were halfway through a cold vigil made even colder by airport authorities. At 10.00 p.m. a loudspeaker announcement had warned, "No arrangements have been made for overnight accommodation of Beatle fans. When the last aircraft departs at 11.00 p.m., the terminal will be closed." When the evil hour came, the 100 gathered fans went out into the storm without protest. All, that is, except two. Nita Martin and Margaret Hartog, both 17, clad in the standard uniform of duffle coat, pointed toe sacking shoes and nylon stretch pants, hid in the ladies toilet as the terminal was being cleaned and managed to elude the security guards all night. They also escaped the carloads of yahoos who set fire to Beatle photographs and mildly intimidated groups of camped fans.

As relentless squalls continued to lash the east coast, there was still no certainty that the Beatles would be able to reach Sydney. Sometime around 4 a.m., a BOAC executive rang the Sheraton to advise that although the plane was in the air, it would certainly be an hour late into Sydney, if it wasn't diverted to Brisbane en route. Jack looked at the storm in disgust, recalling that the long-range weather forecast he had ordered had predicted fine weather. As he dressed and left for Mascot, Kenn went back to bed for an extra hour's sleep. "I was sleeping like a baby until they told me that the plane might be diverted," Neary told waiting newsmen in Macleay Street, "then I couldn't sleep all night." Fourteen-year-old Robyn Ross told *TV Week,* "I live next door to the hotel and police and reporters were making a terrific racket in the street." At one point a cab driver sent Sheraton staff leaping from their beds to scatter fans, when he rang the night bell and it stuck.

At Mascot, few fans had arrived to swell the 150 or so drowned rats huddled in the steel-fenced open enclosure. There seemed little likelihood that even ten per cent of the estimated 20,000 would show up in such tempestuous conditions, particularly when the two commercial TV stations were offering direct telecasts.

Television had held off until the last days, each station carefully monitoring what its competitors were doing. In the end it became an outright scramble for supremacy. TCN 9 had scored a coup at the Chevron Hotel, positioning one camera on the first floor and two more on level six, directly opposite the Sheraton penthouse. Its coverage team comprised David Paterson and Jimmy Hannan at the airport and comedian Dave Allen and hardened actor / TV newsman Chuck Faulkner at the Sheraton.

ATN 7, who claimed they were going to floodlight the tarmac for clearer pictures, sent rock hero Johnny O'Keefe and newsreader John

Drenched but dedicated.

An acid test of fan faith.

Bailey to the airport and then on to the hotel. ABN 2 were a little more restrained, their select filming of the arrival being condensed into a sombre thirty minute special by Kit Denton, for broadcast at 8.30 p.m. as *B-Day*. The stations generally described their coverage as being "on a scale usually reserved for royal tours." It culminated a week of relentless Beatle bombardment on the box, during which every scrap of film featuring them, along with "Around the Beatles," a "Ready Steady Go!" special, "The Big Night Out," "The Mersey Sound" and Morecombe and Wise's "Two of a Kind," all from England, was shoved on air.

By 5.30 a.m. there were 400 fans in the vast, sodden enclosure. A half hour later their numbers were equalled as busloads of police spilled out into the half light of the ravaged dawn. One hundred or so newsmen lifted the tally of shivering waiters to nearly 1000. Amid strewn wrappings and soggy banners, the chanting, skylarking kids resembled a camp of dislocated war refugees. When the Melbourne *Herald's* E.W. Tipping passed through the airport on his way home from the opening ceremonies of the New Guinea parliament, he haughtily muttered to a

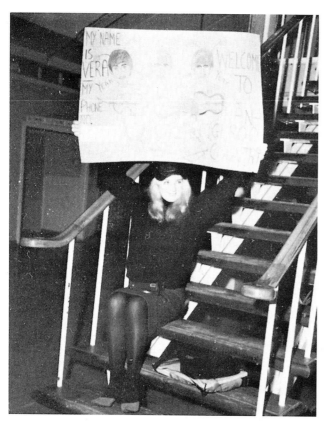

A most optimistic Beatle fan.

colleague, "From a civilised world to an uncivilised one."

Once the 2SM 'Beatle Network' had set itself up at all available vantage points with a team of Garvin Rutherford, John Brennan, Mike Walsh and a cast of thousands, and 2UE's Tom Jacobs had established a link line to his station, the scramble was on for interviews, observations and exclusives. The best comment of all was captured by Johnny O'Keefe, who waded among the signs proclaiming both, "Go Home Insex" and "We Love You Beatles" to ask a young fellow where he and his friends were headed after the arrival. "Well we're not going to school," retorted the lad. "You could catch flu in weather like this."

Mingling with the crowd was a group of twenty students from the University of New South Wales, led by sociology lecturer Dr. Tony Vinson, intent upon examining facets of teenage behaviour. "They will be watching Beatle fans working themselves into an excited state by following other fans," said Vinson. "Their textbooks have told them what to expect, now they will be able to observe it first hand."

Ejected from the warm terminal building, undaunted fans camp right outside the main entrance.

None of the Beatles slept as their BOAC jet cut through the sheets of gale over the Australian heartland. Paul read a James Bond novel, George swotted up on Australia in the BOAC digest and the others played a card game called Russian Bank. Rogers and Searle were in a cold sweat wondering how they were going to get through customs and immigration formalities and still cover the arrival better than each other.

Back on the ground it was rain rather than sweat which ran down the faces of the bored police who stood around, but their Commander in Chief, Supt. Don Davies of the Commonwealth Police, was a relieved man. Genial and considerate, he took pains to speak to the kids (without belittling them), at regular points throughout the morning, always assuring: "We are not here in any way to interfere with your welcome to the Beatles. We don't care how much noise you make, how much you cheer, how loud you sing, or how many banners you wave. Our main purpose here is to endeavour to ensure that none of you are injured because of the thoughtless actions of a few." The fans responded warmly to Davies, the father of three Beatle fans. "He talked to us like he knew us, he's terrific," complimented Pauline Jones, 15, of Punchbowl.

The rain-dampened crowd was almost a disappointment for sixteen-year-old Russell Mills, a junior clerk at the Phillip Street police station. His superiors had decided that his moptop hairstyle and faint resemblance to Paul McCartney might be of value and so instructed him to be at the airport at 6 a.m. wearing a tight-fitting suit, with a guitar slung over his shoulder, ready for decoy duty. "If the Beatles get into trouble I hope I'll be able to help them," he enthused. "I don't care if the girls catch me." Alas, when it appeared that his deceptive dash would not be required, he was sent back to his desk without having met his heroes.

At 7.43 a.m., one hour and eight minutes after the scheduled ETA, the Boeing 707 touched down on the asphalt sea at Mascot International Airport. The fans, who had erroneously bayed at a TAA aircraft a few minutes earlier, managed to come alive under their umbrellas and wraps to deliver a deafening roar that rivalled the backwash of the jet. Once the plane had taxied into position, a special unit of immigration officials went on board to complete formalities. (In those glorious pre-drug days, pop performers were not automatically subjected to intimate body searches and the dismantling of their guitars.)

Given the opportunity of abandoning their open truck journey around the fan enclosure, the four chose to brave the elements. As they moved toward the exit hatch, a TAA executive vaulted up the stairs to hand them each a giant black umbrella. "Nobody had even thought of providing protection for the boys," recalls Lloyd Ravenscroft, "so it was a very sharp move by the airline which had lost the Beatles to Ansett ANA earlier in the piece. Emblazoned right across the umbrellas was TAA, which was subsequently seen by millions all over the world. Ansett, BOAC and Qantas just blew their stacks."

At the foot of the ramp was Brodziak and Neary, almost apologising for the weather. Kenn recalls his first Beatle conversation being a quite off-handed question from Paul to the effect of "We're doing this for you at the old price aren't we?" "He didn't seem to say it nastily," says the promoter.

The journey on the trundling truck was absolutely farcical. Unable to keep a firm hold on the umbrellas and wave at the same time, the Beatles resorted to screaming out unheard salutations to the frantic crowd. They grinned as they moved past a brave mob of malcontents bearing a banner which read, "Go Home Bugs — NSW Anti-Trash Society," not far from another sign proclaiming "Welcome From One Bug to Four Others." One wave too many by George saw his umbrella ripped out of his hand by a vicious burst of wind. Jack Neary dashed over and thrust a hat on his head, which (like the umbrella) was of absolutely no use. All wore batwing capes, black except for Jimmy's fawn.

As the truck hastened towards the Qantas cargo area to transfer the drenched musicians to waiting Austin Princess cars, the press photographers high-tailed it on foot. The four obliged for a few moments before stepping into the warm and dry vehicles, with Paul chiding, "Hurry up fellas, don't you know we shrink when we get wet." All this was being conveyed not only to Sydney's work and school-force as they readied for morning departure, but to Melbourne via TCN 9's coaxial cable. Ambulancemen reported not one casualty, though one officer added, "I bet there'll be a few fans with pneumonia

Dancing to a cracking transistor radio helps the devoted forget the fierce June chill.

or heavy colds tomorrow."

As the motorcade proceeded to Kings Cross along King Street, Florence Avenue, Tunstall Avenue, Anzac Parade and South Dowling Street, and the press drove like maniacs along whatever shortcut they thought would get them there first, TV viewers were shown highlights of the arrival. At the commercial stations, editors were furiously assembling half hour programs for screening at 5 p.m. and suitable segments for the 6.30 News.

Recalls fan club president Angela Letchford, "We had been picked up and taken to the airport by Channel 7 and were allowed to sit inside a kombi van positioned by the barrier. But we felt so guilty that we got out and stood in the rain with the other kids. There was no chance to meet the boys at the airport so we were driven to the hotel in an official car with Aunt Mimi and the other George Harrison, who was trying to convince us that he was George's father."

Not all fans were pleased with the handling of the arrival. Sixteen-year-old Joan Strange of Ryde complained, "I didn't even see their faces. We were all wet and they should have joined us." "But I suppose it was all worth it," chimed in Shirley Comerford, 13, of Ashfield. "If I'd known what was going to happen I still would have come out here."

When the motorcade arrived at the Sheraton, the Beatles were rushed through the back garage entrance, bypassing 300 fans. Bad planning resulted in the lift not being held ready and the four were crushed against the closed doors by clamouring reporters. Bombarded with questions, John remarked, "How could we be disappointed when they came out to see us and stood in all the rotten wind and rain to wave to us. They were great, really great."

Out in Macleay Street, greatness was still in full force. Held behind police barriers, rowdy fans were immobilising the operations of the Chevron Hotel — blocking its doorways, trampling its gardens and deafening its guests. Only one casualty was reported: Seventy-year-old Mrs. J. Walters from Randwick stepped back off the footpath and fell

The Granville Mods came well equipped for their vigil.

Taking a front line barrier position as dawn approaches.

The fan's eye view of the jet disgorging its Liverpool content.

into the churning gutter. Laughing as she was helped to her feet, she said, "I might be seventy but this is still fun."

Seventeen-year-old Brian Frankham of Merrylands sprinted alongside the official car and successfully lobbed a letter in the window. From his six-year-old sister Jeanette, the letter contained an invitation to dinner for the Beatles. A myriad of signs and banners were held aloft to welcome the group, the most amusing being "We Love You John, Even if you are Married." Meanwhile, BOAC hostesses Barbara Riordan, Pamela Bristow and Marigold Lau, were giving their impressions of their celebrity passengers to salivating newsmen. "They never stopped joking, they are terrific wits," said Riordan. "We feel a little let down now that we have lost them. They were engrossed in books most of the way from Hong Kong. Their reading varied from James Bond to a geography book on Australia."

Sheraton manageress Margaret Walpole (Miss Victoria 1950) took the Beatles to suite 801 (where John, Paul and George were booked) on the penthouse level and introduced them to their two Spanish housemaids, Maria Parra and Aurora Martinez. With their luggage in transit from the airport, they were forced to make a brief balcony appearance in saturated and borrowed clothes; all except George who wrapped a towel around his waist (which the press automatically described in print as his underpants) and did a snappy jig. George later explained: "We were watching it all on television and they were saying 'I wonder why they're not coming out to wave' but there was no way we could tell them that we didn't have any trousers, they were out with our capes being pressed. Paul and John managed to get a pair of trousers each from somewhere but all I had was a towel. We went out to wave because they might have thought we were acting a bit funny if we didn't."

Paul then took an M.S.S. man aside, whispered, "Mate, will you get these people out of our room, we want to take a bath," and by 9.30 a.m. the three star Beatles had thrown themselves into bed, clad in underwear or pyjamas borrowed from other guests. As they slept, a few crafty journalists tracked down Aunt Mimi. "They used to practice at my house when they started out," she informed proudly, "and I can't say the music was bad but it wasn't good. Let's just say I think they are getting better every day. Frankly I'm much happier about the success of John's book than his success as a Beatle. He's been writing that sort of humour since he was eight years old."

Admitting that she liked "the heavy kind of music myself — the classics," Mimi conceded, "but I think the music the boys play means something to the young people." Having just "tucked in" her protesting nephew, she said, "They looked like four corpses but they'll be on top of the world again in a few hours. They all think their Sydney fans are wonderful — fancy standing out in all this rain for so long." When *Women's Weekly* photographer Don Cameron remarked that he played his electric guitar in his bedroom, Mimi fixed a cold stare and snapped, "Heaven help your mother young man!" For all her obviously rehearsed replies, Mimi showed herself to be, in Phantom Dave Lincoln's words, "A female version of John. Very witty, very sharp." Though not sharp enough to persuade John to let her go on to Adelaide.

As in Hong Kong, Jimmy Nicol became the tourist Beatle. While the others slept, a second cousin, Mrs. Gladys Richardson, collected

him from the Sheraton in an unobtrusive station wagon and took him to her Arncliffe home to meet (rather distant) cousins Pamela, 14, Suzanne, 12, and Billy, 9. He was reunited with great-aunt Lillian and ninety-year-old Uncle Bill, whom he had last met when they had visited London for the Coronation in 1953. His aunt took one look at his locks and asked, "This mob you're with, they have long hair do they?" Jimmy replied in the affirmative and patiently explained that he had been wearing it in that style for more than three months but had taken to using a lotion to accelerate growth since filling in with the Beatles. After the formalities of reunion, his young cousins took him into the city where he shopped for boomerangs and toy koalas, absolutely unnoticed. He returned to the Sheraton Hotel in the afternoon, just as the other three were arising to face a two-and-a-half-hour press conference. Having not been given a security pass before leaving the hotel, he encountered extraordinary difficulty getting back in, his pleas of, "But I'm a Beatle!" greeted with ill-concealed mirth by the guards. Brodziak's iron rule of 'no entry without a pass' was so inflexible that the man himself was refused readmission when he dashed out without his wallet, requiring him to send a minion (with pass) to his room to fetch it.

When neighbouring schools let out at 3 p.m., Macleay Street once more became jammed with screamers. With urging from George (a common occurrence) the Beatles made a balcony appearance at around 3.30 p.m. Refreshed and in a taunting mood, they looned for a good ten minutes, Paul eliciting the greatest roar by sticking a leg over the balcony railing.

Just before 4.30, Derek Taylor led the four into a packed press reception in the hotel's conference suite. As they took their positions on a mauve semi-circular divan, Taylor heralded formally: "Ladies and Gentlemen, I would like to introduce the Beatles." George immediately leapt on the back of the couch and announced, "Here's picture position number nine."

"The Sydney press bash was seething with a lot of nasty tension," recalls Bob Rogers. "A lot of high-brow newspapers had sent along older reporters who were not quite as starstruck as the rest of us." Dick Lean adds, "They were just brilliant, under any circumstance. They handled the press with a sharp reparte that we'd just never seen before."

After the still photographers had blinded everyone in the room, the TV crews moved in for news footage. Mike Walsh kept up the classic tradition of dumb Australian questioning with, "Paul, what do you expect to find in Australia?" to which John tossed back, "Australians!" When Chuck Faulkner enquired if there was an acknowledged leader of the act, John slyly stabbed back, "No, not really" before the question had even finished. When Buzz Kennedy paid a tribute to the sodden truck ride, John shrugged off, "We thought it was going to be sunny." Walsh leapt in with the probing, "Did you enjoy the rain?" answered by Paul: "Seeing as they got soaked, we didn't mind."

Ernie Sigley, up from Adelaide and knowing John's weakness, asked if Buddy Holly had influenced his music. "He did in the early days obviously." "So did James Thurber didn't he," interjected Paul. "Yes but he doesn't sing very well," John concluded. George was asked his favourite song. "I like . . . (interruption) I like . . . (interruption) I like . . . (interruption) I like *You Can't Do That*." "Has the Merseybeat changed since you've been playing it?" asked a man from the dailies. "We keep saying there's no such thing as Merseybeat," John insisted. "It's rock 'n' roll. It just so happens that we write most of it." Would they be writing songs with Australian themes? "No," insisted John. "We never write songs with themes, just the same old rubbish." Sigley snuck back into the proceedings to get their feelings about the Hong Kong ticket prices. "I wouldn't go and see anyone for five quid," said John. "I wouldn't see you for two bob," inserted George. "What about this film *Beatlemania?*" someone tossed in. "Are you happy with the finished product?" John acidly corrected the title and replied, "It's as good as anybody who makes a film who can't act."

Once the TV crews had shot their film, freelancers scrambled for individual Beatles and the ordered event descended into bedlam. *Sun-Herald* staff reporter Marie Knuckey described the situation with these words: "It was like being caught in the middle of a football match. While a surging group carried me forward to be holed in the spine by a camera, a rush forward meant being jabbed in the face by four or five microphones. Every so often I came face to face with a pair of photographer's feet, perilously perched upon a table among glasses of beer. I had just got within speaking distance of George when someone

Paul McCartney gives Sydney its first Beatle wave.

7.43 a.m., Thursday June 11, 1964. The BOAC Boeing 707 carrying the Beatles to Australia slices through driving rain as it taxies along the runway towards an absurd army of shivering policemen.

demanded a replacement and John changed places with him. John had no sooner reached us than it was decided it would be better if the Beatles moved out into the centre of the room. So we all started from scratch again, surging towards the nearest Beatle.''

George and John debate the wisdom of boarding the ricketty milk truck.

Looning, laughing and making the most of a ridiculous situation.

Arriving at the rear entrance of the Sheraton Hotel.

When George lost his umbrella, tour organiser Jack Neary obliged with a rather inadequate hat.

Official greetings in the Sheraton foyer.

The first official Beatle car, crawling up Macleay Street with Paul McCartney.

Autograph demands were unceasing but the four generally obliged.

And on the questions went. Paul said he was certainly aware of the crowds outside. "I was trying to sleep through it!" What type of girls did he like? "The female ones." Was he an intellectual? "What are they? We are not just four stupid kids who don't know what to do. The old idea that you only have to make a record and the kids will buy it is completely wrong." Did he like culture? "Well I used to read plays, and Juliet Greco is one of my favourite film stars. Is that culture?"

John warned: "At this pace it won't last another year. People in all ages went mad over someone. But now people are going mad over us all at the same time. What is the real difference between fans standing in the rain to see us and a forty-year-old man waiting in the rain to buy a football ticket? Our music's for anybody but it's not basically adult music. It's only older people who can't hear us in concert, the kids manage quite well."

George took time to explain: "When rock'n'roll died and ballads and folk music took over we just carried on playing our type of music.

Shagged out after an arduous flight and a sodden arrival. This photograph made front page throughout the world.

Jimmy, Paul and John safe in the Sheraton foyer.

Awake and refreshed, George, Paul and John check out their pre-press conference lunch with Chef Peter Stross.

When at last we succeeded in cutting a record the people were ready for a change and we clicked." Jimmy even got in a few words. "There isn't much I can say. I've only known the boys since last Wednesday afternoon. I know when this is over I'll no longer be a Beatle but I've got plans. When I go back to London they're fixing up a band for me. I'll do some television . . ." ". . . and he's away," finished John.

Senior radio personality Andrea collared John, pointed proudly to her Beatle brooch and boasted, "Look what I'm wearing." "By gum, clothes!" he shouted in mock surprise. Meanwhile, nobody had noticed a ladder being placed onto the window ledge, nor the teenage girl who summarily peered through the window. Nor did anyone notice the secretary of the Beatles' Fan Club who got tired of waiting in the foyer and slipped past the guards to present her case for an audience. The window girl was removed, but Lynn Andrews was saved from

Aunt Mimi takes on Sydney's media while her boys nap. She admitted she preferred the classics!

Not far from the Beatles, their former lead singer Tony Sheridan was being nursed through a high fever by Billy Thorpe and the Aztecs.

George makes his first Sydney balcony appearance — sans trousers.

Age was no barrier for Beatle worship, as sixty-one-years-old Mrs. L. Howard of Kings Cross exhibited.

The Chevron Hotel was rendered virtually inoperable by fans and film crews.

ejection by a timely intervention of John.

After finally extricating themselves from an insatiable room of reporters who would have cheerfully asked questions till the same time the next day if not shown the door, the Beatles retreated to the sanctuary of their penthouse suite. Fan club president Angela Letchford was summoned from the foyer with her associates for a brief meeting. "I gave them giant sheets of paper and they each scribbled miles of autographs. They seemed honestly interested in the club and asked us lots of questions about how we ran it. They told us to get in touch with England if we had any problems or needed anything. They gave us Cokes and we watched TV for a while."

Exhausted by the afternoon's ordeal, they stayed in their suite to eat dinner and watch Dave Allen on TV. Jimmy again suffered from itchy feet and so made his way to Chequers nightclub to catch Frances Faye. Faye was advised of his presence and within minutes of opening her set had enlisted the audience's aid in enticing him behind the drum kit. Although he had never seen her perform, Nicol picked up every beat and when he rose to return to his seat, a giant cry of disappointment persuaded him to continue. He ended up playing more than two

How the Beatles saw Macleay Street from their balcony.

When radio had the audacity to play records by artists other than the Beatles, fans took matters into their own hands.

Sydney's press photographers used more film on this young miss than the Beatles!

Full-bodied bellows failed to entice the Beatles to the balcony. But then half the fun was the yelling.

Finally, an appearance from above.

Jimmy Nicol being fetched from the Sheraton Hotel by second cousin Gladys Richardson. Mal Evans sees him safely to the car.

Jimmy Nicol working out at Chequers nightclub with Frances Faye.

There were tense moments while this frightened girl was helped down from a high ledge by an equally frightened policeman. She had been attempting to gain illicit entry to the penthouse suite.

Distant cousins Pamela, Suzanne and Billy exhibit proof of their Beatle loyalty to temporary moptop Jimmy Nicol.

hours of a set that normally expired in under ninety minutes. The night was wrapped up with a ten-minute finale that had the house on its collective feet, cheering, clapping and shouting. While head waiter Andre shouted in glee, "This is wonderful, we have a million pound act for nothing," Frances concocted a closer which chanted "Beatles, Beatles, Beatles every day now, it's Beatles all the way now." Asked how he picked up on her repertoire so adroitly, Jimmy said, "She's got soul man."

While Jimmy was bashing away merrily downtown, Paul McCartney was being thwarted in his attempts to take a walk around Kings Cross. All evening the hotel switchboard had been jammed with calls from as far away as London, New Zealand and Tasmania, and tenacious fans had repeatedly tried police patience by climbing trees, edging along ledges, making blind dashes through open doors,

producing amateurishly fake passes and maintaining a constant crescendo of screams.

But by 11.35 p.m. as Paul walked out of the Sheraton lift wearing a raincoat he imagined that most of the mayhem had abated. One look at the fifty fans standing in the rain on the steps of the Chevron changed his mind and he returned glumly to his room.

The night was not entirely without its compensations though. That evening, and indeed every evening of the tour, the Beatles partook of one pleasure they had discovered in Hamburg as unknown teenagers and developed to an obsessive sport over the next three years.

Lennon, in particular, must have been consumed with perverse delight by the grand confidence trick which he and his colleagues were perpetrating upon the whole western world. By day they won the hearts of mum, dad and the garden gnome with their cheeky, innocent

Before the questions flow, photographers pose the four for a seemingly endless shower of shots.

What kind of girls does Paul like? "The female ones."

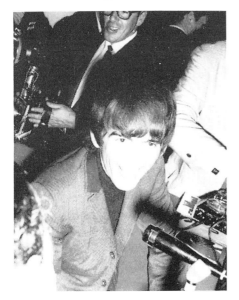

Genial George gushing away to eager reporters.

Besieged on the mauve semi-circular divan of the Sheraton Hotel's conference suite.

charm and by night, according to more than a few observers, they hurled themselves in bacchanalian orgies beyond the comprehension of the humble folk who paid them homage. The "satyricon" scenes which John referred to in an Australian context in his milestone 1971 interview with Rolling Stone's Jann Wenner certainly did occur, though such was the wall of absolute secrecy that only those tour party members accepted into an exclusive inner-sanctum ever witnessed them.

Tour manager Ravenscroft carefully concedes, "They had girls in their room, yes. That was in the hands of Mal Evans, who was very good at picking the right girls. It was all very discreet and well organised. When they were getting involved in that sort of thing I kept right out of the way."

"That sort of thing" is more frankly explained by journalist Jim Oram: "John and Paul, particularly, rooted themselves silly. A seemingly endless and inexhaustible stream of Australian girls passed through their beds; the very young, the very experienced, the beautiful and the plain. In fact, I can vividly remember one spoilt virgin in Adelaide who proudly took her bloodstained sheet home with her in the morning."

"Yes it all went on, and more," admits Bob Rogers, "there were just so many women. The boys never, to my knowledge, repeated the dose. They'd rather have a less attractive woman than the same one

twice. They had become supremely indifferent to it all, as women and girls continually prostrated themselves in their presence. You see I'd always thought that the one great thing about womanizing was the challenge and I couldn't believe it could be so casual. Rather than getting into hallucinogenic drugs, I was convinced that they would all end up homosexuals, out of sheer boredom with conventional sex. There was no pill in 1964 and with the amount of Beatle screwing that went on I just can't believe that there wasn't an explosion of little Beatles all over Australia in 1965. Maybe there was."

Jim Oram has a theory in that regard: "John once told me, 'We've got the best cover in the world. If a girl comes home after being out all night and breaks down under the old man's questioning and admits that she had spent the night with one of the Beatles, he tells her not to lie and goes up the road to kick the bum of the boy next door.' It must have worked because there were no instances of angry parents on the tour, which was almost unbelievable."

One young Queensland girl, who married a prominent Woollahra stockbroker and is now a pillar of Sydney society, kept cocktail party guests amused throughout most of the sixties with her graphic descriptions of being screwed by all four Beatles in the one night. Apparently, advancing years have quietened her boast.

The procuring of sex partners for the Beatles was a carefully

A little bewildered by the attention, Jimmy obliges one reporter with an autograph.
"Actually, it's for my kids . . ."

Paul becomes a gravitation point for most of the female media persons.

In good humour for the first encounter with an Australian press conference — an ordeal known to destroy lesser mortals.

planned procedure. It was usually Mal Evans' job to go downstairs and select the likely candidates. After he had done his "you and you and you and, oh alright, you too" routine, the sweet young things were corralled in a holding room. It was from this reservoir that Derek and Neil allocated a continual supply of carnal delight to the tour members who subscribed to the service. One reporter, who wishes to remain nameless, was midway through a blissful union when Derek Taylor sauntered into the room casually enquiring, "Would anyone like to meet John Lennon?" "The girl slipped out from under me so quickly that I was left doing push-ups on the bed," he wryly recalls.

The odd perversion or diversion was certainly not out of the question. Beginning in Melbourne, some mild excremental sports were apparently engaged in and an amusing variety of copulation locations and combinations investigated. Some of these fringe benefits were generously extended to the less famous members of the tour party, provided they had been admitted into the inner-sanctum. Dave Lincoln of the Phantoms explains: "The supports did get the overspill of girls. We were forbidden to pick up any girls ourselves though. We only had to ask and they were provided, through the correct channels."

Fans on their way to school and unrelenting reporters beat the alarm clocks in the Sheraton penthouse on Friday morning. After breakfasting and packing, John gazed down at the street and confided in a writer, "I wish they'd go to school, they make me feel guilty standing there like that. I mean standing out in all that rain and muck,

well you'd have to be crazy wouldn't you? I think they're wonderful," he added softly, "I wish I could be down there with them."

Over the other side of town, the *Sun's* presses were running off a glowing editorial which declared, "Their press conference showed that teenagers are not necessarily fools when it comes to picking winners. One cannot 'ready' a press conference. Questions are asked and answered off the cuff very quickly . . . they showed considerable insight into the secret of their own success." Quite simply, the four lads from Liverpool had won over Sydney, lock, stock and geriatrics.

The only slightly critical editorial came from the *Daily Telegraph*, which took pains to point out: "Not everything that comes out of Liverpool is a Beatle. Other notable products are Mr. Harold Wilson, likely to be Britain's next PM; Bessie Braddock, Britain's bouncing woman MP; Nicholas Monsarrat, who wrote *The Cruel Sea;* and Tom Bell, the newest British film star. Liverpool also has the Everton soccer team and Brenda Blacker, Miss England 1964. There'll be a Liverpool long after the shrieks have died away."

One point that generally went unnoticed was that, down the hall from the Beatles, in bed with a 103 degree temperature, lay Tony Sheridan, the singer with whom the Beatles had cut their first recordings. In Sydney to commence a tour with Billy Thorpe and the Aztecs and Digger Revell, Sheridan made no attempt to establish contact with his former comrades, nor they with him. A sole reporter who looked him up claimed that he was pleased that his former backing band had done so well but that he certainly wasn't trying to jump on their bandwagon.

The convoy back to Mascot Airport met disaster in the rain when the driver of the first car took a wrong turn into a Kings Cross side street, braked suddenly and collected the other cars up his rear. After an embarrassing ten-minute delay to disentangle the vehicles, the trek continued. In marked contrast to the previous morning, only fifteen or so fans were on hand, well outnumbered by almost 100 reporters and airline personnel. The only notable incident, carried in large headlines in absence of anything more newsworthy, was the actions of fifteen-year-old Arncliffe schoolgirl Mary Kostin, who leapt the barrier in her maroon and grey school uniform and set out for the Beatle car on the tarmac. Moving like a rugby league winger, she side-stepped a series of police tackles before being held just ten feet from the car by a senior Commonwealth Police officer. Screaming loudly, she hurled a copy of John's *In His Own Write* book high in the air, lobbing it quite accidently on George's shoulder. As she was being carted back to the barrier howling, "Did they get my book? Did they get my book?" the four Beatles autographed it and sent it back to her. As it eventuated, Mary became one of the very few Australians able to establish the authenticity of her Beatle autographs. Precious few of the autographed books, photographs, letters, 'thank you' notes and records which emerged from Beatle quarters scrawled upon ever came

With his batwing cape laundered and pressed, Paul arrives in the Sheraton lobby ready to depart for the airport.

A cheerful Friday morning greeting to Sydney: all moptops neatly groomed.

One incorrigible girl had to be bundled into the back of a police car to keep her off the tarmac.

The first fans arrive at Mascot just after dawn to witness the departure to Adelaide.

Commonwealth Police were kept busy all morning by barrier breakers.

near a real moptop. Neil Aspinall could sign John, Paul, Ringo, George or even Jimmy's name with more ease than he signed his own. At a pinch, Mal Evans and Derek Taylor could produce a passable facsimile, a process which was also picked up by Bob Rogers to justify his constant presence. This fairly common procedure is now giving headaches

Sydney press photographers grab final shots on the tarmac.

Neil Aspinall (second from left) hurries his boys past shouting fans to the aircraft.

A last look at Sydney through bleary eyes.

to auctioneers who steadfastly refuse to acknowledge the possibility that their outrageously priced objects d'art might be bogus.

Taking advantage of the distraction, another three girls — who had been put on their honour by Supt. Davies not to create any problems — sprinted into the arms of police officers within scant feet of the aircraft. The girls burst into tears when spoken to by Davies after they had been returned to the right side of the barrier. Indeed, there was precious little else for the twenty Commonwealth and fifty state police

George sneaks back with his new Japanese camera to capture some memories of Sydney in the rain.

Those brave ladies willing to face a boss's reprimand staying at the barriers until the aircraft is in the air.

to do as they stood about feeling silly in the drizzle.

Before leaving Sydney, instructions were sent to Adelaide that four girls be placed on "standby" to accompany the Beatles during "relaxation periods." They were to be "attractive, healthy, typically Australian girls — intelligent, respectable and easy to talk to." Bob Rogers smirks at the seemingly innocent directive. "In Sydney I actually saw a parent encourage his sixteen-year-old daughter to meet the Beatles. I was aghast because I knew just what 'meet the Beatles' could mean."

As the direct flight set out over Botany Bay and headed south west, George Harrison was not a confident man. "Some lightning flashed along the wings and he went as white as a sheet," says Jim Oram. (Interestingly, Dave Lincoln recalls, "George had an incredible fear of being killed, which possibly accounted for the shell he withdrew into. When a kid in Brisbane threw a tin on stage it freaked him right out.") As the flight progressed, George regained his calm and began snapping everyone in the first class cabin with a fisheye lens Nikon camera he had bought in Hong Kong.

The hostess in charge of the Beatles on this chartered Ansett ANA Vickers Viscount was twenty-two-year-old Margaret Paul, an avid Fab Four fan. "The Senior Regional Hostess knew how crazy I was about them so it didn't take too much pleading to get her to give me the assignment," she explains. "They were in the first class compartment with their own people and the economy class section was filled with about thirty newsmen, who kept creeping up the aisle to try and get interviews.

"The airline had prepared all these expensive savouries with caviar and oysters but all they wanted was peanut butter sandwiches.

*Some errant schoolgirls
quite easily deterred
by security men.*

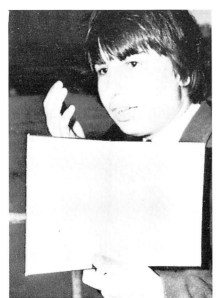

*Paul McCartney's two watches: one set
to Eastern Standard Time, the other to
Greenwich Mean.*

*Mary Kostin displays her autographed
"In His Own Write."*

*George was allowed into the cockpit of the
Ansett ANA jet as it passed over southwestern
New South Wales.*

John came to the galley area himself to ask for them and I nearly fell over. I thought he was one of the most beautiful men I'd ever seen . . . Before they left the plane they all autographed a sick bag for me, which I presented to my fourteen-year-old sister, who promptly lost it."

Jimmy Nicol sat beside Ernie Sigley, quietly revealing that he was not very fond of Ringo as a musician. "I don't think he can play in time," he candidly revealed in a hushed whisper. Meanwhile, John was busy with a pad and pen working out a set for their first Australian concerts. "He quizzed us all on which of their records had been hits where and which were the best known and most popular," says Sigley. "He took all that very seriously."

Paul chatted with Bob Rogers, explaining, "Sometimes I like to go on little sightseeing tours at night. You never know, one day I'll make it." Watching the rain gradually disappear, he quipped, "Sydney wasn't very good weather, was he? I think it must be the mongoose season. But apparently it should be a bit better in Adelaide."

It was. As they peered out of the portholes on descent into the South Australian capital the Beatles were able to clearly read two giant white signs in the quadrangle of Thebarton Girls' High School painted with the words, "Welcome Beatles." Even so, Paul was wondering if there would be anybody at the airport to meet them.

3: ADELAIDE

Initially, it was not intended that the Beatles visit Adelaide during their East Coast antipodean tour. Not surprisingly, Adelaide teenagers reacted with appropriate outrage at the exclusion. The promoters simply stated that the only suitable venue was booked for an exhibition and nothing else was suitable.

Bob Francis, a young Adelaide DJ, described by himself as a "great self-publicist," threw his weight behind the protests and quickly rose to figure-head of the 'Bring The Beatles To Adelaide' movement. Francis had been playing Beatles records religiously on 5AD since late 1963 and had actually received a (supposedly) autographed letter from all four, thanking him for his support.

Late in January 1964, Francis enlisted the aid of fellow jocks Jim Slade (5DN), Warwick Prime and Roger Dowsett (5KA) and launched a petition, designed to persuade Aztec Services to add Adelaide to the tour schedule.

No war, depression or natural disaster could have so galvanised the attention and participation of Adelaide's fine citizens, as did Bob Francis' petition. Eager petitioners canvassed dances, parties, beaches, football matches, city streets and office blocks in search of signatures. A shopfront in the main street of the city (Rundle Street) was converted to a base of operations and reams of butchers' paper hung on the walls for the signatures of shoppers. One brave young fellow dodged cars at a busy intersection to collect a staggering 10,000 signatures from motorists, while a dental nurse demanded a signature from every patient in her waiting room.

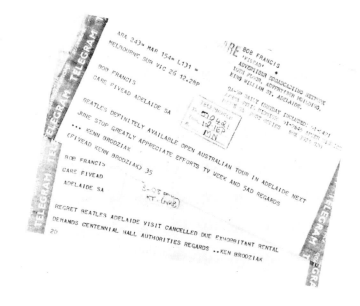

Mail by the sackload poured into 5AD, many letters containing petitions from rural areas of the state. More than 150 high school students bearing "Beatles for Adelaide" placards stopped all pedestrian traffic on mid-city streets each afternoon. The entire city seemed to be ensnared by the excitement; a newspaper street poll of thirty average people reported a support level of twenty-six (including a clergyman).

The enthusiasm was not altogether unanimous. One of the four street dissenters, a 'young woman,' said, "They are crazy, they should be locked up and given a prison haircut," while a correspondent to a daily newspaper wrote, "I earnestly plead with all those Adelaide citizens who still retain any semblance of sanity and who find it painful listening to a group with voices like wailing banshees and heads like old mops, to unite with me and we will present our own petition asking that they go and torture somebody else."

Within two weeks, more than twice the target had been achieved with an incredible 80,000 signatures. Aztec Services' Kenn Brodziak described the truckload of paper as "fabulous, exciting and wonderful" and agreed to "see what can be done." He wired London requesting a one-day extension on the tour and, when positive response was received, telegrammed Bob Francis on March 15 with the good news. Francis went to air screaming "The Beatles are coming to Adelaide!" and there was much rejoicing in the streets.

Eight days later another telegram arrived from Brodziak, stating: "Regret Beatles Adelaide visit cancelled due to exhorbitant rental demands by Centennial Hall authorities." Francis recalls, "I got on air and told the kids that the Beatles weren't coming to Adelaide because of the Royal Agricultural and Horticultural Society. I said 'ring Ron Sedgeman, the boss, and tell him what you think of him.' They did as instructed and within moments he was inundated with abusive calls."

The Society, owners of Centennial Hall, had asked £440 a night for the Beatle shows, somewhat above the normal fee of £65 and considerably higher than the costs of larger venues in Sydney and Melbourne. After Bob Francis' tirade, the Society adopted a repentant attitude. "I have heard from the Centennial Hall people and they are upset at the bad publicity they are getting over the Beatles," gloated Brodziak. "They offered to lower the rental slightly but I don't intend to send the Beatles to Adelaide unless they start talking in terms of £100 a night." The Society declined to comment.

Meanwhile the Beatles were being kept abreast of the South Australian development. A call by Alec Martin, *TV Week's* "Beatle Editor," to the group in Miami, caught Paul exclaiming, "Those Adelaide teenagers must really be something." Brodziak was telegraphing all press headlines to London and felt confident enough to state, "The Beatles are watching news of their Australian tour with great interest, especially in Adelaide, as word of an 80,000 signature petition appears to have thrilled them."

An "extremely brisk and businesslike" Diana Verco, Brian Epstein's London secretary, told a caller from the Adelaide *Advertiser*, "Oh what a shame! I'm afraid that proprietors are putting up the prices of places where the group is to appear. We are getting petitions here every day from all over the world — all demanding that the group sings here or there." Kim Bonython, Adelaide representative of Aztec Services, made regular announcements that he was going all he could to sort out the problems with venue availability and pricing.

No real progress was made until Bob Francis and Ron Tremain took matters into their own hands. Tremain was editor of *Young Modern*, a frighteningly rightist 'teenager' magazine, and also the organiser of a local dance called The Princeton Club which was held in the auditorium of John Martin's department store. He and Francis suggested to store director Ian Hayward that an enormous amount of publicity could be derived from sponsoring the Beatles' visit to Adelaide.

Hayward agreed, although he doubted that any profit could be made on the deal. But, with an instinctive eye for the PR value among the younger end of the market, he empowered Tremain to go to Melbourne and negotiate with Kenn Brodziak. Now, in order to get the Beatles to accept any further dates on top of their contracted agreement, Brodziak had been required to offer a fairly reasonable enticement. That enticement was almost all the profits from the four shows (which came to around £12,000 — more than they were earning for the rest of the tour). So when Tremain came in and said that John Martin's was willing to become the promoter of the Adelaide performances and assume most of the inherant responsibilities (notably financial), Brodziak had no hesitation in accepting.

Bob Francis with Mersey forerunners Gerry and the Pacemakers.

Being an absolute pillar of the Adelaide community, John Martin's was able to sort out the rental problem with the Royal Agricultural and Horticultural Society quietly and decisively. Once the dates were firmed and an agreement signed, the store, Tremain and Francis (an emerging hero of the city) hurled themselves into an unabashed campaign of saturation promotion. Francis became a TV star, presenting a half-hour programme on ADS 7 called "Yeah Yeah Yeah," featuring footage from England. John Martin's respected name lent the overall promotion a great deal of respectability in the eyes of adults, a factor that would have enormous repercussions later.

Ticket sales in Sydney and Brisbane opened on April 13 but, even though the first concerts were in Adelaide, South Australians could not begin purchasing until the following Monday, the 20th. Whereas the eastern state ticket queues had been in the hundreds, Adelaide gave notice of things to come with lines comprising some 3000 campers. Snaking out from John Martin's Rundle Street department store, one queue extended 600 yards down Rundle Street, east to Gawler Place, south to Grenfell Street and east to Adelaide Arcade. A spectacle not previously seen in the small city, it drew a reputed quarter million sight-seers who drove in from all over the state to observe the strange happening. Not even the annual John Martin's Christmas Pageant had ever drawn such a multitude of onlookers.

This world record for Beatle ticket queueing got off to an unfortunate start on Friday evening when two 21 year old labourers began assaulting people in the line outside the North Terrace store. Apprehended by police, they appeared in court the following morning and were each sentenced to fourteen days' hard labour. Good natured larrikinism was prevalent throughout the sixty to seventy hour wait; on North Terrace, passing motorbikes and hot rods tossed mice and stink

The Francis Signature Seekers.

Bob Francis and two of his army of Beatle Brigade followers.

bombs among the blanketed ticket buyers and their sea of transistor radios.

A number of mothers queued in shifts with their offspring, each grabbing a few hours of sleep in nearby parked cars. A Mrs. Hunt of Glenelg revealed that she was not waiting in the line just to help her children — she was also buying a good seat for herself.

The tedium was relieved a little by Bob Francis and his fellow jocks who set up a makeshift broadcast unit from the North Terrace store foyer and ran Stomp Sessions. Speakers were set up on the street and the huge gathering began to resemble an electrocuted conga chain. It was, indeed, as the press described it,"'One great noisy colourful, exhausting, messy spectable. A social event without parallel in S.A."

One man who was not pleased with the frivolity was the Rector of the Holy Trinity Anglican Church, Reverend Lance Shilton. He saw it all as a cheap publicity stunt which capitalised on the susceptibility of superficial teenagers in need of strong leadership. "The community and commercial world which establishes teenagers as VIPs for the purpose of gain should be reminded by Christian people that we are very concerned about the moral implications," he admonished.

By the time the ticket offices opened, at 7 a.m. (thirty minutes early) several fans had been taken to hospital suffering from exhaustion. One sixteen-year-old boy was reported to have suffered a heart attack — an event which gave ammunition to some conservative pockets of the media. Orderly to the end, the bedraggled kids were admitted to the store by police in groups of twenty. The staff at Allans Ltd., the third outlet, were so impressed by the restraint that they extended a burst of spontaneous handclapping.

The first person to buy a ticket was a university student called Judy who had been queueing in shifts with friends since early Friday afternoon. "I've got front row seats," she boasted as she rushed off to a lecture. The first boy to get tickets was seventeen-year-old Bruce Kelly, who had been unrelieved in the line since 2 p.m. on Friday. Although he had slept for only a quarter of an hour during his long ordeal, he insisted, "I couldn't walk straight this morning but I feel better now I've got my tickets so I'm off to work." One girl, after buying her precious passes to heaven, stripped off black slacks and jumper to reveal a school uniform.

All 12,000 tickets, worth £22,000, were sold in under five hours. Police then warned that there would be no box office operating at the shows and that they would be arresting any scalpers or loiterers.

Film of the soggy Sydney arrival and interviews by Ernie Sigley was screened on Adelaide TV on the night of Thursday, August 11, and

Awaiting the opening of advance ticket sales; well equipped with radios, harmonicas, blankets, hot coffee and enthusiasm.

radio announcers were challenging local fans to show a warmer welcome than the Sydneysiders. Police Superintendent J.A. Vogelesang announced that police reinforcements were being brought in from country areas. He also announced that no fans would be allowed on airport property.

As the chartered Ansett ANA jet taxied towards the antiquated Adelaide terminal building at 11.57 a.m. on Friday June 12, the first thing the Beatles spotted, and commented on derisively, was the absence of fans. "Why don't you let the kids into the airport?" demanded John as he stood blinking at the top of the stairs. "Yeah we want to see the kids," George insisted. As the four descended onto the tarmac, washed with bright warm sunlight, Paul spied the Ford Convertible, quadily painted with their names. "It's got Ringo's name on it but he's not here," he complained.

For the next few minutes, the Beatles scrawled upon a succession of autograph books and scraps of paper thrust at them by airway hostesses, ground staff and reporters. Police then called a halt and they were loaded into the car. Two police motor cycles, the open Ford, the Brodziak/Lean/Taylor/Ravenscroft limousine, two vans with Mal and Neil and six ancillary vehicles comprised the cavalcade, which moved towards the rarely used exit gates on Tapley's Hill Road. There the Beatles saw all the kids they wanted and, for the next nine miles, more human beings than they would ever see on one occasion at any point

Early stages of the ticket queues.

The City Council and its street sweepers were critical of the refuse left by queuers.

in their careers.

As the convoy inched down the road towards the Anzac Highway, the red-faced Beatles witnessed a degree of adulation that was new, even to them. Wildly waving and squealing fans of all ages lined the road up to six deep, standing on parked cars and swinging out of trees. Progress ceased at regular intervals as police battled to clear a way through the surging, spilling mass. Police estimates of the motorcade route crowd was 200,000 plus.

EMI National Promotions Manager Kevin Ritchie, travelling in the car with Taylor and Ravenscroft, described the scene: "They were very emotional; 12,000 miles away from home and this was happening. We all felt like members of the royal family as we waved to the crowd — all the mums, dads, kids, babies, and even cripples who had been placed in the front line. Declared or not, I would say that the whole of Adelaide had a public holiday on that Friday — there couldn't have been anybody in any sort of industry or school that day. The whole city had come to a complete halt to welcome the Beatles." Ravenscroft adds: "Nobody wanted to be left out, there were even blind people waving their white sticks at us."

At the Town Hall, scenes of unprecedented, unexplainable and quite unbelievable madness were unfolding. Not even London during the blitz had seen such a cacophonic panorama. The barriers were crowded and beginning to give way at 10 a.m. as thousands of sons, daughters, mothers, fathers, grandmothers, grandfathers, uncles, aunts and spotted dogs battled each other for prime positions. The agile perched precariously on tree branches, building ledges, telephone poles, traffic lights, truck tops and roofs. The police found themselves unable to wade through the seething walls of humanity to order the climbers down.

By 12.30 p.m. all streets intersecting King William Street were closed off by police, as the inner city numbers climbed to around 30,000. Casualties were surprisingly light. A sixty-year-old woman fainted, four girls were trampled, a boy ran into the side of a moving bus, and a girl burned her leg on the exhaust pipe of a police motorbike.

Though it appeared that every upstanding citizen of Adelaide was smitten hopelessly with Beatlemania, such was not the case. Conservative educationalists, employing supression tactics that would not have been out of place on the Gulag Archipelago, managed to remove many thousands of potential welcomers from the front lines.

Adelaide Girls High School students suffered the worst. In (more than twenty) letters delivered to the *News* they pointed out that, although only two streets away from the motorcade passage, they were confined to a small central yard. "I am a prisoner at Adelaide Girls High Prison," one letter read. "They barred the gates and guarded them with prefects. All that was missing was loaded rifles. Inside the school we had demonstrations and even fights. Some colleges came from the other side of town but we girls were not allowed to go 220 yards in our lunch hour. Yet we had to walk more than a mile and stand in sweltering heat for over two hours to see the Queen."

At Walford Church of England Grammer School in Unley 200 senior students staged a sit down strike when teachers confiscated their transistor radios during the arrival description. They sat on the asphalt playground chanting, "We Want The Beatles," until teachers persuaded them to return to classes. Headmistress Miss N. Morrison curtly explained to a reporter that "transistors are banned from the school."

Brighton High School students slow-clapped during assembly and inserted "yeah yeah yeah" into the school hymn. Four students from Port Adelaide Technical High School rang the Education Department three times requesting permission to see the Beatles parade. "They put the phone down in our ears the third time," said one incredulously.

Of course, not every school became an instant internment centre. Quite a few headmasters took advantage of the very obscure Arbor Day to grant their students a half day holiday (to the best of educated opinion, there is no other known instance of Australians celebrating the tree planting day in such a manner).

Plympton High School headmaster Mr. J.G. Goldsworthy sent circulars to parents inviting them to give written permission for their children to leave school grounds to see the Beatles and got a response of ninety-five per cent. "I have no objections at all to these four young gentlemen," he said. "The highway is only a hundred yards from the school and the procession does fall completely within the school lunch-break." Adelaide Boys High students were allowed to line both sides of Anzac Highway and girls from Vermont Technical High School were permitted to walk a mile to the route.

Inspector Wilson of the Traffic Division criticised the lack of control of schoolchildren grouped along the highway, suggesting that teachers should have exercised more control. What he didn't realise was that far more control than was reasonable was being wielded just streets away.

From Anzac Highway, the motorcade wound through West Terrace, North Terrace and King William Street, the estimated forty-minute journey taking a little over an hour and clocking in at a mean 9 mph. From North Terrace the bursting crowds caused nightmarish headaches. Police on foot, motorbikes and horses formed a ring around the car and struggled to clear a driveable space before it. Inch by inch

Moving off the Adelaide airport tarmac toward Tapley's Hill Road in
an open American convertible.

The convoy comes to repeated stops in North Terrace,
as police fight to clear citizens out of the path of the cars.

Creeping along Anzac Highway.

the beseiged vehicle moved toward the beckoning iron gates of the
Town Hall.

"Outside the Town Hall, the kids were physically lifting the cars
off the road," says Ernie Sigley. Adelaide is the most English city in
Australia, particularly around the migrant area of Elizabeth, but it does
have a reputation as 'the city of churches,' a bastion of Victorian
decorum. Such an outpouring of unrestrained fervour was, therefore, all
the more unbelievable. But it was happening, as newsreels, newspapers
and the Beatles themselves would later attest.

Ten council employees were required to edge open the gates and
allow the battered car entry. Once safe inside, the four were escorted
to the Lord Mayor's chambers for their first civic reception in Australia.

Out on the balcony it was as much Bob Francis' moment of glory
as the Beatles'. He scurried about, back and forth, positioning each
moptop and pointlessly urging the crowd of 30,000 to quieten down.
With a reasonable PA set up, he was able to briefly interview each of
the obviously shell-shocked Beatles. George yelled, "Hello! Hello! It's
marvellous, it's fabulous, the best reception ever." Jimmy got a medium
response when introduced, with some booing evident. Carried away by
the moment he gushed, "Oh this is the best I've ever seen anywhere in
the world!" John had real difficulty putting his words together. His

voice wavered emotionally as he declared, "Yes it's definitely the best
we've ever been to, it's great [a huge swell of vocal approval], it's
marvellous." Told there were only a million people in the State, he
butted in with, "and they're all here aren't they?" For Paul, it might
just as well have been another concert stage in yet another nameless
city. Slickly he spruiked, "Hello everybody. How are you, alright?
Thank you very much. It's marvellous . . . this is fantastic, thank you."

Inside the Town Hall, the Beatles faced ninety friends of friends.
In the sombre Queen Adelaide room, normally reserved for visiting
dignitaries, they spent twenty-five minutes chatting to Mayor Irwin and
his wife and were presented with (still more) toy koala bears. Welcoming them, the good Mayor said, "We are delighted to have you in
Adelaide and for having turned on a better day for you than they did in
Sydney." Sipping orange juice and Cokes, the group responded to cries
of "speech" by shoving John forward to state once more, "We are
pleased to be here. It's the best welcome we've ever had."

After the Mayor had got Paul to autograph an Oliphant cartoon
from the Advertiser, the four were smuggled out through a back
entrance of the Land Titles Office into a waiting car on Flinders Street
and off to the squat two-storey South Australian Hotel on North
Terrace. It was twenty minutes before the street throng woke up to the
deception. Meanwhile, police chiefs were beating their chests loudly.
Mounted Police Inspector J.F. Crawley said it was the proudest day of
his life. Deputy Commissioner Mr. G.M. Leane said, "I am proud of the
way in which the police and crowds conducted themselves. It was a
credit to Adelaide." Supt. Vogelesang thanked teenagers for their co-
operation, and Inspector E.L. Calder, in charge of the Town Hall

operations, thanked the Beatles for waving from both sides of the balcony.

Bob Francis went to the hotel with the Beatles and for the next two days made certain he was out of their presence for as little time as possible. He had booked the suite next door to the four and a landline was installed so that he could do hourly interviews and descriptions direct to air. "I had these four large blowups of the boys," he reveals, "and if ever there wasn't enough hysteria when it was time for an on-air segment, I just stuck one of these out on the balcony and the kids went crazy enough for it to sound great on air."

At the press conference John repeated, with a little less visible emotion, "It's the best welcome we've had anywhere in the world." But didn't they say that everywhere they went? "No, we say 'It compares very favourably with those elsewhere.' This is easily the best."

Told that the British police had credited them with helping combat juvenile delinquency, John guardedly replied, "We don't preach to anyone but we are glad to hear that we are helping the problem." Asked who had invented the chant of "yeah, yeah, yeah," he said that many other rockers, including Elvis, had been using it for years. "I forget whether Paul or I thought of using it in a song. It was six months ago, that's a long time." Quizzed about Hong Kong he revealed that he had bought Cynthia a jade ring in the city but added, "I don't know if it's any good." He also revealed that he rang his wife almost every night but that he usually rang "at the wrong times when everybody's in bed. But Paul's rectified this problem by wearing two watches." Did he imagine that there would be kangaroos in Australian streets? "No, but I thought that there would be skyscrapers around the water and then desert inside." The conference was then wrapped up with an assurance that Ringo would be definitely arriving in Australia on Sunday morning and would be waiting for them when they reached Melbourne.

Unlike other cities, where the crowds would substantially dissolve after each balcony appearance, the hordes remained constant outside the Southern Australia Hotel, keeping up a twenty-four hour chant of "We Want The Beatles." "There was no way you could get a good night's sleep," says Kevin Ritchie. "There was the constant noise which drove you up the wall. It was like a Chinese water torture. There was the temptation to check out and go to another hotel across town but the worry that we might miss something kept us all at the nerve centre."

"They'd get bored," related Bob Francis, "walk out on the balcony for a wave, see the crowds, come back in and go 'Fuuuuuuck! What is this all about?' We'd laugh, listen to John tell jokes, drink and play around but we never talked about what was outside the window. John would say, 'We're here so let's have a drink and a chat, nothing's different,' and I'm sure he meant it. George wasn't able to handle it like that, it seemed to upset him a bit."

"I found George wandering around the hotel feeling desperately homesick just after the press conference," says Ritchie. "He was feeling a little bit left out and a bit overcome by the welcome. He said he desperately wanted to get home." George had, it seems, had an argument of sorts with Patti Boyd just before leaving England and the silence hurt the most when the others rang their respective lovelies each night.

But for John and Paul at least, there were the usual diversions to ward off homesickness. "They let the girls they wanted get to them," says Francis. "Top class models and other choice pieces. With all this at their feet their attitude was very cynical. They referred to all the girls who got to them as 'fuckin' molls.' they didn't respect any of them."

Like a great many other media figures who got close to the Beatles in all parts of the world, Bob Francis suddenly had more friends than he could cope with. "People that I hadn't seen in five years would ring me up and say 'Bob, you probably don't remember me but . . .' and ask for free tickets or a chance to meet the Beatles. You see, they'd bignote themselves to their friends by boasting 'Bob Francis — my best mate. He'll introduce me to the Beatles, no sweat,' and they got a very rude shock when I told them where to go . . . to buy tickets that is.

"I did take a few autograph books to Neil Aspinall to see if he could get the boys to sign then. He just looked at me contemptuously and snarled 'Oh fuck man, don't be stupid. I do all the autographs inside the hotels. They don't do any,' and then sat down and knocked them all over in a few seconds. I wasn't naive but things like that came as a great surprise back in 1964."

Australia's first experience of the Beatles in concert (covered in specific detail in chapter 8) was, to put it mildly, unlike any visual spectacular staged before it. Journalists from all over Australia had flown in for the 6 p.m. and 8 p.m. shows and more than one was to be seen skulking out mid-set with a mortified visage and hands planted firmly over ears. Jimmy Nicol was in an emotional state and flayed the skins relentlessly; giving Australia something to remember him by. The other three Beatles were visibly overjoyed at the uninhibited reaction of the Adelaide fans.

That night the Beatles slighted Adelaide society by failing to make an appearance at an exclusive party in the Adelaide hills, twenty miles

The first official public appearance in Adelaide, on the balcony of the Town Hall with king rock jock Bob Francis.

Manning the city barricades on a brilliantly sunny Adelaide Friday.

Inching towards the gates of the Town Hall. Jimmy returns a welcome.

from the city. A Viennese chef had spent more than three weeks preparing some £500 worth of exotic food and had even created two new dishes, including replicas of the four musicians carved out of boiled eggs.

Up in the hills they waited, Adelaide's elite, the four "British Dolly Birds" chosen to be Beatle companions and a vast media/industry pool, including Ernie Sigley, Bob Francis, Alec Martic, Ron Tremain and Jim Oram. But when the food began to get cold and the likelihood of an exalted presence became more remote, Chef Gelenscer declared the party "on" and the guests hungrily tucked into lobsters, hams and caviar.

Unconcerned, the Beatles were in their hotel suite with TV compere Bob Moors and a few of his ADS 7 associates, having a quiet party. "I had told them of the secret society party and they were not enthusiastic," Moors explained. "They said they wanted something more private where they could relax, not be stared at and not have to answer the usual questions. I suggested a little get-together at the hotel and they agreed." Dave Lincoln has a slightly different slant: "They were such regular guys that they didn't want to do a lot of things unless everybody, all the supports and workers, were invited along as well. That's why they said no to that ritzy Adelaide party."

After a midnight meal of soft boiled eggs, steaks, chicken and salad, the Beatles retired at 3 a.m. Out in the street, the faithful were jealously guarding their prime positions, ready for Saturday's balcony appearances. Younger fans bagan arriving at dawn, helping to increase the volume of the endless chant, "We Want The Beatles." Blissfully unaware, four fatigued Beatles slept soundly through till midday and beyond.

In other parts of the hotel, four bitterly disappointed girls were preparing to check out. They had taken two £9 rooms for the night in the hope of meeting their idols. Christine Limpus, 18 of Hectorville and Julie Williams, 16 of Wingfield made it as far as the doorway of the Beatles' suite on Friday night before being ordered back downstairs. As they left the hotel just before noon, without having seen so much as a strand of hair, Julie pouted miserably, "It isn't fair. I bet they weren't even told we were here. And I'll bet they don't know that my birthday is two days after Paul's and that we're both left handed and that we both have brown eyes and hair. I bet they don't!"

The other two hotel guests were just a little bit smarter. Seventeen year-old Heni Timmers and sixteen-year-old Anne Aucott of Mitchell Park tarried a little and managed to collar a security guard. Apparently touched by their blubbering, he made enquiries and secured a meeting for them later in the day.

Thirty miles away, on the banks of the Murray River, steaks sizzled by an elaborate weekender, made from four old Adelaide trolley buses. The barbeque was the second 'official' Beatle social function, approved by John Martin's. It was also the second party that the Beatles themselves chose to ignore, despite some prodding from their inner circle. "I was kind of hoping that the boys would go out," said Derek Taylor. "They hadn't been out anywhere for a couple of weeks and I didn't want them to get stale."

Adelaide had certainly not overspent itself welcoming the Beatles. Charged with new energy, the citizenry mounted another staggering display of worship all throughout Saturday. By noon, the crowd outside the South Australia Hotel was teetering around the 4000 mark. Most of them packed the steps of Parliament House and few even found ways of entering the locked building.

The Beatles arose with ferocious appetites and sent room service scurrying for "a luvly kingside steak, orange juice, cornflakes, and lashings of eggs, sausages and bacon." Outside their window, police were pursuing a lad who had scaled a pole and was heading toward the balcony. The crowd roared support and loudly booed the police when they apprehended the climber.

During the distraction, a girl in tight black jeans and a purple pullover elbowed police and hotel staff and set off on a dash through the saloon bar into the foyer. Unassailed, she tore up the plush old staircase screaming hysterically, "Where are you Paul, I want you." Finally ensnared, she was carried back down to the street sobbing and demanding, "Please let me see him, just once — please, please, please." Pacified, she returned to the street crowd, only to barge back into the saloon bar a few minutes later. But this time the police were a little more prepared. She may not have seen Paul but she certainly made herself momentarily famous. Both the *News* and the *Sunday Mail* gave her the front page.

While the impatient fans awaited the promised appearance of the young messiahs, Lloyd Ravenscroft was busily trading concessions with

Adelaide Lord Mayor Irwin chews the fat with John inside the Town Hall.

Bob Francis whipping up the crowd with needless exhortations.

John surveys the magnitude of Adelaide's welcome from a Town Hall window.

George and John with Adelaide 'Dolly Birds' Robyn McInnerney, Rosemary Carter, Val Wilson and Pat Williams.

An obliging pose with native flowers at the Adelaide press conference.

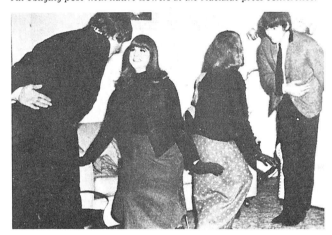

What are they doing? Your guess is as good as ours!

Inspector Wilson, who could foresee chaos when crowds from football matches and other sporting events began to make their way home later in the afternoon. "He said if I could get the boys to come out on the balcony at 4 p.m., he would block the surrounding streets and stop all traffic for fifteen minutes," recalls the tour manager.

They didn't need fifteen minutes. Emerging just before the appointed hour, they spent precisely eight and a half minutes before the assembled mass. As the four smiling, skylarking Beatles acknowledged the tumult, a new type of missile made its debut — the autograph book. A good dozen dropped onto the balcony and the Beatles carefully laid them along the edge without signing any of them.

John and Paul stood together, one playing Abbott to the other's Costello. They blew kisses, pointed smiling to signs of endearment posted on the Parliament House walls, pretended to climb over the balcony, and caught streamers. John realised he had caught one object too many as he tried to remove a sticky sweet from his hand. George and Jimmy stood to one side, waving steadily, George snapping photos with his new Nikon.

Below, the police were successfully holding the crowd behind the barriers by regularly sending squad cars along the line with sirens wailing. Then, short minutes after the madness had erupted, it subsided a few degrees as the four took a low bow and retreated back into the hotel.

"There was a certain sense of propriety among Adelaide fans," says Kenn Brodziak. "There was only a four-foot-high wrought iron gate around the hotel but it was almost religiously respected. Very few fans pushed against it or tried to climb over it."

With the time remaining until their second set of concerts, the group threw a small reception for selected admirers. Local fan club president Stuart Williams (who charged only 5s for membership) and his fellow administrators were granted an audience to present the obligatory boomerangs. Peter Findlay, a twenty-year-old Edwardstown artist, presented each Beatle with an original portrait in oils. A local hide tanner brought along a set of kangaroo skins. The two girls from Mitchell Park got their promised meeting and Derek Taylor expressed surprise at aspects of the crowd behaviour, stating, "We've never had autograph books used as missiles before. Usually the fans keep a firm hold on them."

Of course, Bob Rogers was never far away from his microphone, ready to capture his three entitled spots per day. By this point the group were familiar with the bespectacled enquirer and their responses were witty and casual. "I was just out on the balcony and there were three or four people outside, none of them waving," said Paul. "How many would you say there were John?" "About four million I think Bob." After assuring that it was a bigger reception than New York ("the hotel was a bit taller there") John said they had declined an invitation to an Australian Rules game at Adelaide Oval, extended by the secretary of the S.A. National Football League, because, "We never watch football matches."

John demanded attention while he read a telegram:" 'Did you see

WELCOME BEATLES near landing, please reply, Julie Hodgkinson, Thebarton Girls Technical School.' Well we did see it and we saw you all jumping up and down. We were waving but you couldn't see us. So thanks very much."

John said that he had read news reports about the sit-down strike and "I read also that we were only 220 yards away from one school and the kids weren't allowed out. Some people are like that. Never mind."

Finally a word from bewildered Jimmy on the eve of his final Beatle performance: "I'm looking forward to meeting Ringo tomorrow. I'm not going straight back home though, I fancy going back to Sydney for a few days."

At the hotel desk and the reception area of radio 5AD, fans not fortunate enough to be invited to the informal reception, left advance birthday presents for Paul. The parcels held mulga wood ashtrays, amateur drawings and paintings, cakes, koalas, and a brush and comb set. The hotel switchboard operator was kept busy fielding phone calls from America and all parts of Australia. Two hundred letters a day were also arriving.

By six o'clock, another car was waiting in a darkened laneway beside the hotel, ready to quietly transport the Beatles to Centennial Hall in Wayville. This time twenty fans were in wait, having sussed out the escape route. One girl took a graceless swallow dive from the bonnet of a parked car, landed on a policeman's shoulders and managed to grasp a liberal chunk of George's hair. After a brief tug of war, Harrison was pushed into the car, rubbing his head and muttering unpleasantly. Another girl snatched a dirty fragment of torn cardboard from the pavement and crammed it into her pocket, yelling excitedly, "Paul stepped on it!"

Concerts three and four again went like clockwork, with Jimmy pounding out a perfect beat. Most of the media party braved a second night of ear damage though for Ernie Sigley every moment was pure pleasure. "I was just in love with them," he declares. His recollections of the show focus on a matter of hygiene. "The place stank because the floors and seats were full of piss. Half the little girls were so excited they wet their pants."

Outside the stage door, eighteen-year-old Heather Jolly of Woodville North had arrived with a huge koala wrapped in brown paper. Waving away a proffered ballpoint pen, she produced a tube of nipple

Seventeen-year-old Helen Timmers pushed her luck with a security guard and ended up meeting the Beatles.

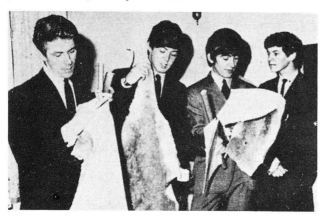

A local furrier brought a range of kangaroo skins to the hotel for Derek Taylor and the Beatles to examine and purchase.

The steps of Parliament House opposite the South Australia Hotel.

The most persistent and agile Beatle fan in Australia. This un-named lady made mockery of security measures on two occasions . . .

pink lipstick and scrawled a message of endearment, then thrust the gaudy bundle at the head usher for delivery backstage.

Before the second show had begun, Dick Lean had left for the airport to catch the last flight to Melbourne in readiness for Ringo's departure from Sydney early Sunday afternoon. Also on the flight was Bob Moors, carrying an opal ring for the drummer from the S.A. Retail Gem Trader's Association and intent upon filming an interview for his "Moors The Merrier" TV variety show.

The Saturday night party was fairly sedate. The local gentry had given up trying to entice the Beatles to their own social events and had left them in peace. Sydney journalist Jim Oram dragged the four dejected "Dolly Birds" with their ludicrous long dresses and gargantuan handbags (what fashion magazine *were* they reading?) up to the Fab Four's suite and finally got them introduced — and got himself an exclusive story.

Before leaving the hotel at 12.15 on Sunday afternoon (the day that Russia and East Germany signed a twenty year friendship pact), the Beatles asked to have their photo taken with local M.S.S. (Metropolitan Security Services) guards. Derek Taylor dashed off two letters on hotel stationery, ostensibly from the Beatles (but apparently not signed by them), addressed to the directors of John Martin's and to the Commissioner of Police Mr. J.G. McKinna — both offering thanks for facilitating an extremely successful tour.

Meanwhile, at the airport, much readiness was being effected for the flight to Melbourne. The Beatles had mentioned a liking for Edinburgh brand cigarettes, so Ansett ANA catering manager Ray Smith arranged to have some packs flown down from Sydney for the flight. He had also prepared an all-Australian banquet menu for the short leg, comprising kangaroo tail soup, Queensland mud crabs and local vegetables. The Tintara Winery sent along eight bottles of champagne to wash down the Aussie tucker (in which the four would have almost certainly been supremely disinterested). Meanwhile, in the town of Mount Gambier, local Ansett ANA officials were going on radio to announce that, despite rumours, the Beatles' plane would be flying direct, with no stopovers. And in Melbourne, GTV 9 was opening the

THE NEWS

SEE INSIDE

Amusements	14	Stars	15
Classified Ads	15	Strips	15
Odd Spot	2	Weekend TV	5

No 12,733   ADELAIDE, SATURDAY, JUNE 13, 1964   Registered in Australia for transmission by post as a newspaper   Phone 51-0351   Price 4d

AMAZING SCENES AS HOTEL BESIEGED

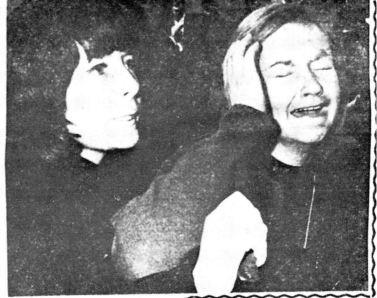

LEFT: Crying hysterically, the girl is led down the stairs by a security officer. ABOVE: Outside with the crowd the girl breaks down and sobs uncontrollably.

Thousands hysterical

Amazing scenes of uncontrolled teenage Jululation erupted into mass hysteria in delaide today as thousands of screaming, anner-waving fans besieged he Beatles' city hotel.

The swelling mob swarmed the steps of arliament House opposite and rattled the indows as the chanting and shrieking rose fever pitch.

Continued, P. 3.

● Pictures — P. 3; Concert r e v i e w; Ringo j u s t got away — P. 4.

DARING DASH

A girl overwrought with the frenzy of the crowd created an incredible scene today when she burst past police and employes to the Beatles' upstairs suite at the South Australian Hotel.

Sobbing hysterically and dressed in tight black jeans and a purple sweater, she dashed through the hotel's saloon bar into the main foyer and then up the plushly carpeted staircase screaming, "Where are you Paul, I want you."

She ran into a wall of Press and television representatives on the first floor foyer outside the Beatles rooms, but tried to force her way through. Police and hotel employes held her and carried her out to the street.

She struggled and cried hysterically, "Please let me see him once—just once—please, please, please."

Within a few minutes of being pacified she again burst back into the hotel and struggled violently before she could be carried downstairs again.

BEATLES SPECIAL

idenoch
unshine

SUNDAY MAIL

MIDNIGHT EDITION

Sunday's estimated max. temp., 62 deg.
Today's max. temp., 53.7 deg. at 1.10.

HIGHEST
CIRCULATION
IN S.A.
224,885

Serve and enjoy
TOLLEYS
SPECIAL DRY SHERI

A JOINT PRODUCT OF ADVERTISER NEWSPAPERS LTD. AND NEWS LIMITED

Adelaide, June 13, 1964

Price in S.A. 8d.

Let me see him... just once!

... and captured front page coverage for her efforts.

Fans besiege the hotel, packed right back to the steps of Parliament House.

coaxial cable and preparing to beam the arrival scenes into Sydney.

Although the police had threatened to switch the route if any fans gave indications of causing trouble, the Beatles retraced their steps back to the airport. This time in a closed car and moving at about 30 mph with police motorcycles clearing the way, the four waved tentatively. Not that they were exactly being ignored. Onlookers were again six deep in the city area, thinning gradually over the nine miles to the airport. A police courtesy car swept ahead, speakers blaring instructions for fans to move off the roadway. Hundreds of cars converged upon the Anzac Highway, causing a huge bottleneck at the intersection of Morphett Road. Freshly painted signs adorned the shoving lines, with such declarations as "Come Back Soon And Bring Ringo With You." (Four girls had already presented the *Advertiser* with a 120-signature petition demanding that Ringo be flown to Adelaide for a few hours sometime during the remainder of the tour.)

As the convoy swung into the top gate of Tapley's Hill Road, a good hundred fans got the better of police and surged through the gate. Police motorcycles rounded most of them up, like a dog would sheep, as they pursued the front car or headed for the waiting aircraft.

At the foot of the aircraft, Bob Francis snatched his final interviews. John told him, "Adelaide is a small place as cities go but it's just been incredible." George added, "Yeah, for a State of only a million people we just can't get over it." Paul seemed sincere when he said, "I nearly cried in the car. Nothing like this has ever happend to us before." Turning to the gathered reporters and officials, John shouted, "Thanks . . . it's been fantastic . . . ridiculous . . . yea, nothing like it in the world."

A closed car waits ready to take the Beatles to Adelaide airport for their flight to Melbourne. Leaving the hotel was a most difficult task.

The final farewells came from some twenty daughters of airline staff, who passed over autograph books for signing as the plane prepared for takeoff. The four Beatles stood at the top of the steps, offered "thanks again Adelaide" and disappeared inside the aircraft, with George wildly snapping photographs all the way. Helen Grimmett, the five-year-old daughter of former test cricketer Clarrie Grimmett, was held up to a first class cabin window by her press photographer father. Tapping her hand on the glass, she demanded, "Hold my hand Paul." The Beatle smiled, shugged and mouthed the words "Sorry I can't."

At 12.59 p.m. the chartered jet barrelled down the runway, the Beatles offering a uniform thumbs-up gesture of farewell. Quite suddenly, the city of Adelaide went dead. Observers described it as "the quietest Sunday afternoon of all time." As the aircraft soared over the Adelaide hills, dozens of families in the Southern suburbs stood in their backyards or on their roofs to watch and wave.

Back in the city, the pieces were being put back together and the platitudes were being mouthed. South Australia Hotel manager Mr. J. F. Byfield exclaimed, "We haven't had anything like this at the hotel since Gracie Fields visited Adelaide before the war." Ian Hayward got carried away to the point of hysteria, gushing, "It's a pity you couldn't see on television the finer shades of their really eloquent facial expressions, the way their eyes sparkle as they react to things. When one was momentarily in the limelight, the others seemed to step back and share in everybody else's enjoyment. And the way they included

Police remove a casualty from outside the South Australia Hotel.

Sounds Incorporated make friends with a real live koala bear in Adelaide.

Jimmy Nicol in everything was a pleasure to see."

Miss Mary Smith, a Liverpool-born psychologist attached to the Adelaide Children's Hospital (and not another of John's relatives), offered her opinion of the spectacle which the city had just witnessed. "The prime attraction is sexual," she claimed. "With their tight pants and long hair the Beatles really look asexual. They could almost be either boys, or girls in tights, so they have an attraction to both sexes. I think there are few women of any age who could resist a baby face like Paul McCartney's. It appeals to the mother instinct. But those girls who called out for Paul — if he were to answer their pleas a great many of them would have run for their lives."

The following week's press was scattered with revelations, confessions and tasty titbits concerning the tour. Most were clumsy attempts by media figures to link their names with the departed superstars. But one 'secret' stood out above all the others. *TV Week* magazine informed all its readers that John and George had gone to church before departing on Sunday!

Bob 'Beatle' Francis with John at the airport.

SOUTH AUSTRALIAN HOTEL LIMITED
A D E L A I D E

JUNE 14TH, 1964

To the Directors of John Martins,

Dear Sirs,

We never get time to write letters, but this is one we all want to write, to say thank you as sincerely as we can to you and your company for bringing us to Adelaide for this wonderful start to our Australian visit. You made your teenagers and thousands of grown-ups very happy, but you have also made the Beatles very happy.

It was a wonderful welcome, the audiences at our shows were fantastic, and they showed us what they thought of John Martins for bringing us to Adelaide. We love you too and we only wish we could have visited your great store. We know about your famous Pageant too...you really like people don't you?

So, Mister Directors of John Martins, for this memorable experience and wonderful start in "Aussie" we say

Thank you again, and again, and again

THE BEATLES.

Jimmy Nicol's signature is almost certainly legitimate. The same cannot be said for the other three. Did Derek Taylor strike again?

Ernie Sigley (right) leads the press rush to George at the Adelaide press conference.

4: MELBOURNE

Sunday June 14 saw Beatle madness on three fronts. By dawn, boisterous crowds were assembling in Melbourne, Sydney and Adelaide, all planning to catch sight of one or more moptops.

As the indefatigable citizens of Adelaide were mounting one final burst of affection for the departing heroes and a goodly portion of' Melbourne's population was taking up vantage points from Essendon to the city, five thousand Sydney Beatle fans were back out at Mascot terminal waiting for Ringo.

Having finally been discharged from hospital, Ringo had set out with Brian Epstein for San Francisco on Saturday morning, after discovering that a route via the US would get them to Australia almost twenty-four hours earlier than planned. An hour before departure, when Brian asked Ringo for his passport, he winked and said, "I haven't got it." After briefly pondering and rejecting the possibility of a joke, Epstein organised a car to pick it up from Ringo's home. However the car was just not fast enough and officials had to arrange a special clearance for Mr. Starkey to travel without it. "After all, a Beatle's a Beatle all over the world isn't he?" commented an official. On the steps of the plane Brian asked Ringo if he would like to meet Vivien Leigh. "Who's Vivien Leigh?" he retorted. The actress certainly knew who Ringo was and pumped his hand furiously.

The change of planes in the gay city on the bay caused a riot, with 300 fans at the airport and five hospital cases. Ringo agreed to meet the San Francisco media in a brief press airport conference but this broke down into a wild melee when TV cameramen rushed the startled drummer demanding autographs for their daughters.

Reunited with his passport, Ringo boarded a Qantas jet to Sydney on Saturday afternoon. As he left, more than 100 fans were milling at Mascot. Airport manager Mr. G. Inglis had announced that arrangements would be similar to the previous Thursday so the hapless devotees were once more thrust out into the cold at 11 p.m., guarded by twenty Commonwealth policemen. One of the first to arrive was sixteen-year-old Fairfield schoolgirl Mary Jackson who told a reporter she would wait all day if necessary. "I got wet waiting for the Beatles on Thursday," she said, "so it would take a lot to stop me waiting for Ringo. I don't mind having to stay up all night. Every minute will be worth it if I see him."

Most of those waiting did see Ringo as he disembarked, stepped into a Holden and passed through customs with the other passengers. Twenty-year-old Edward Beard of Brighton-Le-Sands got sufficiently carried away to sprint towards the landing aircraft and paid a heavy price for his impulsive act. Arrested by Commonwealth Police, he was charged with trespassing, resisting arrest and using indecent language. In Redfern Court on the following Tuesday, a Sgt. Headland told Mr. J. A. Letts S.M., "He was stopped by a Qantas security guard but broke free. I grabbed him but he broke away and had to be held by two other police. He kept yelling, 'I'm not going to be taken by you mug coppers.' At Mascot police station he resisted being placed in the cells and used indecent language." After being told by the Crown Solicitor that the Civil Aviation Department wanted the matter treated seriously, the S.M. fined Beard £23 with £7. 7s costs and placed him on a £50 good behaviour bond, adding to good measure, "It is difficult to understand this type of conduct by young people." Outside the courtroom, Beard said, "I won't be going to the Beatles concert now. Tickets cost money." However his biggest regret was, "I was only a few feet from the plane door when they grabbed me. They took me away and I didn't get to see Ringo at all. Now I don't think it was worth it."

Inside the Sydney domestic terminal, Ringo faced his first Sydney press gathering, with most questions coming from 2SM's Garvin Rutherford. Ringo declared that he had switched from Scotch to Bourbon, itemised every piece of his personal jewellery and assured all present that he was still very much in possession of his tonsils. Some of his captured quotes included, "I've heard that you've got a bridge or something here. No one ever tells me anything, they just knock on my door and drag me out of bed to look at rivers and things. At the moment I love it all, I think we all do, I mean wouldn't you if you got off a plane to all this?" To the endless and idiotic question "Do you ever have your hair cut?" he curtly replied, "Of course, it'd be down by my ankles if I didn't."

After about ninety minutes in Sydney, Ringo and Brian flew on to Melbourne, encountering the beginnings of the crowd that would greet the others later in the day. The operation was reasonably smooth until the car pulled up in front of the front doors of the Southern Cross Hotel in Swanston Street. The crowd by that point was around 3000 and, in retrospect, it would have been far wiser to have taken Ringo in by the laneway garage entrance.

Dick Lean, who met the pair at Essendon Airport, recalls the moment vividly. "Mick Patterson, the police inspector, decided to put Ringo on his very broad shoulders and make a dash for the entrance. It seemed like a good idea until our PR lady Elanor Knox began bowing and waving to the crowd, then tripped and fell down right in front of this piggy back. Well Mick stepped on her and down came Ringo, right into the grasping claws of hundreds of kids. When we finally pulled him out and got him inside he was as white as a sheet and the first words he said were, 'Give us a drink, that was the roughest ride I've ever had.' Then he went straight to his suite to lie down."

As a shaken Ringo Starr was resting safely inside his hotel room, the remainder of the group were heading towards Melbourne in an Ansett ANA Fokker Friendship, and it was a case of out of the frying pan into the fire. The Fab Four, although they didn't know it, were about to ignite an explosion of human emotions which would certainly equal, if not eclipse, that which had occured in the South Australian capital.

Alarmed at the events in Adelaide, the Victorian police force had made a last-minute decision to call in the army and navy to assist with crowd control. Initially seen as a chronic case of over-reaction, the move proved to be a wise one.

After taking a breather for lunch, the crowd that had welcomed Ringo began to swell appreciably until 10,000 were thronging Exhibition Street at 2 p.m., two hours before the rest of the group were due. By three o'clock the first barriers were knocked down, as the crowd pushed towards the hotel chanting, "Ringo, Ringo" and "We Want The Beatles." Half an hour later, the combined unit of police, army and navy, forming a human barricade at the front of the Southern Cross, began to lose control.

At this point the first casualties began to occur, requiring mounted police to retrieve unconscious girls from the midst of the mass and carry them to a first aid station established in the Australia-American Centre, across the road from the hotel. The faintings were jointly attributable to nervous exhaustion, hysteria and hunger, as many of the girls had first taken up vantage spots early on Saturday morning.

Out at Essendon Airport, 5000 fans were on hand to shriek to the heavens as Paul McCartney bounded down the aircraft steps onto the tarmac, madly waving to the horde before him. At least another 20,000 packed the mile motorcade route to the city, offering a welcome even more raucous than their Adelaide counterparts. The procession of vehicles was stopped repeatedly as crowds spilled onto the road.

As the procession inched closer to the city at around 4 p.m., the madness heightened and even the police became flustered. The carefully planned exercise was thrown into chaos by a young constable on point duty at the corner of Elizabeth and Victor Streets who let the entire convoy across the intersection with the sole exception of the car carrying Brodziak and Derek Taylor. Meanwhile, the twelve police motorcycles at the front of the parade made radio contact with the hotel nerve centre and were told to abandon plans to send the four musicians in through the front door. Instead they were to create a diversion, along with a special dummy police car, by pulling up at the front door with sirens blaring – allowing the actual Beatles' car to sneak into a laneway garage entrance. The car left at the intersection did not disgorge its passengers for another half hour at least.

Unaware of the eleventh hour change of procedure, the 20,000 strong crowd pushed closer to the hotel, crushing steel barricades as if they were damp matchboxes. Assistant tour manager Malcolm Cook recalls, "the front of the Southern Cross was all glass panels and it was terrifying to watch thousands of fists beating against the glass and thousands of bodies throwing their weight into it – it was bigger than a Victorian football grand final. And I remember Tony Charlton from Channel Nine doing a live coverage, staring in horror at the scene before him saying into his mic, 'Mothers, if your child is out there you should be ashamed.' "

Staff at University College Hospital in London farewell Ringo as he prepares to depart for Sydney via San Francisco. "I've got a bottle of stuff with me in case I get any twitches," he told reporters.

Fans gathered at Sydney Airport in the early hours of the morning to await Ringo's first steps upon Australian soil.

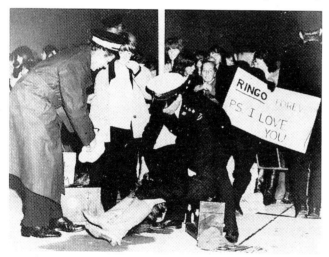

A St. John's Ambulance officer shoved this fan's head between her legs. He probably stopped her screaming by snapping her spine!

Sydney police put their backs into the support of a Beatle barrier on the second of five wearying occasions.

Ringo displays his elusive passport in Melbourne. Tour official Jack Neary looks on.

An official car swept Brian and Ringo direct from the Essendon tarmac to the Southern Cross Hotel.

During his brief Sydney stopover, newsmen introduce Ringo and his aching tonsils to cold Aussie beer.

Brian Epstein and Ringo Starr make their first Melbourne appearance.

On the other side of the endangered glass the conditions were even more petrifying for any poor soul bearing the responsibility of keeping the peace. The police contingency had grown to 300 but, even bolstered by a military force of 100, order was a lost cause. As the first field hospital was filled to overflowing, another was established in the foyer of the Southern Cross. Doctor Ivan Markovics, a hotel guest, played Florence Nightingale, muttering, "I've never seen anything like this." Neither had one policeman, who described the situation as "frightening, chaotic and rather inhuman." The gentle, festive character of the Adelaide adoration had been somehow superceded by a more brutal, determined clamouring, not at all disimilar to a VFL grand final.

In the midst of the sea of bodies brawls erupted and expired within the space of a few seconds. One youth fell ten feet from a tree branch which gave away; an expensive Italian sports car was crushed from boot to bonnett by hundreds of scrambling feet; one slightly-built young girl commenced hitting a hapless man on the head with her stiletto shoe when he blocked her view; fainted girls were carried along in the crush, held upright like sardines; elderly people attracted by the spectable were trapped inside the crowd, some crying in fear, and a fleet of ambulances took forty of the more serious casualties to Royal Melbourne and St. Vincent's Hospital. More than 150 fans received medical treatment. "The mounted police did a marvellous job," recalls Kevin Ritchie. "They could get right into the heart of the crowd, drag fainted kids up and over the front of their saddles and take them off for treatment. Nothing else could have done it."

Within ten minutes of their successful secret entry into the hotel, and midway through a boisterous reunion with Ringo, all five Beatles were rushed out into the first floor balcony in order to ease the crush on the front doors. All appeared to be cold, with Ringo approaching a shade of blue in the icy winds. The deep resonant roar obliterated any words that the objects of the adulation proferred, so John held one finger to his upper lip and threw a series of Nazi salutes, shouting "Sieg Heil." Below, the surge increased instead of abated. One policeman later explained, "they pushed forward twenty feet so we mustered all our strength and moved them back fifteen feet — then it started all over again."

Before the repeated five foot losses of ground could bring the fans to the glass walls, the Beatles retired from the balcony and the satisfied mass quickly dispersed, leaving a loyal core of a few hundred stalwarts. When fainted girls awoke to find that they had missed the appearance, they became hysterical, some rolling about on the floor weeping and screaming, "I hate the Beatles, I hate the Beatles!"

Back inside the hotel, John admitted that it was all "a little frightening" naming it "the greatest reception we have received anywhere in the world," breaking his own code of protocol. At a press conference later in the day, the five Beatles were photographed together for the first and last time. After which, Jimmy was sent to his room to pack.

If Jimmy had felt like an outsider throughout his stint with the group, he might as well not have even existed when Ringo came upon the scene. "He obviously felt quite uncomfortable with John, Paul and George," recalls Bruce Stewart, "and spent most of his time with Sounds Incorporated and the Phantoms." Dave Lincoln of the Phantoms remembers that some of Jimmy's comments to the press had irritated Brian Epstein, who had already given the instruction that the drummer was most definitely *not* to return to Sydney to play again with Frances Faye. As Nicol himself would later comment, "The boys were very kind but I felt like an intruder. They accepted me but you can't just get into a group like that — they have their own atmosphere, their own sense of humour. It's a little clique and outsiders just can't break in."

During the press conference, John and George spoke with Alan Lappin of 3UZ, who put to John: "One place you haven't been is the Soviet Union," to which Lennon replied, "They think we're some kind of capitalist trick. But it doesn't really matter, I don't think they can afford to buy records there." Asked if any of the Beatles had ever undergone National Service, John tersely clipped the question with, "No we don't like armies or things like that." Did he ever get a haircut? "Yes, in fact I need a trim at the moment but I can't find anyone I trust."

Lappin and George engaged in a deep discussion on the pirate radio situation in England, which Harrison supported enthusiastically. "It's about time we had commercial radio without having to go out of the five mile limit," he said. "We could do with a couple of stations right in London."

The reunion with Ringo was considered reasonable excuse for a party so the press were earnestly assured that the group were going to bed at midnight. After all but those booked into the hotel had departed, four hand-picked Melbourne lovelies were ushered into the Beatles' master suite and the merriment began, raging through to 4 a.m. with only one reported outside the inner sanctum tweaking to it. At 2.30 a.m., a dejected Jimmy disobeyed Epstein's curfew and borrowed a car for a drive through Melbourne, ending up at the seaside suburb of Beaumaris. At 8 a.m. he slipped quietly out of the hotel without saying farewell to the others ("they were still asleep. I didn't think I should disturb them") and went to the airport with Epstein. Before Nicol departed for London via Brisbane, Brian presented him with his promised fee of £500 and a gold watch engraved "To Jimmy, with appreciation and gratitude — Brian Epstein and The Beatles." He arrived home to an embarrassing silence, with the only shrieks coming from his five-year-old son Howard.

Although John had confidently predicted at the Sydney press conference ". . . and he's away," Jimmy's post-Beatle career was simply a non-event. The Shub Dubs, the group re-formed around him, failed to set the world on fire, as did his terrible cabaret-style single *Husky*, the flip of which seemed to sum up the situation neatly — *Don't Come Back*. According to Dave Lincoln, "He had big plans to become a big star, to cash in on his Beatle association, but he only ended up putting himself in big debt." Ironically, one of his parting comments in Melbourne had been, "When I get home I won't have to run a group on £15 or £20 a night anymore."

Monday was a public holiday and the Beatles were inundated with offers of visits to football matches, race meetings and barbecues and, as usual, turned them all down. While their heroes were all shagged out in deep repose, a few hundred fans were at the wrong end of a fire hose down in the street. Hotel workmen let loose the jet of water when a roller door lock was sprung at the carpark entrance. "We regretted having to do it," said a maintenance man, "but they were pushing against the door while we were trying to fix it and ignored our pleas to stop."

A European freelance photographer who took pictures of the hosing was chased into an alley and mauled by forty enraged fans until police dragged him clear of the drenched fury. To add to their misery a thousand fans had to flee for shelter later in the afternoon when rain began to fall. At least half of them had been there since dawn. Three girls, one celebrating her seventeenth birthday, slept the night on the concrete floor of the basement carpark. Hotel management gave them a breakfast of bacon and eggs and then turned them back out into the street. Up on the roof were more fans, hiding successfully under the base of a water tank. Those who weren't at the Southern Cross were possibly part of the 100 person queue at the Police Property Office sifting through mountains of shoes, baskets, radios, thermos flasks, watches, purses, coats, hats and other sundry items which had been detached from their owners during the Battle for the Southern Cross.

The first official Melbourne engagement was an EMI Records reception in the Epsilon Room of the hotel, organised by the company's Victorian Manager Cliff Baxter.

"It was the first and last time we ever had a hundred per cent

acceptance for an artist reception," confides Baxter. "My most vivid memory of it, apart from having to forcibly move people around the room and away from the smothered Beatles, was John Lennon in an absolutely livid fit of anger because EMI here had designed a different cover for the *With The Beatles* album. I had to keep explaining that it was done at the Sydney headquarters and had nothing to do with me at all. I also found it very difficult to stop people interviewing the boys."

Stan "The Man" Rofe, Melbourne's premier rock jock with a record collection to match his excellent taste, was literally forced upon the Beatles at the reception. "Cliff Baxter was getting very tired of one particular woman reporter who was chasing John and Paul around the room with a shorthand notepad, so he asked me to get them in a corner for a chat to keep her at bay.

Waiting for the Beatles in Exhibition Street.

The army had to be called in to control the Melbourne street crowds.

Arriving in high spirits from Adelaide on the morning of Sunday, June 14.

The airport crowds were small compared to other cities. Most fans were in wait at the Southern Cross Hotel.

Part of the Essendon Airport crowd.

Sailors, soldiers and police could barely contain the crush towards the plate glass front windows of the Southern Cross Hotel.

St. John's Ambulance Brigade manned the front lines and removed the casualties during "The Battle of the Southern Cross."

Injured fans being ferried off to field hospitals located in the lobbies of nearby buildings.

A startling perspective on the extent of the street crowd.

Once safely inside the hotel, all five Beatles made a public appearance on the large ledge. They were vastly outnumbered by tour officials, chambermaids, newsmen and hotel management.

John "Adolf" Lennon and Paul "Herman" McCartney salute Melbourne.

"It's funny when I think about it now, but I told them that if they ever ran short of material I had lots of blues records they might be interested in. They seemed to be quite knowledgeable about the type of music I liked so we swapped addresses." Rofe also gave Sounds Incorporated an indulgent hour on his 3UZ shift, allowing them to play little else than Jerry Lee Lewis and Little Richard tracks.

Brian DeCourcy, manager of Merv Benton and another maniac record collector, was introduced to John in Melbourne. "We shook hands and he said, 'You've got a grip like a fuckin' bear, I'll bet you're no poofter,' which startled me a little I must admit."

Kevin Ritchie was also berated fiercely over the cover change incident. "I thought I was doing the right thing giving them copies of their new album but it just started the tirade again. I was dismissed by John on the spot and he was going to contact the Chairman in London and have me fired and the whole of the Australian company was going to be sacked. I copped it because I was the only one accessible to them. Everyone at EMI was hiding behind closed doors, thinking 'oh dear here's the biggest thing to ever come out of the company and we've done the wrong thing by them.' As soon as it passed John had forgotten it and everything went along smoothly again."

Bill Robinson, then EMI A+R Manager, explains why the change occured. "We would have gladly used the British cover if we had been able to. You see in those days there was no such thing as importing film negatives for covers, the unions wouldn't allow it. We had to reshoot everything from the overseas covers that we were sent. But the *With The Beatles* jacket was very shadowy and soft and our printers — all we had was letterpress printers then — made a complete botch of it, so we had to make up a new jacket with nice clear, sharp photographs. We tried to explain all this to the Beatles but I'm sure they didn't believe us."

The Beatles' own view of the worshipping mass.

A rare shot of all five Beatles paying their respects to Melbourne. (L-R) George, Jimmy, Ringo, Paul and John. Tour promoter Dick Lean can be seen behind John. The black and white photograph does not reveal that Ringo was blue with cold.

Ritchie observed, like everybody else, that the Beatles never indulged in the copious amounts of exotic food liberally laid on at press conferences and receptions. However, he was one of the very few Australians to find out why.

"After the reception I followed them to another room and watched in amusement as hotel catering staff wheeled out this ornate silver trolley covered with nothing but bread and raspberry jam — the boy's beloved jam butties, with a slight variation. The chef had prepared this simple fare like the most expensive hors d'oeuvres. The bread was cut into every shape imaginable; squared, circles, half moons, crested stars, butterflies, everything. Then there was gallons of milk to wash it all down. The four of them were as excited as little kids as they tucked into their favorite food."

That night, after the first two Melbourne concerts at Festival Hall, filmed by the Nine television network and broadcast as "The Beatles Sing for Shell," the four agreed upon a rare excursion outside their hotel. They were taken to a private party in the ritzy suburb of Toorak where Paul fell into conversation with a nineteen-year-old girl in whom he confided his dislike of civic receptions. He was not aware that the eager listener was Elizabeth Curtis, a daughter of Melbourne's Lord Mayor.

On Tuesday, the battle-scarred police closed off Collins and Swanson Streets at 12.30 p.m., to accommodate the estimated 15,000 fans who gathered in the streets to catch a glimpse of the four on the balcony of the Melbourne Town Hall. They arrived almost thirty minutes late, creeping their way through a snowstorm of ticker tape. At one point hysteria swept through the more gullible sections of the crowd when someone joked, "they must have had an accident" and some distraught young things were seen to sink to their knees on the pavement, sobbing "Oh no, oh no." Absenteeism and truancy levels for the day set a new record that is probably still to be broken.

Within minutes of being bundled from their Rolls Royce into a side entrance they were on the Town Hall portico whipping the assemblage below into a fine state. John, wearing a leather jacket and pink shirt, refrained from his Hitlerian gestures and contented himself with demure waves.

Leaving the balcony, the Beatles were confronted by a nightmare scene. Originally confined to 150 guests, the reception had swelled to around 350 as a result of Mayor Curtis' action in granting invitations to 200 fans who had written, phoned or asked him. Even moved from the tiny second floor reception room to the lower Town Hall Chamber, the function was still potentially disastrous. Called upon for speeches, Ringo was thrust forward to mumble sarcastically, "I wish you'd had this reception a little earlier instead of dragging me out of bed at this early hour." (It was 1.15 p.m.)

Once the "no autographs" rule was breached by the Mayor himself, the stampede began. The famous and the unknown clawed at each other to get to a Beatle, buffeting, shaking, kissing and pawing the furious celebrities. Derek Taylor spotted a man making his way towards Ringo and shoved him aside as he was about to grasp a handful of hair.

Departing the Southern Cross Hotel for the Town Hall in a VIP Rolls.

Mayor Curtis encourages Paul's boomerang technique.

"You bruised my ribs," the man shouted. "That doesn't matter" Taylor retorted as he shoved him over four large pot plants and called in an MSS guard, who also had to deal with an over-enthusiastic eighty-year-old woman. After a girl pushed aside the Lady Mayoress to plant a violent kiss on him, Ringo demanded that the four of them leave immediately, so the Mayor took them to his wife's chambers on the second floor. Here the mood changed drastically as the Beatles and the Curtis family sang around a piano and listened to university student Noel Kemp play the didgeridoo. They stayed half an hour longer than scheduled and Brian Epstein later described the session as "the most happy informal moment since the tour began." However the press had seen only the hasty departure from the lower chamber and so whipped up giant national headlines which read: "Beatles Walk Out! Anger At Rude Guests."

One of the Lord Mayor's invited guests was fifteen-year-old Malvern schoolgirl Annie Cooper. "My mother wouldn't let me go to the Southern Cross on Sunday," she relates, "and I had to content myself with watching it on TV. But on Monday I received an official-looking envelope from the City Council which included a very formal

The now-famous photograph of the first Town Hall balcony appearance, with Lord Mayor Leo Curtis and his elated twelve-year-old daughter Vikki.

Acknowledging the teeming crowd from another Town Hall location.

A cheesy Lennon wave from the balcony.

A sing-a-long in the Lady Mayoress' chambers, with Paul hitting the high notes for the Mayor's children (l-r) Peter, Elizabeth, Mrs. Julian Metzner, Vikki.

Swanston Street greetings.

invitation from the Mayor to attend his civic reception for the Beatles. It turned out that a lady who knew how Beatle crazy I was had written on my behalf asking for tickets, but hadn't told me.

"What I remember best is arriving at Swanston Street, seeing all those thousands of people in the streets and being able to walk right in the front door. When they made their speeches and the Mayor said they would be mingling with the guests, my friend and I stood frozen for about ten minutes but we finally got enough courage to shake their hands. I think we ended up shaking hands with each of them about six times. If they did notice our recurring faces they never gave any indication."

Persistent attempts by influential and important people to get close to the Beatles was commonplace throughout the tour, but no-where was it more pronounced than in Melbourne, where the absolute upper crust of society descended upon the Southern Cross.

"There were streams of these people in furs and jewels just waltzing into rooms, ordering large amounts of alcohol and charging it to the occupant," Bob Rogers remembers bitterly. "I got a bit tired of it so I rang the desk and told them not to admit any more people to my room. Then, ten minutes or so later, in troops another fifteen people that I'd never seen before in my life. So I got onto the desk manager to demand an explanation and he said, almost in tears, 'Mr. Rogers it's

more than my job is worth to ban those people from the hotel, they a the backbone of Melbourne society.' I had to chase them out myself."

The Beatles put certain portions of this privileged cocktail party set to practical use though, as Cliff Baxter explains: "They were determined to get into the pants of as many Australian VIP daughters as possible and I believe they were most successful. It was almost a competition between the four of them; looks didn't matter, they just wanted to see how high up the social ladder they could go in bed."

Road assistant Ron Blackmore adds, "There were times when th weren't as discreet as everybody would have you believe they were. I saw lines of girls in passageways at the Southern Cross and recognised more than one face. Nowdays it's a status symbol for girls to boast about but back then screwing a rock star was something that remaine a close secret, so only those who actually saw it knew that it happened."

Epstein's stay with his number one boys was surprisingly brief. After just three days in Melbourne he decided to depart for Canberra on undisclosed business. He and Derek were supposed to fly up to the national capital on Wednesday morning but this was abandoned when Taylor slept in and they missed the flight – provocation for one of their many famous yelling sessions. "Epstein walked around the room like a great while God," recalls Johnny Devlin. "He didn't seem to tak

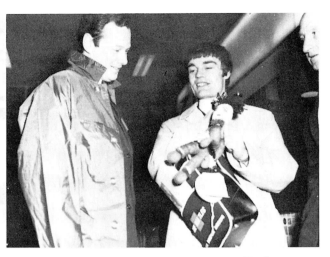

While the four Beatles slept, stand-in drummer Jimmy Nicol was escorted to Essendon Airport by Brian Epstein and tour manager Lloyd Ravenscroft, given £500 and a gold watch and sent on his way.

An almost cruel contrast to the previous day's street scenes.

With Melbourne fan club president Suzette Belle. She later married one of the Masters Apprentices.

Concert compere Alan Field shares John's distaste for the Australian-designed cover of "With the Beatles."

much notice of anything going on around him. He left it all to Derek."

Derek Taylor was the central strength of the tour party. "He never slept," says Malcolm Cook, "he operated like a crisis centre in a disaster. He handled the press beautifully, nothing was ever beyond him. He got printed exactly what he wanted printed without ever really upsetting any journalists.

"There was a very definite line of control. Neil Aspinall and Mal Evans were closest to the Beatles and it was impossible to break down their system by going direct. They vetted everything that came near the group and knew exactly when to lower the veil of privacy to protect them."

On the Wednesday, Lloyd Ravenscroft offered the four an opportunity to drive MG sports cars in the Dandenong mountains outside of Melbourne but only George accepted. In order to evade the press, who had set up a twenty-four-hour "watch car" in the basement (covered with transmitting aerials) the tour manager enlisted the aid of a policeman who owned a 1936 Hupmobile. At a carefully specified time, one of the security men parked an Austin Princess in the centre of the garage floor and raised the bonnet — neatly obliterating the view of the media car. This accomplished, George was loaded into the Hupmobile and spirited out of the basement and up to the Dandenongs for his afternoon's motoring.

Throughout the tour, all the Beatles were angered by the multitude of BMC advertising that used their name. Here John attempts to remove an offending car door sign outside the Southern Cross Hotel.

While George saw the sights, John, Paul and Ringo subjected themselves to hair trims in their suite. Val Behrens, 20, and Grace Ferrigno, 22, were fetched from a Collins Street salon and spent two hours snipping away.

"For most of the time they fooled around and jived to Little Richard records," said Val. "We cut their hair, shampooed and dried it but they never stopped clowning around." That night, two eighteen-year-old workmates took the clippings to Festival Hall offering them to fans for tickets or money. There were no takers.

As in most cities where they would tour during the height of Beatlemania, cripples and handicapped people were cruelly thrust before the group in Melbourne for what seemed to be a rather sick "laying on of hands" ceremony. One incident however was handled tastefully. A teenage niece of the Police Surgeon, suffering from cancer with only weeks to live, was allowed to meet her idols.

Thursday morning, 600 police were taking their positions in Sydney, exactly one week after the first arrival. The previous day another task force, comprising senior officers from the Police Rescue Squad, Traffic Branch, Radio Communications Squad and the Mounted Police Division had met at Police Headquarters under acting Metropolitan Superintendant M.W. Chaseling to examine filmed coverage of the Adelaide and Melbourne welcomes.

Sydney's teenagers were being lectured from all corners. New South Wales Premier Jack Renshaw appealed to parents to warn their children of the dangers involved in greeting the Beatles: "I don't want to see a repetition of the near riots which occurred in Adelaide and in Melbourne particularly. I am confident that with the co-operation of the children who are Beatle fans the NSW Police Force will be able to do its job and will make it possible for the children to see the group in safety and reasonable comfort."

Judge Adrian Curlewis, Chairman of the Youth Advisory Council, chimed in with his admonishments as well: "Show the world that the warmth of your welcome is equal to your sense. At all times act sensibly and give everyone a fair go." Mr. A.W. Doubleday, regional director of Civil Aviation at Mascot, announced that the arrival plans would be identical to those adopted the previous Thursday: "We do not care how much noise is made but those on the tarmac must not crush the barriers. If that happens the program will be cut short and the Beatles whisked away very quickly."

The press was a little less overbearing, however. The *Mirror* decided to match the *Sun* in the area of Beatle editorials with the bold statement: "The Beatles come back to Sydney tomorrow and we are happy to welcome them. They bring fun and games wherever they go. Whatever the explanation of this phenomenal Beatle cult, it has a dynamic effect on young people and even the grumpiest old ones admit the lads from Liverpool have a special kind of magic."

John never refused to autograph a copy of "In His Own Write."

Passing the long hours of hotel room confinement.

A gift for Paul left at the hotel front desk by a frightened fan.

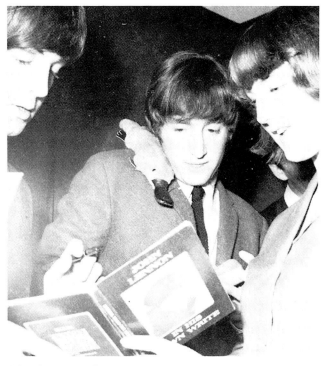

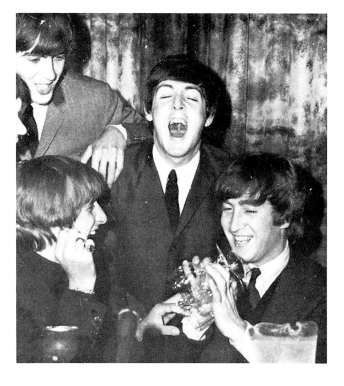

John adopts a toy platypus at the Melbourne press conference.

5: SYDNEY: THE SECOND TIME

The Sydney authorities were not to know, but the real madness of the tour was over. Sydney, graced with five separate visits from various combinations of the Fab Four, seemed to divide the intensity of its welcome accordingly.

The drive to Essendon airport was relatively uneventful, although some twenty girls invaded the tarmac as the car pulled up at the floor of the aircraft stairs. Police scrambled from a riot wagon to converge on most of them but a few managed to make it to the door of the car when it stopped. For a few moments there existed a surging tumult of police, M.S.S. men, reporters, photographers and squirming, squealing girls. The plane, which had been held twenty minutes to allow the Beatles to finish their breakfast at the Southern Cross, was in the air and northbound by 10.20 a.m.

Though grey skies loomed ominously, the Sydney the Beatles encountered as they touched down at 11.40 a.m. was nowhere near as intimidating as it had been a week earlier. No more than a hundred fans had camped overnight and the welcoming committee, estimated by various press organs to be 400, 1500 and 3000, was actually around 1200 — a far cry from the turnouts in Adelaide and Melbourne. Centre of attention was Paul McCartney, that day celebrating his twenty-second birthday.

After the other passengers had alighted, Ringo was the first Beatle to appear, followed by George, Paul and John. The 300 police on duty handled the crush easily and one girl who clambered over the barrier as her idols descended from their aircraft was instantly returned to the rightful side of the fence by two officers of the law. In the midst of the screaming girls was one excited sixty-eight-year-old woman wearing an "I Love the Beatles" pin-on. She claimed to be a staunch fan with tickets for that night's concert.

The four clambered upon the same flat bed truck, sans umbrellas, for another ceremonial lap of honour. As it drove past the press enclosure, John spotted an attractive blond woman reporter and swung a leg over the railing as if to jump off. After passing the waiting crowds, the truck driver, instead of heading off over the tarmac as planned, continued along the barrier until an unenclosed section was reached, enticing scores of fans onto the tarmac. There followed a mad dash as the truck belatedly headed for sanctuary in the cargo area.

The drive to the city was uneventful and as the cars swung from Darlinghurst Road into Macleay Street in Kings Cross, there were only 500 or so fans in the street, another far cry from the southern cities. Even so, the 300 police were once more concerned for the safety of the Chevron's front glass panels and also were keeping stringent guard on a gaping forty-foot excavation site by the side of the building.

Not all the meagre fan contingent was there to pay homage to the Beatles. Students from the University of NSW had descended upon the Chevron Hotel with giant placards proclaiming, "We want Arthur" and similar. The greetings were directed to pianist Arthur Rubinstein, who had unfortunately clashed his tour dates with the Fab Four's. As the students were trading friendly insults with the younger fans, Rubinstein appeared on the balcony waving and bowing. He later stated, "I am pleased the students staged a demonstration in support of musical sense." He added that he would like to meet the Beatles but they would have to come to his hotel. Ringo responded to this with: "Maybe we can meet him halfway across the road."

After being greeted by their Spanish handmaidens once more and settling back into their old suite, the four faced another round of press, somewhat less bestial than the previous Thursday. Paul managed to grab most of the headlines by bringing up a very sensitive subject — the

Them vs Us.

The Front Lines.

hotly debated White Australia Policy. It all began when he was approached by a Nigerian journalist and commented, "I didn't think that Australia allowed coloured people to come in. I remember reading about this in geography at school — which I failed — and I thought it was a bit off. I thought you were the only country in the world to do this. Apart from koalas and kangaroos my biggest early impression of Australia had been this 'white-only' business. In fact John and I were talking about it only this afternoon. So when I saw you today I thought, 'Hullo, we'll get onto the government right away.'" When the journalist told him that there were more than 3000 Asian students in the country and that he himself had found no real discrimination, Paul answered, "That's good, because there is in Britain and America."

A radio newsman sidled up to Ringo and boldly declared, "I'm from Perth, Western Australia" and got back: "Are you bragging or complaining?" "I have flown 2000 miles to record this interview," he persisted. "Gee your arms must be tired," commiserated Ringo, who then recounted his own woes, pointing out that his hands had become blistered as a result of his stint in hospital, away from his kit.

Paul, his eyes notably accented with mascara, told a newsman that he was feeling a little homesick on his birthday, the first he had ever spent completely away from home, and that he was going to ring his father at about 1 a.m. He confided that he had rung Jane Asher before leaving Melbourne. "No we're not secretly engaged," he recited, "but I do miss her. I told her all about Australia and said that she'd enjoy it here. Jane likes water so I told her that she would just *love* Sydney." Later he added, "Birthdays have never meant very much to me. Big parties are always a bit of a drag and since we've become famous I don't enjoy them because of all the commotion."

Asked what presents the other Beatles had for Paul, George pointed out that the four never usually exchanged gifts, adding, "I think you only give presents to people you don't know so well."

Paul would probably not have noticed the absence of offerings from his fellow Beatles, submerged and surrounded as he was by literally hundreds of gifts which flowed into the Sheraton from fans all over Australia and the world. Stuffed toy koalas headed the list but the oblations included swimsuits, ties, boomerangs, troll dolls, amateur portraits and books. One little old lady arrived at the front desk with a plate of freshly baked cakes and biscuits, insisting they be sent up

"before they get cold." Two crates of bananas and uncountable cartons and packets of cigarettes also arrived.

As Paul prepared to assess, examine and selectively open his mountain of birthday gifts, most of Sydney's press were clamouring in the corridor for an interview with the 'birthday boy.' Paul agreed to speak with the reporters briefly but when he made his way towards them his eyes set upon seventeen-year-old Kerry Yates, the Lois Lane of the *Women's Weekly.* "I had long blond hair and a pink sweater and I must have stood out from all the grey and brown suits because Paul made a beeline right for me and invited me up to his room. He let my photographer take shots of him surrounded by his presents and the next week we ran one of them in colour on the front cover with my 'exclusive' story inside. For years I've been asked what I had to do to get that scoop, which really did help my career. I know what everyone wants to know but I'm not saying if I did or if I didn't."

That night, the revolving stage at Sydney Stadium (which John, like most other performers, said he had considerable trouble orienting himself to) was showered with gifts, as well as the usual torrents of jelly babies. Wrapped boxes with ribbons, a bouquet of roses, some toy koalas and a whole roomful of boomerangs were collected by Mal Evans after the show and added to the pile.

All the gifts were ceremoniously opened and all but the foodstuffs were forwarded by the promoters to the English fan club headquarters, from where they were distributed to orphans and handicapped children. Where possible, the fan club acknowledged the gift with a letter or photograph. One donor who managed to receive his thanks in person however was the zany Mad Mel armed with his completed 'Sydney to Perth' scarf.

This time around, Mel was not about to be thwarted. Rejected by both his own station and the tour organisers in his repeated requests to present his many miles of wool to the Beatles in person, he commandeered the elevator control booth on the roof of the Sheraton as a headquarters and laid in wait for a live moptop.

"I finally caught Paul in a corridor and when I showed him the scarf he said, 'Yeah, sure, come on down.' They were all really knocked out by it and we became great friends within a few moments. Now, by that point, all the money that the station had paid out wasn't doing them that much good because the Beatles were getting well and truly

As John forges his way through the police parade, George plants a kiss on a hostess and Derek Taylor discusses strategy with Brian Epstein.

Delectable twins in twin sets bid an enthused welcome alongside a left-over Sinatra bobbysoxer.

The staunchest fans arrived during the night to secure vantage positions.

tired of Bob Rogers.

"The guys adopted me as their number one Sydney DJ and ordered that I be given free access to them. So I delivered mail from my listeners, recorded interviews and spent lots of time talking with Paul. It got to a point where 2SM were asking my permission to get to the Beatles. After forbidding me to go near them, they were asking, 'Can you get us in?'"

Even more gifts were delivered in person by the Sydney fan club, the leadership of which was granted a second audience so that they could meet Ringo. Angela Letchford remembers being shocked by the callouses on the drummer's hands. With the fan club came Horace, the giant stuffed koala bear who was able to make the acquaintance of a five-foot-high stuffed toy kangaroo of no specific name which was a present from a group of 2SM listeners. Good Guys Mike Walsh and Phil Haldeman would occasionally spirit away the inanimate bounder and parade it on the balcony.

"It was fun to hear the kids go berserk," Walsh admits. "It gave us the tiniest idea of what it would feel like to have the power of the Beatles." They and all their fellow jocks were at the Sheraton for the first birthday party of the day, taped for later broadcast. Walsh, who gave Ringo an impromptu lesson on his trademark instrument — the kazoo — remembers that a girl tried to crash the party and got stuck on a drainpipe.

However, the main thrust of the birthday celebrations came from the *Daily Mirror* newspaper which organised an exclusive party at the Sheraton — approved and supervised by Brian Epstein and Derek Taylor, who had flown up to Sydney a day early. "This Easy Contest Offers The Chance Of A Lifetime" howled the headlines, above a neat coupon that girls between sixteen and twenty-two could fill in and append with a fifty word essay on "Why I Would Like to be a Guest at a Beatle's Birthday Party." The judging was in the hands of Derek, Irish comedian Dave Allen, Sunday *Mirror* editor Hugh Bingham, promotions manager Leicester Warburton, and cadet journalist Blanche d'Alpuget. More than 10,000 entries flooded the newspaper office, from as far away as Brisbane, Bendigo, Hobart and Canberra.

After great deliberation and searching interviews, seventeen girls were chosen for the honour, with another fifteen runners-up promised a brief backstage meeting the following night (one of which was later Miss Australia, Sue Gallie). The party contingent was initially intended to be fifteen, but was extended by Beatle decree to allow inclusion of girls from the cities of Canberra and Newcastle.

The winners were Glennys Smith, a secretary from Cremorne (20); Jenny Lamb, a sales assistant from Vaucluse (18); Sandra Linklater, a student nurse from Earlwood (17); Caroline Styles, a secretary from Henley (21); Ines Truse, a mannequin from Canberra (21); Evelyn Mac, a model from Concord (21); Patricia Thompson, a student from Newport; Christine Buettner, a student from St. Ives (16); Claire Hogben, a secretary from Pymble (18); Carolyn Keirs, a librarian from Newcastle (19); Carmel Stratton, a showroom assistant from Bondi (18); Anne-Marie Alexander, a secretary from Collaroy (18); Marcia McAtamney, a student from Strathfield (17); Delphine Dockerill, a university student from North Bondi (18); Jannette Carroll, a student from Ultimo (16); Nancy Haddow, a secretary from Cremorne (22); and Sandra Stevenson, a teacher from Cronulla (21). For Glennys Smith and Claire Hogben (the editor's daughter), it was a double celebration, as they also had birthdays on June 18.

Jannette Carroll, an inner-urban Sydney-ite among some fairly daunting silver spooners, was the youngest winner and now, as a school teacher in her thirties, remembers vividly the event which altered the course of her adolescence.

"It was my eleven-year-old sister's idea to enter. I thought it was rigged and that only politicians' daughters would win but I was bored one Sunday so I sent in two coupons. I had read John's book so I composed my entry in that sort of language. I felt a bit silly about doing it so I didn't say anything to my friends.

"Then about a week later mum came up to school to say that I'd made it into the final and I had to go for an interview at the *Mirror*. We rushed into the city so I could get my hair done and then I was shoved into this room at the *Mirror* that was entirely full of men. Derek Taylor was there but most of the questions were from Dave Allen. They asked me why I'd entered and I said I didn't have anything else to do at the time. That must have amused them because I was chosen over a whole lot of rich debutantes that were streaming in and out of the place while I was there.

John spots a good looking blond reporter at the barrier.

Tossing back into the crowd what appears to be an overcome airline hostess.

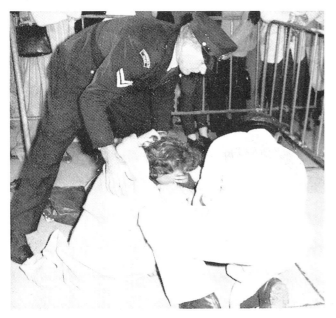

An early casualty.

"On the night, we were all dropped off at the *Mirror* by our parents and then driven to the Sheraton Hotel in big black limousines. Along the way there were girls by the side of the road booing us and throwing things at the car.

"We got there first and waited for the Beatles who were coming from their second show at the Stadium. They came in to meet us before the press were allowed entry and they weren't anything like I imagined superstars would be. Paul, George and Ringo came around to talk to each of us personally but John seemed to hang back a little, as if he was shy. Because of that I went out of my way to talk to John and I think I ended up monopolising a lot of his time.

"Once the press and the other performers were allowed in and the party got underway, I danced with Paul, George and Ringo a couple of times each but I noticed that John wasn't dancing at all. So I got a bit cheeky and went up to him and said, 'Don't you know how to dance? I thought all English people could dance.' He started laughing and got up and danced with me and we got along great for the rest of the night. I was wearing a bright red dress so he christened me the 'Red Devil.' They were all really sensitive, soft, intelligent guys but John was the most amazing of all. He opened my mind with some of the things he was saying, things I'd never talked about before.

"After about an hour, all the reporters were sent away and the party became much less formal and restricted; it became just like a gathering of good friends. Ringo and John became very funny; like whenever a photographer came near me, Ringo whipped the glass of Scotch out of my hand and replaced it with a salt shaker. Then once the photographers had gone they became much more relaxed. When one tried to sneak back in, George gently kicked his camera out of his hands.

"They seemed to be a little infuriated with Little Pattie, who kept putting Beatles records on, because they really wanted to hear the Rolling Stones and Motown stuff [Little Pattie denies this]. But apart from that they were in a great mood and the party went on until about 2 a.m. I didn't notice much of the other performers, except Johnny Chester who poured a drink all over the front of my dress.

"As we were leaving Paul shook all our hands and by this time I was even braver so I said, 'I'm not used to shaking boys' hands on their birthday' and offered him my cheek. He very gently took my chin, turned my face around and gave me a beautiful kiss right on the lips. I know it sounds corny, but for about two weeks I washed every part of my face but my lips."

The Beatles themselves seemed to be in enormously good spirits throughout the midnight bash. "Ee, it's a proper do isn't it?" Paul had quipped when he first walked in the room. "Hey Ringo, don't get yourself plastered," instructed George. "Shurrup kiddo, watch hows yer speaks to yer elders," he retorted, adding later, "I love these Australian girls mate, they're smashing." "You'd never meet such marvellous girls from a contest like this in England," smoothly offered Derek Taylor. "Their reasons for wanting to attend the party were excellently explained. I couldn't write better myself — and that's my job!"

Bob Rogers (who was allowed to stay throughout) has his own recollections of the party. "The thing that sticks in my mind the clearest is how absolutely rotten drunk Ringo got. At about 3 a.m. he passed out on his feet and just slowly sunk to the ground where he stood." This incident was not witnessed by special guest Patricia Amphlett, who had departed some hours earlier. After all, she was only fifteen, hit record or not.

As Little Pattie, the diminutive Eastlakes schoolgirl, Miss Amphlett had scored a freak hit record over Christmas 1963 with the charming novelty song *He's My Blond Headed Stompie Wompie Real Gone Surfer Boy* and was on the charts with her second hit, *We're Gonna Have a Party Tonight,* when the Beatles arrived.

"I went to see them at the Stadium on Thursday night with my friend Noeleen Batley [then Australia's most successful female recording artist] and one of the security men that we knew offered to take us backstage to meet the Beatles. I was absolutely terrified because I was very very shy and I only looked about twelve. But they were marvelous; they'd heard about my first record and wanted to know what a 'stompie wompie' was — something which I had great difficulty explaining.

"Ringo was extremely warm and friendly towards me and he insisted that Noeleen and I come to the party. I rang mum and she said yes so I went back to the hotel in their car. I think I spent most of the night sitting in a corner though."

Riding the milk truck under much more agreeable conditions than the previous Thursday.

One gentleman spent most of the evening locked in his room, although he was somewhat unaware of it. According to Lloyd Ravenscroft: "The M.S.S. security guard got stuck into the grog and started causing problems, so we carried him down to his room, blind drunk, took away the key and I rang Devon Minchin (the M.S.S. Managing Director) to say I'd sacked the man and wanted another. He was so upset that he got in his car in the middle of the night and came straight to the hotel and announced that he was replacing the man personally for the remainder of the tour."

Dave Lincoln saw the second half of the party that the press were forced to miss. "After all the journos and officials left, we all went back to our rooms, changed into dirty jeans and the like and rocked on without having to look over our shoulders. It was a great party, just like being with your best mates at the local."

At one point, guests Evelyn Mac and Carmel Stratton gave their hosts a crash couse in the dancing of the Australian Surfer's Stomp. Ringo and Paul caught on quickly, George gave up after a few clumsy attempts and John wouldn't have anything to do with it.

Among the afternoon media guests had been Dale Plummer of *Woman's Day*, who delivered a white fondant fruit cake baked by

Just altogether too much to handle.

cookery expert Margaret Fulton. With the candles blown out (in four attempts) before the concerts, it became a handy photo prop later in the evening. The astute Ms. Plummer noted that while George and John were consuming the "Beatle Drink" of Scotch and Coke (described in a national magazine by Jim Oram as "a hideous concoction"), Paul was partaking of vodka and tonic because "vodka leaves no smell."

Alcohol may not have tainted Paul's breath, but his kiss had devastating effects on one of its recipients, Jannette Carroll. "The next day I was an absolute celebrity at school, with kids queueing up at the canteen to ask me questions. But I think I lost as many friends as I gained. One close friend got really angry and said, 'Why didn't you tell me you'd entered. I would have too,' and then didn't speak a word to me for six years. After a while, getting mobbed in the playground wasn't much fun, in fact it nearly got me expelled from school — the very staid Fort Street Girls High.

"A reporter from the Sunday *Mirror* came out to interview me and

Getting in early with seasonal wishes.

took a photo of me in my school uniform. It appeared on page three with a heading of 'Pals Make It Hot For Red Devil' and on the Monday I was called before an absolutely furious headmistress who was threatening all sorts of things."

Seventeen-year-old Sandra Linklater also found that meeting the Beatles had more repercussions than she had imagined. A student nurse at Royal Prince Alfred Hospital, then the biggest hospital in the Southern Hemisphere, Sandra entered the competition when a close friend won two concert tickets and refused to give one to her.

"RPAH had a hard rule that training nurses couldn't be photographed in their uniform but that was the only shot I had so I sent it to the *Mirror*. A few weeks later I got a call at home from a livid Matron Nelson who demanded to know why I was on the front page of the *Mirror* in my uniform. When I got to work I had to go and see her and try my best to explain it. Then a few days later I went to the newspaper office with my mother for an interview and the next day I was on the front page again!

"In 1964 a seventeen-year-old girl was a little more protected than she is now. My father thought the Beatles were totally disgusting and he rang the *Mirror* demanding to know where this party was going to be held and who was going to be there. Matron did the same thing. At first they refused to tell him but when he said that he wouldn't allow me to go, they told him it was at the Sheraton. On the night he drove me to the *Mirror* and then followed the convoy of limousines to make sure they were telling him the truth. Matron gave me strict instructions not to be seen with a cigarette or glass of alcohol in my hand, because the reputation of the hospital was at stake.

University of New South Wales students taunting Beatle fans with platitudes to classical pianist Arthur Rubenstein.

Spanish handmaiden Maria Parra attending to the Beatles' sleeping comfort.

The Beatles forcibly alter the hairstyle of their constant shadow Bob Rogers.

Macleay Street, Potts Point.

John flanked by two friends of a friend of a friend . . .

Mad Mel finally entangled the Beatles with his incredible scarf offering in wool.

Braving the June freeze to the tinny accompaniment of Beatle-dominated transistor radios.

"When we got to the hotel, I was really terrified because all these screaming girls started banging on the car, abusing us. I didn't know those sorts of things happened. I can't remember much about the party itself except that we all danced a lot. At one point a girl fainted and someone said, 'you're a nurse, take care of her.' I took her pulse and helped her into the toilet to freshen up.

"The most memorable incidents happened after the party. A car took me to the hospital at about 5 a.m. — and in those days there was a 10.30 p.m. curfew. I started work at six and at nine Matron called me into her office and had me recount everything that happened, though she pretended not to be really interested. Over the next week I must have told every detail to at least 200 people. Wards from all over the hospital were ringing in to ask if I could come and talk to their patients. For literally years afterwards I was known to everyone in the hospital as 'The Beatle Nurse,' I got so used to it I never even thought about it."

"The Sunday Mirror was quite ingenious," says Dick Hughes. "If

The after-school crush outside the Sheraton Hotel.

you drove around Sydney and looked at the street posters you would read 'Vaucluse Girl At Beatles Party,' then 'Bondi Girl At Beatles Party' and so on. They printed up a poster to cover the suburb of each of the seventeen girls."

The Sunday Mirror also carried pages upon pages of comments from the girls concerning their night with the stars. According to Nancy Haddow, who was "adopted" by Ringo for the night: "Ringo's a bit shy but full of fun. He called me 'luv' all night and told me that he would never get married because he is scared stiff about walking down the aisle. He's a beaut dancer, he taught me how to do the Monkey and the Banana — apparently nobody does the Twist in England anymore. He let me read his palm and I found he had the longest line of fame I have ever seen." Carolyn Styles was amazed by her host: "Paul had memorised every small detail he could about all the girls so that when he met one he was completely at ease and could ask her straight off about her job or something she was interested in." Jenny Lamb, who gave Paul a bottle of Scotch, was amused by Ringo: "When he went to the bar to get drinks for the girls, he would make all kinds of grimaces and mutter 'work all day, work all night.' He also went around asking everyone if they were foreign and when they said no he would shake his head sadly and walk off." Delphine Dockerill gushes: "Paul is the most divine person I have ever met. I thought he would be terribly conceited but he was natural and friendly. He is the most fantastic dancer, the way he moves is amazing. And when he danced cheek-to-cheek with me I thought I'd faint!"

But that was on Sunday. On Friday, the dailies were more interested in the quarter empty houses at the Stadium, an occurrence in keeping with the relatively quiet airport turnout.

"To this day," says Kenn Brodziak, "I'm really not sure why that happened. I tend to think that the sort of hysterical coverage which the Sydney press liked to run, frightened a lot of parents who thought there would be some kind of wild riot." Derek Taylor sought to save face by stating: "We took a look at the Stadium when we arrived and didn't expect to fill it for six shows. Why that's almost 65,000 people!" When it became evident that nobody's sons and daughters were being trampled underfoot, the backlash eased off and the remaining four shows were jam packed. The Beatles awoke at 4 p.m. to read all about it.

The three days in Sydney were relatively uneventful. Each day there were the regular morning and afternoon balcony appearances, prompted by George and approved by John. Their song publisher, Jack Argent of Leeds Music, dropped by for a meeting with Brian Epstein, who introduced him to the group. "Gone were the four looning guys," he recalls. "I felt that they had immediate respect for anyone that

A rare balcony appearance. This time George found some trousers.

M.S.S. Patrolman Peter Munday keeping track of Paul's birthday gifts and letters inside an armoured car.

Derek Taylor (left) and comedian Dave Allen with Evelyn Mac, one of the 17 girls chosen to attend Paul's 22nd birthday party on June 18.

John accepts a slice of smoked ham from Carolyn Keirs.

Janette Carroll, the 'Red Devil' (left), watches Carmel Stratton plant one on Paul as he attempts to cut his cake one more time for the benefit of photographers.

Sunday Beatle

Happy birthday, Paul!

SUNDAY MIRROR SOUVENIR

Sunday Beatle

WORLD BEATLES SCOOP

YOU ... COULD GO ... PAUL'S BIRTH... PARTY!

GIRLS! How would you like to go to Beatle Paul McCartney's 22nd birthday party in Sydney on Thursday?

This easy contest offers the chance of a lifetime

Beatle Birthday Party entry form

NAME
ADDRESS
OCCUPATION
PHONE NUMBERS
PARENTS SIGNATURE:

"WHAT SMASHING BIRDS..." PAUL

A TOAST FOR PAUL.

EASY DOES IT! Paul cuts a big slice from his cake, watched by Glennys Smith, 20, of Cremorne, Caroline Styles, 21, of Henley, Claire Hogben, 18, of Pymble, Jenny Lamb, 18, of Vaucluse, and Marcia McAtamney, 17, of Strathfield.

ALL TOGETHER NOW! Paul hardly has room to cut his cake as everyone crowds around him, waiting for a piece.

THAT CAKE AGAIN. Paul is helped by Glennys Smith, Delphine Dodwell, 18 of North Bondi.

BEATLE

WHERE'S MY LIPSTICK says Paul as Nancy Haddow

PAUL DIDN'T FORGET THEM ...

...young girls just missed ...among the lucky 17 ...and Paul McCartney's ...party.

...didn't forget them ...ort them

...ranged it and Paul ...the girls after the ...Friday night

NORMA SHIRLEY, 18, Manson. VIVIANE BERLING, 19, Lane Cove. JENNIFER ADELSTEIN, 21, Clovelly. KAYE JAGO, 17, Manly. KAY ALBURN, 20, Seven Hills.

SUE GALLY, 19, Bondi. JUDY HANDMAN, 17, Lindley Vale. SUE EDWARDS, 18, Seaforth. MERAN AMORY, 16, Malabar Rd. SANDRA MILLER, 18, Pymble.

SUSANNE CATHMAN, 18, Chatswood. JUDITH McELNEY, 18, Lane Cove. SUSAN CATLEY, 17, Wollstonecraft. SUSAN GRIFFITHS, 16, Cronulla. KATHERINE TROUTC, 17, Watsons Bay.

...IRROR

GIRLS!

...Sydney: P.2

...were chosen from more than 10,5...
...Mirror and Sunday Mirror Beatle par...
...the most enthusiastic response to a conte...
...tries set so high that the judges had...
...when it came to picking the...
...FULL STORY, PAGE 3
...s' pictures: Pages 24 and 2

...e lucky girls for the

WHAT A NIGHT IT WAS!

Beatle Paul McCartney is in the swing at the party held to celebrate his 22nd birthday last night. And enjoying this moment with him are Glennys Smith, Jeanette Carroll and Delphine Dockerill, three of the 17 girls chosen from 10,000 applicants by the Daily and Sunday Mirror to attend the party. For Glennys the Beatle party was a very special occasion. It was her birthday yesterday, too.

YEAH—YEAH

Anne-Marie Alexander, 18, secretary, of Collaroy. Glennys Smith, 20, secretary, of Cremorne. Ines Truss, 21, mannequin, of Canberra. Evelyn Mac, 21, model, of Concord. Patricia Thompson, 18, student, of Newport.

Carmel Stratton, 19, showroom assistant, of ... Marcia McAtamney, 17, student, of Strathfield. Claire Hughes, 18, secretary, of Pymble. Carolyn Keirs, 19, librarian, of Newcastle. Sandra Linklater, 17, nurse, of Eastwood. Caroline Styles, 21, secretary, of Manley. Christine Buettner, 16, student, of St. Ives. Delphine Dockerill, 18, university student, of North Bondi. Jeannette Carroll, 16, student, of Ultimo. Jenny Lamb, 18, sales girl, of Vaucluse.

29 DAILY MIRROR, THURSDAY, JUNE 18, 1964. 29

Brian personally introduced them to. They took him very seriously indeed." Argent had issued a commemorative song folio as a tour souvenir, at a time when such integrated promotion was not commonplace. He sold more than 120,000 copies. The Beatles also met with the aged EMI board of directors for some fiscal chit-chat and formal photographs. Apparently John refrained from bemoaning the fate of his precious *With The Beatles* album cover.

Still the security screen remained virtually impenetrable. To Ravenscroft's credit, the protection system he had so carefully planned and executed was one of the very best the Beatles would ever have applied to a tour. Nobody came and went without his knowledge, not even a Beatle. When George wanted to go bowling after midnight, it was Ravenscroft who arranged for the Rushcutter Bowl to be specially open and then ferried him there and back in his own car without vigilant fans being any the wiser. The tour manager says the biggest problem he had was the thousands of autograph books that were thrown, left, dropped or handed over in the vicinity of the Beatles. "All the ones with addresses inside we returned, signed or not," he claims. "The rest had to be discarded."

Television was still struggling to capture every muscle spasm of the Liverpudlian musicians. On the Thursday, ATN 7 did a live telecast of the airport arrival from Melbourne and the hotel balcony appearances. Then at 5.30 p.m. they had crossed live to Bob Rogers

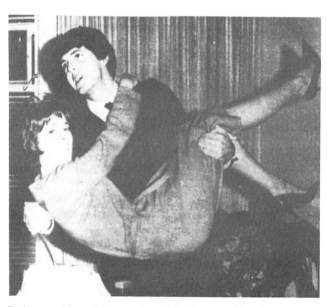

Paul sweeps Women's Day reporter Dale Plummer off her feet.

outside Sydney Stadium for one of the most bumbling, disastrous and hilarious moments in television history.

"The station decided at the very last moment that they would slot in a half hour live program just before the news and score an exclusive," recalls Bob. "I was to stand at the front side door while the camera was positioned in the upstairs room of a milk bar across the road. My cue to go to air was a flashlight beam. But what nobody had counted on was the double decker bus that parked right in front of me at about 5.28 p.m.

"Somehow I got it started and was busily interviewing people going into the concert when I was moved on by a Police Inspector — live on national television and this cop tells me I'm causing an obstruction and have to leave! So I went over and stood on the ledge of a closed doorway so that I was technically not on the footpath. That worked reasonably well until I was interviewing Harry Miller and we both had to balance on the ledge together. Occasionally we'd tip onto the footpath and have to jump back before the Inspector spotted us. I just wanted it to be over, it was the longest half hour of my life."

At the final show on Saturday evening came a sign of things to come, as Dave Lincoln explains: "As Johnny Devlin was taking a bow an egg missed him by a whisker and scored a direct hit on Pete Watson's bass, splattering the whole group. We warned the Beatles before they came on and they noticed the remains as they walked onto the stage.

"Nothing happened for a few songs and then another egg hit John on the foot. Without missing a beat he turned toward the direction of the throw and yelled, 'What do you think I am, a salad?' That was pure Lennon."

Meanwhile, back at the hotel, all was not well with the Beatles' shadow. "It really was becoming difficult," Bob Rogers explains. "The Beatles were getting tired of me obviously. In Melbourne, Paul was saying good naturedly, 'Oh no, not you again Bob, how about giving some of the other fellows a chance?' I'd have to say, 'Sorry but we've got three of these a day to do, now what on earth are we going to talk about?' What made it worse was that every day was another round of grovelling and begging the tour officials to let me to the Beatles, who themselves never knew that it was happening. This daily subservience was humiliating and on top of it, I had little sleep and was living with the constant fear of being scooped by one of the other interviewers. I was also finding it very hard to explain to my three children why I couldn't spend any time with them even though I was in Sydney. When Brian Epstein decided to go sailing on Pittwater on Saturday I had to

Paul (note the eyes) and Ringo with the 2SM 'Good Guys' (left to right): John Brennan, Mad Mel, John Fryer, Mike Walsh, John Mahon and Bob Rogers.

go in case he said something newsworthy, which he didn't. I didn't have a single minute to myself.

"I had a great relationship with Derek and John but I didn't hit it off well with Epstein at all. I ended up having an ugly screaming argument with him outside the lifts at the Sheraton, as he was departing for Hawaii on Saturday night. I wanted to introduce my two daughters to the boys and we were mucked around and mucked around until I got so angry I told him where he could shove his tour.

"I honestly felt like I was cracking up and I just couldn't face going to New Zealand, so I packed my bags and quietly walked down the back steps late on Saturday night to my car. I realised that if I went home they'd know where to find me but I was too confused to go far so I just drove into the Chevron car park and booked a room there for the night. Very early in the morning Bill Stephenson and Kevin O'Donohue from the station (2SM) found me and persuaded me to go to New Zealand. I felt better after a night's sleep and I always prided myself on meeting my commitments, so I agreed to go."

While Rogers had been skulking down the stairs, another personage had been scaling the outside wall heading for the penthouse.

Peter Roberts, a young British immigrant, succeeded where all others had failed, landing himself on the balcony of the common sitting room of suite 801.

"We were each shoving our dirty rags into a case," detailed John, "when I heard a knock on the window. I thought it must have been one of the others mucking around so I didn't take any notice. But the knocking kept on so I went over to the balcony and there was this lad who looked just like a typical Liverpool lad. I knew before he opened his mouth where he was from, because I knew nobody else would be climbing up eight floors. This lad Peter walked in and said, 'hello dere' and I said, 'hullo dere' and he told me how he'd climbed up the drainpipe from balcony to balcony. I gave him a drink because he deserved one and then I took him around to see the others who were quite amazed. They thought I was joking when I told them."

The Sunday morning saw the biggest Sydney airport mass of all. The *Sydney Morning Herald* claimed the crowd to be 10,000 while

still see nothing. But somehow we've come to accept being stuck in our hotel rooms. It just seems part of the job, part of being professional. To be completely honest we were not looking forward very much to our Australian trip. But there was nothing personal in it. The tour involved a lot of flying and we hate flying. It also meant a long time away from home and we hate that too. You know you people of Australia are more hospitable than any we've ever known, in a funny sort of way. We are grateful that we weren't 'organised' too much, in fact we've only had two civic receptions on the whole tour. There doesn't seem to be any 'white tie' set-up here, like there is at home in Britain." Ringo added, "The way people have received us in Australia has made all the difficulties of being a Beatle worthwhile."

Talking to Dick Hughes, John admitted to serious doubts about Sydney. "The crowds outside the hotel here were nothing like those in Adelaide and Melbourne and neither were any of the airport crowds. We were really afraid that it might all fall through here after those empty seats at the first shows. Then we got full houses on Friday night and we knew we were right then."

The Women's Day birthday cake.

Jannette 'Red Devil' Carroll in the school uniform photo that gave coronaries to the conservative Fort Street Girls' High, where she was a prefect.

an airport spokesman said that only the Queen and Billy Graham had drawn comparable numbers in recent times; leaving the way clear for an historian to point out that more than 10,000 saw Ross Smith land his Vickers Vimy in 1920 and Southern Cross in 1928. Even Amy Johnson's solo flight from England in 1933 had been a bigger drawcard, he insisted.

With Superintendant Davies on duty once more, the fans were in high spirits and fine voices. The official car was kept on the far side of the tarmac while a minor aircraft fault was checked and then brought around in a long slow run along the barricades. Davies gave a running commentary over the loudspeaker system and cooled any pockets of disorder. Subsequently, the team of thirty ambulancemen and nurses had only ten casualties to attend.

A *Sun* reporter travelled to the airport in the Beatles' car, capturing impressions of the Australian concerts. George told him, "We haven't been out very much. It seems wrong to come so many miles and

As the Beatles ascended to their TEAL Electra, an Auckland ex-serviceman presented them with a giant toy Kiwi as a good luck token for the flight. From the barriers could be heard pleading cries of "Don't go, don't go," and "No, no, no, no."

Placed in a rear compartment with three Sydney businessmen, the four had little else to do than mouth utterances into Bob Rogers' ever-waiting tape recorder. Again it was George doing most of the talking, trying desperately hard to prove that he was not "the quiet one." He lightly dismissed the egg incident with the words, "All the way through the act I was ducking and looking around for eggs but, as luck would have it, nobody seemed to throw any at us," but became gravely serious over the matter of jelly babies. "I don't like them at all. They're so dangerous when they come in big numbers like they do at a show. If you get one in your eye you're blinded for life." And the infamous revolving stage? "It was a bit off-putting but you get used to if after a couple of days."

6: NEW ZEALAND

Beatlemania wasn't really understood in New Zealand early in 1964. True, the Beatles were dominating the charts, and their television special "Around the Beatles," shown in early June had whipped up considerable teen interest. But to Norman Glover, Associate General Manager of the Kerridge organisation, promoting the New Zealand leg of the tour, a repeat of the hysterical scenes of the first American tour seemed most unlikely.

He predicted, "We do not expect the frantic clamour that has been associated with Beatle tours overseas. We found during the Cliff Richard tour that the teenagers here are not troublesome and are no problem." They were, indeed, famous last words.

Tickets for the tour, with dates in Wellington, Auckland, Dunedin and Christchurch, went on sale with postal bookings a month before the Beatles arrived, and sold out within days. Glover feebly defenced the prices charged, at £2.11s ($5.10) a seat, were well above Sydney seat prices of 37s, 27s, and 15s ($3.70, $2.70, $1.50). "The Beatles are a very expensive group," he said, "and at Sydney Stadium people are on hard benches, with some of the audience a long way from the stage."

Four security men, one of them a 21 stone human mountain, were hired to be with the Beatles throughout the New Zealand leg of their Australasian tour. "Even in sedate New Zealand we can't take chances," said their leader. Local recording group the Howard Morrison Quartet commemorated the pending arrival by releasing a parody disc called *I Wanna Cut Your Hair.*

When the group arrived at Wellington Airport on Sunday June 21 the sedate New Zealanders went wild. At the airport there were 7000 fans, mostly screaming girls. Nobody fainted, which caused Ringo to comment, "The kids are far wilder everywhere else." Five Maori girls were on hand to greet the Beatles and indulge in an orgy of nose-rubbing – passed off as "traditional welcoming kisses." John told one

girl, "My wife will kill me for this," while Paul queried, "I thought only Eskimos rubbed noses." A lavish smorgasbord was laid on in the VIP lounge for the celebrity arrival but George wasn't interested. "All I want is some bacon and eggs," he pleaded.

About 3000 watched their limo drive into the Hotel St. George in the city, while back at the airport ambulance men packed off to hospital a girl who badly sliced her thigh trying to climb a mesh fence.

At the hotel, the Beatles were smuggled through the bottle shop, while outside, teenagers pushed over the damaged two police motor-bikes and applied such a surge against one of the Beatles' cars that, even with the handbrake on, it was pushed backwards.

The Beatles made a brief balcony appearance, then went to face a short-back-and-sides Kiwi press corps. What did they think of the Australians? "They've come on quite a lot since they were let out," said Paul. How long did the group take between haircuts? "It depends how close we are to the barbers," McCartney continued. Did they know that their welcome in Wellington was bigger than Royalty had ever got? "They should have cut a few good records," said John. What did they think of a description of them in the House of Commons as "nearly illiterate"? "It was a good plug," Lennon added.

George Harrison, asked what he would have been if the group hadn't become stars, said, "A poor Beatle." Asked if before becoming a Beatle he was so shy he found it hard to talk to people, Ringo Starr quipped, "That's what they keep telling me, so I'm beginning to believe it myself." What sort of meat did they like? George: "Beef, pork – oh, and mutton, yes, I like mutton. New Zealand mutton is marvellous mutton." Ringo: "And butter." Paul: ". . . and butter. New Zealand butter and New Zealand mutton, love that."

At the early Wellington concert on Monday night, police cautioned several girls who leaned over the hall's balcony rails, scream-ing and waving. But the first rush at the stage didn't occur until the late show, when fifty policemen had to force girls back into their seats. One youth ran on stage and almost knocked a bemused Ringo off his drum stool before being hustled backstage, while Paul was almost dragged into the audience. Wrote one reviewer, "As the Beatles finished, everyone in the hall was standing and it took the National Anthem to restore calm." Paul later commented, "It got a bit exciting towards the end. We were hoping they'd be up on stage dancing but the police got them back." One can only presume he was being facetious.

If the house PA systems in Australia had been barely tolerable, the primitive sound facilities in Wellington Town Hall were virtually useless. Recalls Johnny Devlin, "The sound at the six o'clock show was just shithouse, so low that it couldn't be heard even when the screaming took a rare break. The houselights were also left on. So when the Beatles came off stage, John screamed, 'What the fucking hell is going on here?!!' I told him not to worry, that I would get it all straightened out in time for the second show. Now Derek Taylor really didn't have a club about anything other than the press, and Brian Epstein was in Hawaii, so I elected myself to confront the PA operator. It turned out that he was terrified to turn up the sound because he thought it would blow the diaphragm out of his precious speakers — he had never had to handle anything like the Beatles before. So I calmed him down, set him straight, and the second show was a killer. A bunch of air force guys in the audience measured the sound and described it as a Boeing 707 on landing. Derek Taylor came to me, thanked me sincerely and asked if there was anything he could do in return. I could have asked for a lot but I only wanted my photo taken with the guys, which he arranged."

Asked about the problems later, Paul said, "We have sung through worse mics but not very often, usually during the early days; we expected better here. Actually Gerry [Marsden] warned us about Wellington. The fellow said he had put a new set in since then but the new mics sounded as bad as the old set." Ringo added, "A few kids were shouting 'speak up' but it had nothing to do with us. If they've got crappy mics what can we do?" Ringo had sung at the two shows, after refraining in Melbourne. Though he had been doing *I Wanna Be Your Man* since the American shows in February, the New Zealanders got *Boys*. "We always do whatever song is the most popular where we are," Paul explained on his behalf. "Did you notice the enormous reaction when John moved the mic over to you?" Bob Rogers asked. "Yea, they thought he was going to hit me with it," Starr quipped.

After the show there was an obligatory hotel party to which the Beatles invited as many non-hysterical girls as possible. Annabel Wigley, 18, was a guest at the hotel who found herself ushered into the Fab Four suite. She later complained to a newspaper that the four took little notice of the entry of her and her two friends and dared to remain seated in front of a TV set while their guests had to park themselves on the floor. "I suppose it didn't matter much to them," she said. "there were plenty more girls where we came from!" When a supper trolley was wheeled in, the discourteous young Liverpudlians apparently "looked after themselves and left their visitors to attend to their own supper." To make matters worse, "The Beatles knew little about New Zealand and had not bothered to read up about the Dominion." Tsk tsk.

That night the errant musicians almost got their just deserts. At 3 a.m. a raiding party intent on cutting off Beatle locks was disturbed by a maid as they tried to force a fire escape lock. The shadowy figures disappeared into the night as their unharmed targets slept on unaware.

Yes, as difficult as it was to comprehend, there were actually people in the world in 1964 who *did not* like the fluffy, British bundles of joy. Lyndal Cruickshank, Miss New Zealand 1964, was a good example. A twenty-one-year-old kindergarten teacher heavily into Wagner, singing opera and acting Shakespeare, she also happened to be a guest at the St. George. "I don't like them and have no wish to even see them, let alone meet them,' she said curtly, before flying out to the Miss Universe contest in Miami (which Beatle fans were delighted to find she didn't win).

Tuesday was relatives day at the hotel. John was reunited with Aunt Mimi who came by with a tribe of distant cousins to announce that she would be staying at the dairy farm a little longer than had been first intended and would therefore make her own way back to Liverpool. Ringo was confronted with three Starkeys, cousins who had emigrated from Liverpool late in 1963. He warmly welcomed Christine, 16, Patricia, 13 and Theresa, 12, though he found it difficult to pinpoint their lineage cross with his own.

Ringo addressing fans at Sydney Airport before leaving for New Zealand.

Before departing for Wellington on a TEAL Electra, the Beatles are presented with a giant stuffed Kiwi bird made by New Zealand disabled servicemen.

Bob Rogers, an Auckland ex-serviceman and the Beatles bid Australia farewell.

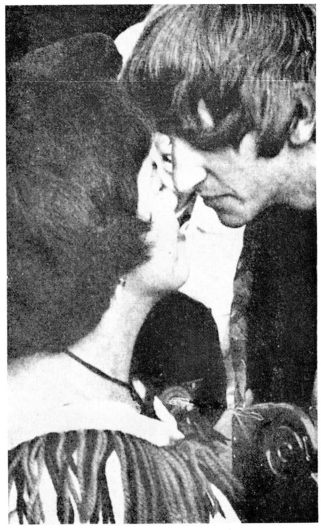

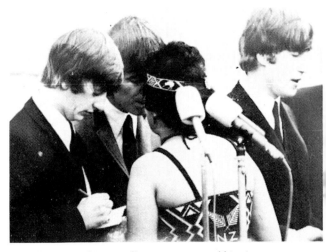

While Ringo rests his nose, George gets some rubbing in.

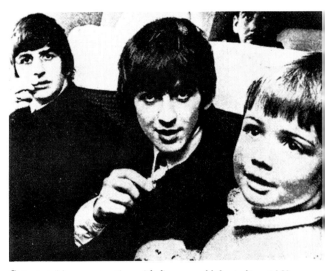

Ringo assaulting Maori maiden Nancy Manurui with his sizeable snoz at Wellington Airport.

George making conversation with five-year-old Australian girl Kaye Peebles on the flight to Wellington.

That night there was a heavy drama in Mal Evans' suite at the St. George, with a girl being found in the room with slashed wrists. A policeman spotted the girl through a window from the fire escape, after Evans had reported that he could not gain entry to his room. The door to the suite was then broken down. She was treated and discharged from Wellington Hospital the same night.

Beatles press officer Derek Taylor insisted there was absolutely no connection between the Beatles, or any of their party, and the girl. He suggested she had gained admission to the room by masquerading as a relative of a member of the party. No police charges followed the incident, which the press announced as, "Girl Tries to Die for Beatles."

Both Bob Rogers and Lloyd Ravenscroft now admit that the disclaimer was hastily concocted to avoid a scandal. Ravenscroft says, "Yes we tried very hard to keep it from the press," while Rogers adds, "She was in her mid-twenties and looked a lot like Angela Lansbury. She had booked into the hotel in an attempt to meet the Beatles, something that was quite common in every city, but had only managed to get into bed with a member of Sounds Incorporated. We all played room swapping a lot, because the switch girls used to listen in on the Beatles' phone conversations, and these two were in Mal's room drinking champagne. When he told her that he couldn't get her to the Beatles she became hysterical and when he went out to the show she locked herself in, broke the top off a champagne bottle and cut her wrists. When the police were called they showed up with an actual battering ram and smashed the door off its hinges. They'd been watching too many movies."

Meanwhile in Auckland, a storm was breaking out over the question of whether the Beatles should get a mayoral welcome. At a city council meeting on June 22, Mayor Dove-Myer Robinson and some of his council clashed over spending $120 to welcome the group.

Councillor Tom Pearce said, "Recently I welcomed home a fine bunch of athletes [the All Black Rugby team] who had been playing football for New Zealand. They didn't get a mayoral welcome. If we are going to pander to the hysteria, the adulation, the screaming, and the rioting, I think we should at least honour our youth. I find it difficult to get excited over these bewigged musicians."

Told by Mayor Robinson that the welcome had been suggested by newspaper reporters Pearce snarled, "Well, they're not responsible people." An English-born councillor, Tom Bloodworth, said, "I wouldn't go anywhere to see them. It's hard to believe they're typical of my native land."

Ringo spoke for his comrades when he mocked, "Oh no, my God they should be broke after that. Look, I've read about it but it doesn't bother me one way or another. We either go or we don't." John added, "I mean we never ask for civic receptions and we don't expect them. If people do it we're flattered. That's that."

Pressmen flew on the plane with the Beatles from Wellington to Auckland on Wednesday but Derek Taylor said the four were too tired to talk, adding, "They're finding New Zealand pretty quiet, though the response from the fans at last night's Wellington concert pleased them." Paul had described Kiwi fans as "very different from Australians, who are a much wilder people. It's very exciting to do a show in Australia but here it was a different kind of thing because they're all very conservative. Mind you, the New Zealand people thought it was wild." To which John added, "Compared with most other places they're very quiet."

Johnny Devlin's reward for sorting out audio problems at Wellington Town Hall: a photo.

Auckland press conference . . . going better with Coke.

In Auckland, Ringo is presented with a souvenir greenstone Maori tiki emblem by eighteen-year-old Auckland Regional Queen Deidre Gribble.

A small group of fans admitted to Auckland's Royal International Hotel to meet the Beatles. Declared young Debbie Davis: "I like Ringo best."

John (the would-be Messiah) attempts to quieten the crowd below from the balcony of Auckland Town Hall. Pictured centre is Wes Hunter of Sounds Incorporated.

At Auckland's Whenuapai Airport about 300 fans who had waited for up to three hours got only a very brief glimpse of their idols. Airport manager B.E. Parkinson called a quick conference with promoters and police, and it was decided the Beatles should be spirited out through the crash gates at the end of the runway after their plane was halted in the maintenance area, about 400 metres from the passenger terminal. The fans called the move "a mean trick" and Taylor said later, "The Beatles are very sorry to have disappointed people. They would have liked to see more fans."

At the Royal International Hotel in the middle of the city about 2000 people were on hand to see them arrive and later wave from a balcony. Three girls fainted in the crush but, according to an *Auckland Star* reporter, most of the crowd were "not genuine fans but lunchtime strollers."

Lloyd Ravenscroft remembers Auckland as possibly the most difficult of the entire tour. The city's hostility extended far beyond the councillors who opposed a civic reception. "As soon as we arrived, I went with Norman Glover to meet the Inspector of Police. He was one of those great bulky characters with a giant stomach bulging over his belt. His opening remarks were, 'We didn't want 'em here and I don't know why you brought 'em.' We had a lot of problems trying to get him to protect his public from themselves and a lot of trouble getting around Auckland.

"The Royal Continental was rather inconveniently located on a hill with a laneway running behind it and a tiny car park descending from the lane. On one occasion our Cadillac got to within thirty feet of this entrance and, because there was only a handful of police on duty, it stopped dead in the middle of a surge of people. So Mal, Neil and myself squeezed out, locked the boys inside and pushed it inch by inch

towards the garage door, a process that took about twenty minutes.

"All through this, girls were fainting in the middle of the crush and we were passing them over our shoulders to safety, only to discover five minutes later that we were handling the same girl. We managed to get the steel door open and we carried about 200 fans into the garage with us. So we kept the Beatles locked in the car until we had removed them one by one."

Somehow the fans did get their hands on the group, as John told American interviewer Jim Steck in August, "It was a bit rough. I thought definitely a big clump of my hair had gone. I don't mean just a bit. They'd put about three policemen on for three or four thousand kids and they refused to put more on. 'We've had all sorts over 'ere, we've seen them all,' they said, and they had seen them all as we went crashing to the ground."

Dave Lincoln expands, "That was the one time I saw John really lose his temper, particularly as Ringo had got a bit hurt. He virtually went on strike, refusing to play any more shows until he was assured that there would be enough police when they needed them. It was times like that he showed very clearly who the leader of the group was."

That night there were two capacity concerts at the Town Hall. The *Auckland Star* sent two reviewers to the show. One, John Berry, seemed to see the Beatles as musical Boy Scouts. Wrote Berry, "There is one element about the Beatles which overshadows all others — fun. It was rock'n'roll certainly — but healthy rock. The delighted squeals of the fans, the hand-clapping, the foot-stamping, the driving rhythm and the noise — all these were identical with the American brand of rock'n'roll which shook, rattled and rolled the world with a young Elvis six years ago.

"But with the Beatles there is an important difference. There is no underlying sense of savagery or overtones of sex which made parents shudder with the first wave of rock. Not once, as the Beatles breezed through their numbers, was there a trace of a curled, defiant lip. Pelvic bones did not rotate. Youthful exuberance here; not teenage rebellion."

Berry was also happy with the attitude of the supporting acts, particularly veteran New Zealand rocker Johnny Devlin, though he was less than impressed with the "gaudy blue suits" of the Phantoms. Alexander Wollcott he was not.

The other reviewer, Pat Booth, was as typical of his way as Berry's hopelessly out of time view of what rock and roll was about. Booth's review was a heavy-handed joke about audience screaming. "Yes, they certainly did Auckland proud, that audience which provided squeals of such volume, the uproar and the footwork under the seats. The Beatles? After all, you can't watch everything at once."

That night the Beatles partied on, with only George showing signs of wear. "They almost weren't human," observed Bob Rogers. "They just kept on and on, rarely sleeping, always up to something. At about seven in the morning I got a phone call and this strange English voice said, 'Hello Bob, it's Neil here, hows about coming around for a drink?' Now I knew it wasn't Neil but I was fascinated so I went around to the suite and I found John, sitting wide awake in bed, dressed in Chinese silk pyjamas downing his second bottle of red wine. He'd obviously run out of people to party with. No songs were written in Australia, it was one long party."

On Thursday, before two more Auckland concerts, the Beatles attended another press conference at which they were a little more serious than they had been in Wellington.

What type of music did they play? "Broadly speaking, coloured music," opined George. "It's closer to rock and roll than anything else," offered Paul. "When we first became big business the promoters didn't like the term rock and roll because that was supposed to be dead. So they called it the Mersey Sound, whatever that means." Their favourite performer from the early era of rock and roll? "Chuck Berry," insisted George. The other three nodded agreement. What about Elvis Presley? "Yeah, his early material. Not his more recent numbers," said John.

Why had the new British sound sprung from Liverpool? "Because we lived there," quipped George. Paul hastened to correct, "No, he means the pop upsurge generally. I think it's partly Liverpudlian humour. But then, Liverpool has always been a great city for talent. Lots of comedians have come from there." Was it true none of them could read music? "It is," said John, "but you only need to read music if you want to write it down. You see, we don't need to write our songs down. Paul and I work them out, then we play them. And that's it. We can't be bothered to learn to read music." Paul said he had piano lessons when he was young, "but it involved playing a lot of stuff I wasn't interested in. It was such a drag."

Was writing their own songs one of the reasons they were successful? John answered firmly, "Yeah, it is. Too many groups try to get there by copying other people's material, and it doesn't work." What about the haircuts? the press concluded. Paul responded, "The funny thing is that our hair didn't start off as a gimmick. In fact Brian Epstein had us trim our hair at first. But as reporters obviously took notice of the hair it became a gimmick and we let it grow longer."

That afternoon the Beatles were on show for nothing. At the mayoral welcome outside the Town Hall 7000 fans turned up to see them rub noses with three Maori girls in native costume and pretend to attack Mayor Robinson with Maori pois. Slight drizzle didn't deter the crowd, who got waves but no words from the Beatles, described by the

Those not invited by the Mayor to meet the Beatles in Auckland attempting their own means of entry.

mayor as "the best in the world in their field." Later he would also praise the behaviour of the crowd.

"It was one of the quickest and most pleasant we've ever been to," John confided later. "We went out on a balcony and waved to the crowd, some Maoris danced for us and away we went. The mayor was very nice, he said 'I wouldn't have blamed you if you hadn't come, with all the fuss they've been making around here.' He was very good."

During the concerts that Thursday night, the portly inspector rang Ravenscroft at the hall to inform him that he had received a warning that a bomb was to be placed on board their early morning plane to Dunedin. But it was not the standard rounding up of the usual suspects for this officer of the law. Presuming the culprit to be within the satanic tour party, he personally oversaw the packing of all stage gear after the performance and had a police truck cart it around to head-quarters for safekeeping until the morning. As the tour party checked out of the hotel, every piece of personal baggage was opened and examined by policemen. This process was repeated at the airport.

Thirty minutes behind schedule, the plane got off the ground and managed to stay airborne and intact until Dunedin. That night, at their late show, they got probably the loudest reception of the whole tour. Halfway through their thirty minute act George and Paul both appealed for less noise, but the audience only responded with more screams.

Johnny Chester recalls the Dunedin concerts vividly. "Policemen there wore bobby helmets and they trooped out in front of the very high stage and linked arms with their hands behind their backs. As it turned out, Dunedin was about the only place where the kids didn't try to rush the stage — because it was so high. But what they did soon wake up to was the fact that the police had made themselves quite powerless with their chain-link stunt and were unable to move independently of each other without full-scale discussion and mutual consent. So the cheeky ones began dancing up and down the aisles playing football with the helmets they were knocking off the embarrassed cops' heads. It was one of the few laughs we all got in New Zealand."

Dave Lincoln remembers, "The New City Hotel in Dunedin was probably the only one where we got any peace and could sleep without the constant chanting of 'We Want The Beatles, We Want The Beatles.' The kids didn't seem to know we were there."

That night the Beatles found themselves once more faced with Bob Rogers' microphone but by this point in the tour the interviews were more relaxed, less serious, usually hilarious and often obscene. Paul and Bob were keeping their distance after a hotel room incident involving a nude girl which Bob, John and Ringo had perpetrated against Paul. "He was really furious about what we did but he couldn't take it out on his friends so I copped the lot. John was able to placate him but relations between us were strained from then on."

During some fascinating discussions about their music, Ringo revealed that Carl Perkins had been in the studio when he did his vocal on *Matchbox*, just a few days before his collapse. He admitted to being very nervous about the presence of the song's writer. Asked about why he didn't write any songs, Ringo revealed that he had written one, called *Don't Pass Me By.* "I keep trying to push it on them [John and Paul] every time we make a record," he pointedly stated, causing John to respond almost apologetically, "We always try to do it but unluckily there's never quite enough time to fit Ringo's song in because he never finished it." "It is finished!" Ringo vigorously asserted. (The song finally appeared on the 1968 *White Album.*)

Rogers also asked them what they thought of topless swimsuits. "It's a joke," said Paul. "It sounds like a vaguely good idea but I wouldn't have my wife or any of my friends wearing them," said John. "I'll have you know I've been wearing one for years," smirked George.

Told that the Vienna Boy's Choir was also in New Zealand, an uncommonly cutting Paul offered, "Oh I must go and see them, must go, I've heard they're a rave." George joined in with, "I believe they're wild, you've got to watch it when they're on!" Then Paul continued, "Hey they don't half blow up a storm those fellows. Have you seen 'em, shakin' their 'eads, aw go mad they do!" "Vienna Boys Choir mania I'd call it," finished John. At the same time, the Austrian warblers were being asked about the Fab Four. All twenty-one of them claimed they'd never even heard of the Beatles.

Paul noted scornfully that some New Zealanders were chanting, "We Want Arthur," after reading the press reports from Sydney. "Mind you, for all I care they can definitely have Arthur," he added disdain-fully. Asked what he thought of New Zealand food, Ringo thought carefully before replying, "Well, the Scotch is alright."

Next stop on Saturday, June 27 was Christchurch, regarded as New Zealand's most staid city. The Beatles turned it on its head. At the airport the by-now-familiar routine of meeting the plane at the perimeter was followed by 5000 but at the Clarendon Hotel in the centre of the city came the first really frightening fan incident the Beatles themselves would witness.

Ringo and George while away the long hours of hotel boredom in Christchurch.

A thirteen-year-old girl flung herself at the bonnet of the group's limo and bounced off onto the road. Luckily the car was travelling very slowly and the young fan recovered quickly enough to be taken inside the hotel to share a cup of coffee with the group.

Shortly after arrival at the hotel, the four made their way out onto the balcony but were forced to flee back inside as rotten eggs showered down upon them. Policemen protecting the front door were powerless to prevent the stream of missiles being hurled from the back of the crowd and parapets of the building opposite, and themselves became targets. The eggs crashed on the hotel wall and windows for almost four minutes. Mildly aggravated, the Beatles passed it off as a one-off incident. They were to be proven wrong.

"Christchurch had the youngest police inspector in New Zealand," says Ravenscroft. "His name was Twentyman and believe me, he was worth twenty men. He gave us a hundred per cent co-operation." Ravenscroft cites Christchurch as a prime example of the high degree of advance security planning that was implemented throughout the tour. "I had drawn up five different exit routes from the Clarendon Hotel. One of them would have required the Beatles to climb a ladder over the back fence, scurry over a tin roof, go down another ladder into a shop, enter a picture theatre and come out the front door into a fleet of taxi cabs."

On Sunday afternoon the rather bored troupe left for Auckland, where they transferred to a Sydney flight early in the evening.

Bob Rogers was not sorry to leave. He would later write in his column for the Sydney *Sun-Herald* newspaper, "The general attitude of the New Zealand general public was one of complete indifference. Australians would be surprised at the extremes to which they have gone to give the Beatles a cool reception. Police refused to provide escorts, claiming 'The Beatles are not Royalty,' and at one hotel this apathetic attitude was repeated to the point of sheer rudeness."

The Fab Four departed New Zealand without any major dramas but the overall impact they created has never been forgotten. Jack Croft, head of security for most of the New Zealand tour, says now, "We weren't ready for that mass hysteria. We'd never seen it before. And you know, we've never seen it since."

Auckland Mayor Mr. Dove-Myer Robinson observes John's prowess with a Maori poi, ceremonial dance ornament, at an official reception.

John and Paul on the Auckland Town Hall balcony.

7: BRISBANE

One of ten girls who broke through the barrier and dashed across the tarmac. Retrieved by a sympathetic policewoman.

The four Beatles being escorted across the Sydney tarmac to a domestic aircraft, out of the sight of fans.

Commonwealth Police were called in to restore order at Sydney's Kingsford Smith Airport as the Beatles changed planes for Brisbane.

The Beatles arrived in Sydney from Christchurch on a TEAL flight at 9.35 p.m. on Sunday June 28. Four thousand fans, waiting patiently most of the afternoon, were rewarded with little more than a brief glimpse of the four as they walked 150 yards along the tarmac to a chartered Ansett ANA aircraft. Mournful pleas of "please don't go!" blended with the obligatory wall of screams and regular snatches of sung Beatle verse. Ten girls broke through barriers and were swiftly retrieved, while one persistent devotee was locked in an ambulance after three separate dashes. At 10.07 p.m. the thirty-two minute frenzy was over, as the flight headed out over Botany Bay northwards to Brisbane.

The capital city of Queensland is not misrepresented by its international reputation as an ugly, sprawling cultural backwater. As with many isolated ultra-conservative cities lorded over by landed gentry, Brisbane's youth have long embraced an almost reactionary (if transient) stance in the face of constant niggling repression by a police force considerably larger than those of more populous states. .

As the Fokker Friendship prop jet landed at Brisbane Airport eight minutes into Monday June 29, the Beatles had no reason to expect a reception any less adoring than those extended in other cities. Certainly the throng of 8000 was dominated by Beatlemaniacs,

but secreted within the mass was a core of antagonists who would turn the red panic crimson.

An hour before arrival, workmen from the Department of Civil Aviation had urgently installed iron struts to the steel fence supports, which were fast giving way under the surge of humanity resulting from the abandonment of a 500 foot temporary wooden barrier — thrown aside to ease a crush that was generating a steady stream of unconscious fans, passed hand-to-hand over heads to a fleet of ambulances. One tragic young girl was rushed to hospital after being pressed unconscious to the fence for an hour.

The pandemonium eased off a little when the DCA announced that the flight would be diverted to another airport if some degree of order was not restored. Even so, the police were kept busy breaking up brawls and reprimanding several girls for throwing smoke bombs, fire crackers and bottles onto the tarmac. A dozen or so of the more vocal "Beatlehaters" were ordered to leave the airport area by police at least an hour before the plane arrived.

As the four young gods appeared in the hatchway, beaming huge grins and waving almost as furiously as their fans, thirty policemen threw their backs into the buckling fence. Paul and John clambered first onto the flat-top truck at the foot of the stairs and launched into an impromptu dance, George lay on his back on the truck tray, looning like Spike Milligan.

As the truck inched toward the fence, a fierce and sudden black rain of projectiles crashed down upon the unsuspecting Beatles. As eggs, tomatoes, pieces of wood and rotten fruit showered the open truck, George took refuge behind the cabin, while the others ducked and kept smiling. Cretinous placards made an instant appearance — the likes of "Haircuts Only Five Bob."

Rescued and rushed to Lennons Hotel, the angered Beatles declared, "No more unscheduled appearances, we've had enough eggs. For as long as we're in Brisbane, it's the hotel and hall for us." Derek Taylor challenged the pelters to "take us on, face to face" — an edict carried with glee by the morning papers.

Despite the unlikelihood of a balcony or window appearance, 1000 fans waited outside the hotel in freezing conditions from 12.45 a.m. to 2 a.m. At 3 a.m. a nineteen-year-old male shinnied two storeys up the drainpipe of an adjoining building and crossed roofs to the hotel. He was apprehended on the fourth floor.

At 6 a.m. five girls crawled in through a laneway grille and made their way into a service lift before being escorted out. Four hours later there were still sixty kids in the street.

At a morning press conference George withdrew Derek Taylor's challenge, "We're not that keen — really," while Paul declared, "We're not disgusted or dismayed — just disappointed. It was all so pointless." John then chimed in with, "Every nit in the world will start throwing eggs for the next month or so, until some other nit thinks up a better trick." Asked if they would feel like caged animals, Lennon quipped, "Oh no, we feed ourselves."

But caged they were. The ever-vigilant police had gone to great pains to warn the hotel management that any Beatle under twenty-one (George just scraped in) could not be served liquor. At 4 p.m. the four made a careful public appearance, behind a heavy plate glass lobby door. Later in the afternoon they ventured out on a balcony — within throwing range — but encountered no problems.

The boisterous but not yet violent Brisbane crowd.

Sweet young things, hoarding eggs, rotten fruit and chunks of timber.

In Brisbane, the Beatles faced some of the most intelligent questioning of the entire tour, at the hands of 4BK's young beat buff Tony McArthur. He and George chatted at length about their common interest in Motown music and the youngest Beatle revealed, "I like most music if it's good. I like classical music, on a guitar. I'm not keen on classical played on a piano." Paul said that, if he had the power, he would stop the release of the early Tony Sheridan Hamburg material. (*My Bonnie* had just dropped out of the US and Australian top thirties,

Cry For Shadow was top ten in most parts of Australia, and *Ain't She Sweet?* was just moving toward the top thirty in England and Australia.) "I think they're a bit old hat," said Paul. "We signed those contracts when we were about eighteen because we had no manager and we didn't know what we were doing. Consequently we can't do a thing about it."

It was in the Queensland capital that Kevin Ritchie witnessed one of the cleverest attempts by a fan to get to a Beatle, possibly ranking second to Peter Roberts' Sydney climb. "This young man had saved up his pocket money for months and bought a perfect professional waiter's uniform. Armed with an empty tray, he managed to make it into the Beatles' floor without so much as a question from the security force. But he didn't know which room the boys were in so he knocked on my door asking if I had a drink order. Well I became suspicious, so I rang Lloyd Ravenscroft to warn him and a few minutes later the boy was being carried bodily out the front door. He hung around the hotel the next day and so I took him aside, gave him a photograph and told him he'd better leave before he got arrested or something. He was quite a nice kid really."

Paul, looking fatigued at the Brisbane press conference.

The night's two concerts, before a total of 11,000 at Festival Hall, were subdued by southern standards — though inaudible as usual. The 'nits' turned out in force, lobbing a steady stream of food and drink containers, coins, sweets and rubbish onto the stage. At one point during the second show, two youths raced down the centre aisle and hurled a large metal biscuit tin on stage, swiftly returning from whence they came to avoid apprehension.

One press report claimed the Beatles "ducked and gestured angrily at the audience," while the thirty police at the base of the stage confiscated streamer rolls from little girls and blocked photographers. The ambulance crew had a fairly easy time of it, with only six true faintings.

Between shows the Governor of Queensland, Sir Henry Abel Smith, with Lady May Smith in tow, visited the Beatles backstage and proclaimed them to be quite decent chaps. The police added to the cheery picture of official delight by praising the restraint of the fans — who managed to stay close to their allocated seats until the end of the second show.

That night, twenty Brisbane lovelies attended the after-show party and danced to Motown records. Despite the day's antagonist antics, the four were in quite high spirits and made plans to take advantage of the superb sunny weather (uncommon for June) by undertaking a day trip to the Gold Coast beaches, just an hour's drive from the city. Ringo was presented with a grey kitten which he was forced to quietly decline.

On Tuesday morning a Peter Rossini rang Derek Taylor claiming

Ringo and John oblige a cameraman . . .

. . . and oblige themselves.

Departing Lennons Hotel in the dark hours of the morning.

to be a student and a representative of the egg hurlers. He claimed that the barrage was a protest against materialism and that the Beatles were a product of advertising. Taylor invited him to present his views to the group in person, later in the day. In Taylor's own words, "Three very polite students arrived at the hotel at five o'clock and they were let in, sat down and given Cokes. But, as it turned out, they were only there to apologise for the University of Queensland. Five minutes later the porter announced that four egg throwers had arrived with their spokesman. They were shown into the room and given no chairs or Cokes. So we had four Beatles, three apologising students and myself sitting on one side of the room and four students and one spokesman who never said a single word during the entire meeting — standing on the other side."

Paul later related the gist of the meeting to a reporter, stating, "We had a bit of a chat with them — more of a debate really — and we all ended up friends. We asked them why they threw eggs and they said they were sick of hearing our songs on the radio and sick of kids screaming at us. So John asked them why they didn't throw their eggs into the crowd if it was Beatlemania they were against."

Taylor's version added, "Paul told the leader, 'We'll give you a few years and you'll be wanting all the suits you can get your hands on.' It broke up then with no progress being made in what was just a fundamental argument on the clash of materialism and idealism."

With that out of the way, the Beatles secretly left the hotel in two hire cars for what was the best kept secret of the entire tour — a visit to the Gold Coast. According to their personal M.S.S. guard: "We set out just before lunch and got back to Brisbane just before the first show. We spent most of the time on the coast between Broadbeach and Surfers Paradise and because it was a school day they went virtually unrecognised. It was also a fairly sunny day.

"They weren't terribly good swimmers but they seemed to enjoy themselves. I don't think they'd ever seen such a long stretch of white sand beach, they were quite overawed by it. I was overawed by the fact that they went into the water with their socks on — they claimed they had soft feet.

"Personally, I had much more time for the Rolling Stones. Once they were out of the public eye they each became just one of the boys. When I took them to the Gold Coast, they had me out of my uniform while I was still in Brisbane. When they ate, I ate. But with the Beatles it was very different; I could do a whole fourteen hour shift without hardly a word or a bite to eat. Everything was very officious with them, and a security guard was only there because he had to be. Ringo was the only one with any real personality. The only thing they seemed to be interested in was the very young girls that we were regularly instructed to let past the security screen around their hotel rooms."

After their final Australian concert, George retired to his room early to write a column for a London newspaper, while the others busied themselves with whatever dalliance Mal was able to arrange until about 3 a.m. Three hours later they were awakened, bundled into a Rolls Royce and onto a plane to Sydney. They posed for shots on the aircraft steps and shook hands with Festival Hall manager Bert Potts. A few hundred fans waved goodbye from behind a police-guarded fence, under a clump of tropical palm trees.

89

Brisbane Police, not the world's most humanitarian species of life, taking no chances at the first Beatles concert.

Arriving at Brisbane Festival Hall in a Rolls Royce.

The final wave.

A balmy, tropical farewell from the city of the north.

Festival Hall manager Bert Potts was on hand to bid the Beatles farewell at Brisbane Airport.

Fans stopped by the airport to catch a last glimpse on their way to school.

8: THE CONCERTS

Brisbane Festival Hall

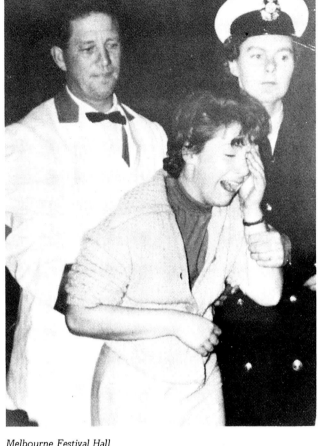

Melbourne Festival Hall

Adelaide Centennial Hall

Sydney Stadium

Tour manager Lloyd Ravenscroft leads the group through the back door of Sydney Stadium.

Despite Ernie Sigley's recollection of John compiling a song list on the flight to Adelaide, the set delivered in Australia was identical to the ones in Denmark and Holland:

I Saw Her Standing There, I Want To Hold Your Hand, You Can't Do That, All My Loving, She Loves You, Till There Was You, Roll Over Beethoven, Can't Buy Me Love, This Boy, Long Tall Sally or *Twist And Shout.*

In Wellington the group were embellished once more with the voice of Ringo and returned to a standard eleven song set with the addition of *Boys.* Never on stage for more than thirty minutes, the Beatles used almost identical patter at each performance. Paul delivered most of the taunting, teasing lines, with the ad libs coming from John. Musically they were adequate, occasionally descending to abysmal. As can be observed from the film of the 1966 Tokyo concerts, George Harrison was not a particularly impressive live player at any time. Ringo freely admitted that he could rarely hear what the others were playing and simply guessed the progress of the songs (accurately as it turned out!)

In 1964, at least in Australia, there was no such thing as a concert sound system in public halls, and stage foldback was just unheard of. Ron Blackmore, later to become Paul Dainty's partner and to supervise PA's for such tours as the Rolling Stones (1973), explains that the hall

sound facilities provided for the Beatles were exactly the same as that used for wrestling, boxing and revivalist meetings. "There was one amplifier, of about 100-150 watts, into which ran an average of eight microphones. There was no mixer; the singer balanced the sound by moving back and forward on the mic. In the case of a rock concert you swallowed the thing. There was a volume knob and a tone knob and that was it. All this was usually locked away in a back room somewhere, although at Sydney Stadium it was under the stage.

"Out front it was even worse. At the Stadium there was a cluster of three tin AWA horns on each of four posts which were aimed at the four seating sections. Festival Hall in Melbourne used, to the best of my knowledge, Altec 'Voice of the Theatre' boxes like they used to have in old picture theatres. There were about six of them stuck up on top of a canopy over the stage and angled toward the audience. This was what the Beatles' voices were carried through, though it wasn't altogether as bad as it sounds. Groups in the sixties usually learned their harmonies so well that they could be put in separate rooms and still keep in time with the other guys. The Beatles' harmonies weren't bad at all."

On stage, the three guitarists had a single Vox 60 watt amp each, and the drums were expected to be loud enough without any electronic assistance. Today, it is worth noting, an indoor concert PA for a major rock act pumps out around 40,000 watts of sound.

But, for the older generation, the sound emitted from the Beatles' concerts was something akin to sacrilegious. In Sydney, the *Daily Telegraph* sent a technician to the early Friday concert with a decibel meter. Under a heading of "Beatle Fans Scream Like a Jet in Flight," they reported that the pre-interval proceedings clocked up 90-100 decibels, the same as a Boeing 707 at 2000 feet. Johnny Devlin and Sounds Incorporated occasionally managed to push the needle up to 110 and it hit 112 with anticipatory screams as the second half opened. The Beatles took it to 114 and never let it slip below 110 — the equivalent of an industrial lathe from three feet.

Bob Taylor, a young New Zealand piano player with the Kiwi Four, who would become a member of Johnny Devlin's Devils just six weeks later, sat eight rows back from the stage, with a "mature lady of seventeen who tried hard not to scream. I'm positive I didn't hear a note of music," he says. "All I heard was ear-splitting screams. Particularly when the stage revolved around in my direction and a thousand voices shrieked, 'He's looking at me — aaaah!' " Devlin gives a vivid description of just what effect an innocent gaze from a real live Beatle could have: "I saw girls in Adelaide lying on the floor, bashing their heads into the seats until they bled. Just gone, completely gone. It was frigtening then and the thought of it is still quite disturbing."

The shows were opened and compered throughout by Alan Field, who was followed by the Phantoms who then stayed on stage to back Johnny Devlin and Johnny Chester. Sounds Incorporated closed the first half and the Beatles occupied the entirety of the second.

Field, to put it plainly, was a disaster. His slightly risque adult-oriented northern English dialogue might have been understood by British kids but the culture gap was just a little too wide for him to

The primitive facilities and revolving stage of "the old barn" — Sydney Stadium.

The long walk from dressing room to stage.

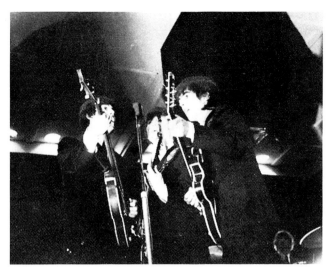

Paul, John and George share lead vocals on the gentle "This Boy."

George lets fly on his solo lead vocal – "Roll Over Beethoven."

connect down under. "I had to cut back his time every night," says Ravenscroft. "He went down like a lead weight. His material just wasn't for the kids." Bruce Stewart adds, "He just died slowly every night."

Field compered in every city except Adelaide, when Bob Francis had been assured the honour as reward for his valiant efforts. The first Adelaide concert was recorded (with sound engineering by Bob Rogers!) by 2SM and broadcast over the (legitimate) "National Beatle Network" early the next week, actually clashing with the second Sydney concert. It does not stand up to the passage of time well, though it is of historical value due to the presence of Jimmy Nicol.

The Phantoms, resplendent in electric blue suits, played, like most Australian instrumental units of the period, a compelling blend of the Shadows and US west coast surf music. They had scored two instrumental hits in Melbourne before the tour and were among the more polished and imaginative outfits of the stomp era.

Devlin, with a reputation for being outrageous, pulled out all stops for the tour. He spent a reputed 150 guineas on a black leather suit which, one unkind reviewer suggested, made him look like "an over-stuffed suitcase." His frantic set was comprised entirely of Fifties rock'n'roll chestnuts and went over surprisingly well, scoring him encores in New Zealand (of course), Adelaide and Melbourne. "The Beatles used me as a barometer to what the audience was like in each city," he says, "and sometimes watched my set from the wings."

Chester, a little more restrained, sang similar material but added his own peculiar touches. "I wanted to do things a little different to the other acts. So I took my own lights with me, packed in a suitcase. I carted them on and off planes myself and almost got a hernia. When I did *Fever* I had this red spot trained on me and the effect, on a show where there was no other special lighting, was quite dramatic. When I came off stage one night, John came up to me and said, 'That was fabulous, I've never seen anything like that before.' He seemed incredibly impressed."

The most puzzling aspect of the concert reviews was the complete and absolute absence of critical comment on Sounds Incorporated. They performed vibrantly and competently, got excellent audience reactions in every city, but were almost completely ignored. Even the Phantoms got more ink. Bruce Stewart, for one, was greatly impressed by their set. "They worked very hard and always pleased the audience. What I remember best is a weird, wild dance they went into during Stevie Wonder's *Fingertips*. I'd never seen anything like that."

In every city, there were two shows a night; one at 6 p.m. and the other at 8 p.m. Rather than face the daunting difficulties of returning to the hotel, the Beatles waited backstage between sets, often observing their support acts. Stewart remembers, "They were incredibly clean. They often washed and shampooed their hair between shows." Devlin recalls the four, with Ringo on makeshift corkboard drums, improvising a rough backstage version of the then-unreleased theme to *A Hard Day's Night.*

Though they exchanged jokes with the boys, received visitors or caught up on James Bond's progress, the backstage wait was generally

unpleasant. The "dressing rooms" tended to be draughty, deteriorating wooden boxes, stinking of sweat and liniment and occasionally infested by cockroaches.

One notable exception was Sydney Stadium. Dawn Miller, wife of manager Harry Miller, completely redecorated the backstage area prior to the concerts. The dingy grey walls were painted white; two olive green lounge suites and light wood coffee table and cabinet were installed; gold Thai silk curtains were hung; there was a dining area with purple upholstered chairs; and four monogrammed towels were provided. The supports made do with the standard deprivation.

Such opulence may have been laid on to divert the Beatles'

John explains "You Can't Do That."

Ringo returns to singing with a croaky "Boys"

Getting the show underway with "I Saw Her Standing There."

Beatlemania proves a little overwhelming for the very young . . .

. . . and the very old.

attention from the curse of Sydney Stadium — the revolving stage. Ron Blackmore explains: "Because the microphone cables ran up a centre pole, the stage couldn't go around continually in the one direction. It went one turn and then a little man by side-stage with a lever sent it back the other way so that the cables could untangle."

The audience response at the Australian concerts was fairly uniform, with one dramatic exception — Melbourne. There the screaming and hysteria reached a pitch that justified the over-reaction of the daily press. The Victorian fans did not stop for a single breath, they roared and howled during introductions, ballads, announcements and dedications. Paul had to take around three cracks at every introduction and at one point abandoned the pointless exercise with the words, "It's like Christmas." The return of Ringo, highlighted by Paul on two occasions each show, certainly added to the enthusiasm. The final Melbourne show saw a rare cheerio from the stage, as Paul thanked the local fan club presidents, sitting at ringside, and dedicated *Long Tall Sally* to them.

Entering and departing the various halls was often a major tactical operation, though one Sydney policeman claimed, "We had more fuss than this for Johnnie Ray." Extensive traffic jams usually occurred as the first show's patrons spilled out into the street as the second shift were arriving. The turmoil, in Sydney at least, meant lean trading for souvenir hawkers, who were left with most of their stocks of placards, plastic wigs, 'I'm a Beatle Fan' badges and official programme books.

In Melbourne, one bumbling hall attendant opened the rear double doors at Festival Hall (which served as both an emergency fire exit and stagedoor) as a show ended, flooding the rear street with milling fans who mobbed the Beatles as they made their getaway. So severe was the clamour that a rear door of the Austin Princess was torn completely off its hinges and left lying on the roadway.

Ravenscroft employed the now-common trick of letting the audience think they were getting an encore, while the group were rushed straight off the stage and into a waiting car. "By the time they had realised they weren't coming back," he smirks, "the Beatles were in their hotel room with their feet up."

Even when the kids didn't fall for the mock encore trick, there was always one other failsafe buffer. In the irreverent Eighties it's hard to comprehend but, as the Adelaide *Advertiser* dutifully reported: "At the first sounds of *God Save The Queen,* the huge crowd stood silent and still. And as the last sounds of the anthem died away, they all started screaming again."

At the first Melbourne concert, over-zealous security men took to forcibly ejecting from the ancient hall any fans who appeared to be enjoying themselves too much. Two young men were tossed out for screaming too loud just before the final song, and spent the duration of *Long Tall Sally* pounding on the back door in a tearful state of near-collapse. They were Ronnie Burns and Ian 'Molly' Meldrum, two celebrities-to-be of Australian music.

Burns was the mop-topped lead singer of Melbourne Beatle clone group the Flies (who opened the Rolling Stones concerts the following year). He and Meldrum, a medical student infatuated with every aspect

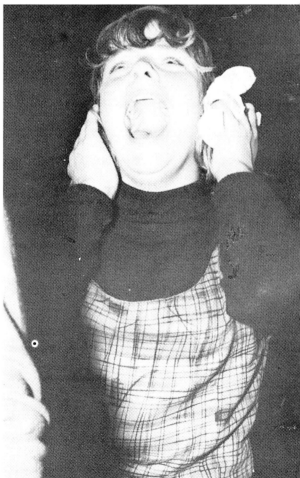

of the beat revolution, lived in the same house and were inseparable friends.

"I spent two days in the ticket queue for ringside seats and I was at the front of the barriers at the Southern Cross Hotel," recalls Meldrum. "Those four days made me realise how important rock was to me." Soon after, Ian became a member of the "Kommotion" team, a reporter for *Go Set* and a remarkably intuitive record producer. In the late Sixties, his adolescent dreams came true when he became a staff member at the Apple headquarters in Saville Row, London, and a close friend of the Beatles. He had been invited to stay with John and Yoko at the Dakota just a few weeks before the murder.

Symptomatic of the novelty position that "pop music" held in the Australian adult-dominated community in 1964 was the generally supercilious critiques handed out to rock concerts. With the Beatle shows, every arthritic swing devotee able to hit a typewriter key and twitish cadet journos who wouldn't have known what they were hearing, were handed tickets and ordered to review the event. The coverage reached its lowest ebb in New Zealand (see that chapter) but there were certainly no Pulitzer Prizes earned in Australia.

ADELAIDE: John Miles from the *News* saw the Friday concerts as ". . . the greatest audience-participation show Adelaide has ever seen and heard. The Beatles provided the Liverpool sound at Centennial Hall and the audience responded with the Adelaide sound, which was much louder. They screamed, shrieked, yelled, whistled, stomped their feet, clapped their hands, cheered, cried, waved, shouted 'Yeah yeah yeah' and threw streamers onto the stage . . . Dozens of girls sobbed with excitement and one girl swooned away. St. John Ambulancemen treated her for what appeared to be a state of sheer ecstasy. In spite of an early promise not to scream through the songs the audience forgot itself and did . . . 'Thank you very much for signing that petition to bring us here,' said Paul and everybody screamed . . . From a milling mass the audience suddenly stood still and silent for *God Save the Queen*. They then gave just one final fabulous, delighted, grateful scream."

Such was the blueprint for most reviews. The *Sunday Mail* reported "At five minutes past seven 3000 teenage boys and girls crashed through the sound barrier and stayed there for half an hour," while the establishment tabloid the *Advertiser* shook a wrinkled finger and exaggerated, "Hysterical screaming fans stormed the stage in a near riot as the late Beatles' show drew to a close last night. The closing incidents marred what was otherwise an orderly evening of screaming, shouting, stamping and singing." The paper quoted a senior police officer as saying: "It could have got out of hand at any time," and highlighted a short grey-haired woman at the back of the hall trying to view the show through a pair of binoculars, who clambered up on a reporter's seat and balanced on an ambulanceman's shoulder to obtain a clear view.

The *Advertiser* also sent writer John Horner, who tried terribly hard to treat the event as he would a chamber recital. "The Beatles sang properly. Their tunes were melodious, warm and folky — but not 'folksy.' Their harmonies were firm and effective, and sometime had odd modal touches. The chord on the flat seventh, of all things, enriched a cadence now and then." Imagine that.

A nameless *Sydney Morning Herald* representative sent back a workmanlike report, which referred to the well-known hit *She Was Just Seventeen*. As naive as he was ill-informed, he deduced: "The Beatles, unlike other rock'n'roll groups, have no rehearsed movements and when John Lennon started to climb a piano, the crowd went wild."

Dick Hughes, covering the opening shows for the Sydney *Daily Telegraph*, was at least witty: "There was a participation sporting event, billed as a concert, in Adelaide's Centennial Hall tonight. The participants were ninety per cent of the audience of 3500. The remaining ten per cent were 'squares' like myself, trying to find out what makes this Mersey Sound tick. We didn't stand a chance because most of the time you can't hear it . . . to qualify as a participant, your squeal, when combined with those of other participants, must leave an after-ring like the din of a million or so cicadas . . . as with so many sports, Australians seem to have a natural flair for it."

Melbourne: The *Age's* John Gevegan, kept up the Adelaide standard by managing to review both the Monday Melbourne Festival Hall shows without mentioning a single song title. Starting off with the supports (rare in itself) he thundered, "Johnny Devlin looked and behaved like a skin diver with St. Vitus Dance. He finally accomplished whatever he was trying to do by lying full length on the stage. They screamed at Johnny Chester, who sang the same songs as Mr. Devlin."

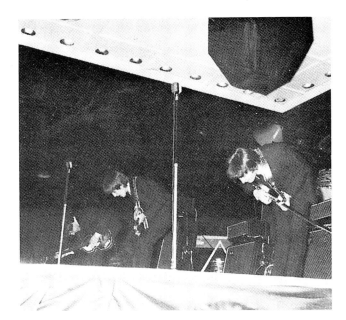

The final bow.

Paul and John unstrap their guitars.

George ventures a little too close to the catwalk on the way back to the Sydney Stadium dressing room.

Road manager Neil Aspinall leads the way to backstage.

The audience at Sydney Stadium crush toward the exit ramp to catch a final glimpse of a Beatle.

But Gavegan's sharpest barbs were saved for the Beatles and their audience. "Prolonged screams, pitched somewhere between an air raid siren and an automatic paper towel dispenser, rent the air for a total of sixty minutes tonight. About 15,000 people saw the two shows, including adults curious and slightly shamefaced among an audience of mainly devoted teenage girls . . . the nymphets of 1964 in their uniform of black slacks, duffle coats and purple sweaters, who showed the orgiastic devotion due to the young men from the damp and foggy dead end of England. The girls wept, screamed, grimaced, fainted, fell-over, laughed, threw things, stamped, jumped and shouted. So did a few matrons old enough to know better. As though this were a religious rite, every high-pitched Beatle 'ooh' sent the noise to a new crescendo. These were the high priests of pop culture taking homage from a captive, hypnotised, hysterical congregation.

"Paul perspiring, flashed his naughty eyes. George looked bored, John looked cynical. Ringo bobbed up and down like a golliwog dervish. The songs were rapped out slickly and indifferently. Songs of shout, scream, twang and thump. Somewhere in the Aeolian shades, Beethoven must have rolled over."

The *Herald* was a little less offended: "A record crowd of 7500 made Festival Hall a solid block of stunning, overwhelming sound tonight. The music, carried through giant (!) amplifiers, rarely rose above the hysterical screaming. Several teenage girls fainted, scores had to be pushed or helped back into their seats. One hundred and fifty policemen ringed the stage and patrolled sections that threatened to get out of control. Girls who occasionally tried to reach the stage were stopped within yards of their seats. Hall manager Mr. Lean said it was 'the biggest noisiest, most excited crowd we have ever had here.' Police whisked the Beatles out of the hall while the crowd stood for the National Anthem."

Sydney: In the harbour city there were almost more reviewers than fans at the first and third nights. The standard of their reports ran the gamut from peurile to refreshingly serious.

The *Sydney Morning Herald* sent two writers to the opening Thursday concerts, only one with a byline. The anonymous newsman devoted considerable ink to the recognition by the crowd of Paul's birthday, continuing with, "The Beatles band could be clearly heard in all numbers except one. That was when George Harrison (actually Paul McCartney) looked at his watch and announced in a thick Liverpool accent, 'The clock says this next number will have to be our last,' and

Sounds Incorporated delivering their frantic set

Mrs. Harry Miller provided monogrammed towels for the Fab Four. John got red, Paul blue, George purple, and Ringo had yellow.

The hardest part of every show — the departure.

Paul under the protection of the local constabulary.

swung the long-haired four into *Long Tall Sally*. Thousands shrilled, shouted, clapped and jumped in a final frenzy. Delirious teenagers rushed toward the departing Beatles but found thirty police forming a guard."

Craig McGregor, later to become one of Australia's better contemporary writers, gave a sole serious appraisal of the performance, without once mentioning what was happening on the other side of the stage. "The Beatles showed themselves last night to be every bit as polished, as exciting and engaging in person as they are on records — and, what is more surprising, a great deal gentler. This quality is somewhat unexpected in a Liverpool beat band whose music is raucous R&B, only slightly mellowed by a native English interest in harmony and musical colour . . . It was unexpected to find them singing numbers like *All My Loving* and *I Saw Her Standing There* with such warmth and romanticism . . . Yet, the Beatles were, without a doubt, the wildest, swingingest and ravingest quartet of pop musicians to hit the stadium since Little Richard, whose far from silent shade lingered over the entire show and must have approved of the finale — an up-tempo version of his *Long Tall Sally*, with left-handed bass guitarist Paul McCartney supplying a high, wild vocal lead."

The *Sun's* Ron Ford reported, "It hit the tin roof of the Stadium and thundered round the empty bleachers: 'She Was Just Sev! En!

Teen!. . .' The first real live Beatle song in Sydney. And that's all they got out before the shrieks took over for thirty minutes solid. It was hard to believe that these four frail and largely lifeless looking lads could whip up such a scene. Round and round went the baffled Beatles, with a 'stop the stage I want to get off' look on their faces, going through the motions of ten top pops. Odd things happened when the Beatles burst into top gear. A middle-aged lady was helped out in a state of collapse while they sang *She Loves You;* some of the ushers held their hands over their ears; a man of at least forty-five, in charge of three children, suddenly lost control and began pelting the Beatles with pieces of streamer. Afterwards, I stumbled towards the Cross with a dong-dong ringing in my ears. It must have been the stadium but it seemed like the whole town had been belting the devil out of a piece of galvanised iron with railway hammers."

Ford's sentiments were echoed by Wendy Thomson, also from the *Sun.* "Wanted: One new set of drums, ear drums. Even today, more than twelve hours after the first Sydney concert, I've still got to tilt my head to hear properly. But I can't blame the Beatles, it's the fans — they sounded like a very high-pitched swarm qf locusts descending on a ripening crop . . . One frantic teenage girl screamed, 'John, John' and her idol raised his eyebrows and grinned. She closed her eyes in ecstasy, sank back into her chair and pounded her heels on the floor."

All three Sunday newspapers carried extensive reviews of the fifth and sixth concerts on Saturday night — the first to have house-full signs up before the headliners hit the stage. The late show was the

Souvenir sellers having a lean time out front of Sydney Stadium.

Not all Beatle screamers were teenyboppers.

The social event of the season.

balltearer of the tour and even the out-of-touch reviewers managed to realise it, though not one of them managed to include a song title in their screeds.

The *Sun-Herald* waffled along with the usual adjectives describing the crowd reaction, a few lines of which included, "Thousands of girls under sixteen who occupied the most expensive seats seem to be in a state of delirium . . . laddering their stockings and losing their shoes. Many were hurried off to the first aid room, too excited to stand any more. Mothers with over-wrought young children left mid-way."

The *Sunday Telegraph* took a more exploitive line. "Screaming teenagers last night turned the Beatles' last two concerts into near riots. Police and Stadium attendants fought to control the capacity crowd while the Beatles were on stage. Those packed inside warmed up by screeching as Johnny Devlin and Johnny Chester went through their

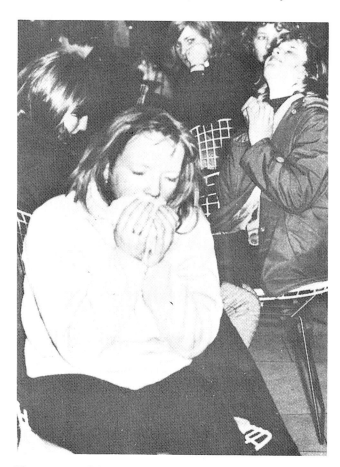

When screaming fails . . . pray!

bumps and grinds . . . The Beatles, though flanked by policemen, were mauled and grabbed as they entered and left the Stadium and the stage . . . The voice of the English compere was drowned by the yelling for the Beatles. Couples with young children left as the screaming grew louder and louder and the crowd grew wilder and wilder."

The *Sunday Mirror* approached it from a quite novel direction. They sent actor John O'Grady, star of *They're A Weird Mob,* to the Stadium to review the proceedings. He rose to the occasion admirably, supplying almost a page of copy, from which comes these extracts: "Most of the Beatle friends are girls — very young and very pretty — who specialise in the Stadium Sound, which differs from the Mersey Sound in that it has no beat. If you've never heard the Stadium Sound you should hire a Boeing 707 and ask the pilot to gun up its engines in your living room. The volume of sound may not be as great as at the Stadium but the quality will be similar.

"Beatles have thin legs and long hair, and would be very useful in a house for cleaning cobwebs off ceilings. The noise they make would be useful in the Riverina for scaring cockatoos and galahs out of the wheat paddocks.

"If you're looking for me in the next few weeks, I'll be on a poultry farm up Thirlmere way, listening to the quiet, gentle sounds made by about 10,000 cackling chooks and crowing roosters. Be very peaceful, I reckon. You'll find me combing jelly babies out of my beard, with one foot going stomp, stomp, stomp in a sort of Beatle hangover."

Finally came the highbrow critique, delivered in *The Bulletin* by Charles Higham, who would later do his best to convince the world that Errol Flynn was a Nazi spy. Generally disdainful of the proceedings he wrote: "The whole evening threatened to resemble Saturday night at the RSL. Even the absurd, impossible Phantom outfits (sky blue suits spangled from head to toe with sequins and pillar-box red guitars) didn't provide compensation . . .

"Introduced by a flabby compere named Alan Field, Johnny Devlin looked fat, well past the dreaded bourne of 30, and far from the condition that once won him the title of Mr. West Coast of New Zealand. Nevertheless he was, for my money, unquestionably the best performer of the evening. Clad in pitch-black leather from toe to tippet, he looked at first like an animated suitcase; then he unzipped, screamed, shook from head to toe and turned into a blackberry jelly with legs . . .

"But excitement was followed by bathos as Johnny Chester, wearing boots the color of cherries with pointed toes, a pallid suit and a cerise tie, sang *Fever* in the dark with luminous blue cuffs and a face that, because of some trick of lighting, now matched both boots and tie . . .

"Three of the Beatles — John, George and Ringo — looked distinctly nervous as they hit the spotlight; grotesque figures like escapees from a Beardsley illustration of the Yellow Book, respectively solemn, ravaged as though by mice, and greedily lupine. Only Paul, an accentuated choir boy with licorice eyes, seemed at all assured . . .

"The Beatles' appearance, certainly, is their strongest suit. The hair fringes, by Ish Kab (of the old Kay Kayser Band) out of Larry in the Three Stooges, curtaining dead-white faces, the funeral suits of tight grey, black ties and elastic sided boots, look at once mannered and not too riskily unlike their (British) audiences. Their arrangements and singing, whatever music critics may be paid to say about them, are strictly routine rhythm & blues, rather below the level of say, the Joy Boys. They move in a very limited way, evoking the loudest screams only when they make deliberately sexual gestures with their phallic guitars. Their legs move slowly and jerkily, like those of marionettes. Only Paul, jolly and enjoying the applause, seemed to be alive and having fun. The others looked tired, jaded and old."

Every reviewer, high or low brow, seemed to be oblivious to the regular doses of wonderfully bad taste pantomine being delivered on stage by John Lennon — possibly reinforcing the supposition that they all left after the first three songs. But it's hard to understand how a giant scandal didn't erupt after the national television screening of 'The Beatles Sing For Shell,' filmed in Melbourne. There, in graphic close-up was John engaging in his cruel and legendary spastic imitation, complete with contorted face and ill-aimed handclaps. Nary a letter to an editor was forthcoming, almost as if naive Australia was simply not aware of what it was seeing.

9:BEATLEMANIA

The Sensational **BEATLES** Australasian Tour Souvenir Album

CHAINS
LITTLE CHILD
DON'T BOTHER ME
I WANNA BE YOUR MAN
PLEASE MISTER POSTMAN
THERE'S A PLACE
HOLD ME TIGHT
THIS BOY

AUTHORISED FOR SALE ONLY
IN AUSTRALIA AND NEW ZEALAND
☆ ☆ ☆ ☆ ☆ ☆

LEEDS MUSIC PTY. LTD.
☆ 324 PITT STREET, SYDNEY, N.S.W.

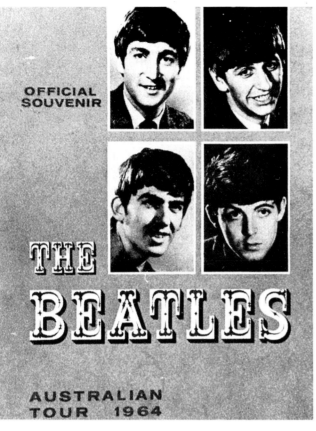

OFFICIAL SOUVENIR

THE BEATLES

AUSTRALIAN TOUR 1964

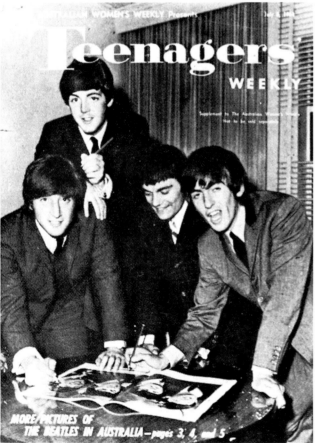

Australia's business community was no less opportunist than America's when it came to merchandising, marketing and heavily promoting Beatle spin-off products.

Once Seltaeb Inc. had laid down the ground rules, there was a mad scramble to saturate the market with paraphernalia before the arrival of the group. Basing most merchandise on Seltaeb-approved designs, Australian companies unleashed tons of plastic and paper, crafted into plastic wigs, autograph books, desk calendars, bracelets, pencil cases, drink tumblers, powder puff compacts, stockings, miniature figurines, scarfs, paper napkins, boots, dolls, stickers, posters, serving trays, fans, hairbrushes, brooches, pendants, mock postage stamps, face masks, wallpaper and school bags.

From all indications, a great amount of this cash-in material was left lying on store shelves. Australians were obviously not as obsessed with the acquisition of physical emblems for vicarious worship as the Americans. One newspaper reported that Beatle dolls were slashed in price from 39s 6d ($3.95) to 19s 11d ($1.99) the day after the group left Australia.

In the publishing area, there were countless exploitation examples, from cheap'n'nasty books of foggy photos, to souvenir liftouts in Sunday papers, to Beatle cooking recipes in women's magazines.

EMI's contrition did not extend to repentance. With the Beatles safely back in England, they created completely new covers for the *Beatles for Sale* LP and *Further Requests* EP, using Sydney Stadium photographs by Tony Merrick.

From leading cartoonists to humble 'letters to the editor' writers, most Australians seemed to want to have their say or give their impressions of the Fab Four. A small sampling of such outpourings follows.

A silk Beatle scarf

A section of Beatle wallpaper.

Barbara of North Nowra:

"My whole life revolved around the Beatles, from my hair cut down to my boots. My Beatle mug was the only thing I would ever drink my tea out of. I wore Beatle brooches and sweatshirts and kept big scrapbooks full of newspaper clippings.

"The day they arrived in Australia I was glued to the TV screen hours before the plane landed. The moment the door opened and they walked out onto the steps, I burst into tears. I did a lot of screaming and crying that week, especially at the concert. I wrote in my diary that Paul waved and smiled at my girlfriend and I. Even though we were right up the back, it made us happy at the time to think that we'd been noticed. I came out of the show totally hoarse and exhausted but I'd had the best time of my life.

"The ticket cost me a £1 of my pocket money, which I saved by not spending a penny at the school canteen for weeks. The day we bought our tickets, Billy Thorpe was in the same store autographing copies of his new record. We had the choice of buying one of them or getting our Beatle tickets but we only thought about it for a fraction of a second before lining up at the booking counter. I really wanted to enter the competition to go to Paul's birthday party but I was only fourteen and the age limit was sixteen. Boy, how I hated those girls that won!

"After the tour I sent away to 2SM for a piece of Paul's bedsheet which Mike Walsh was giving away. I treasured it over the years and only recently threw it out when Mike revealed that most of the pieces weren't authentic at all. I'm glad I didn't find out back then, I would have been shattered."

This exclusive Australian EP featured Sydney photographs, taken at a Stadium concert and EMI gold record presentation.

Two rare six track Thai bootleg EPs which cause collectors' pulses to race.

GEPO 70015

Further Requests

The Beatles with the Gold Records presented to them in Sydney by E.M.I. (Australia) Limited.

SHE LOVES YOU
(Lennon-McCartney)

I WANT TO HOLD YOUR HAND
(Lennon-McCartney)

ROLL OVER BEETHOVEN
(Berry)

CAN'T BUY ME LOVE
(Lennon-McCartney)

The Beatles

Front cover photographs taken by Tony Merrick at an actual performance in Sydney Stadium.

PARLOPHONE 45 R.P.M. EXTENDED PLAY MICROGROOVE RECORD

Copyright Record — All Rights Reserved

MADE AND DISTRIBUTED IN AUSTRALIA BY E.M.I. (AUSTRALIA) LIMITED, SYDNEY, NEW SOUTH WALES

2SM TOP 100

THIS WEEK			Last Week	Times In
1	ALL MY LOVING	Beatles (Parlophone)	1	3
2	LOVE ME DO	Beatles (Parlophone)	2	11
3	ROLL OVER BEETHOVEN	Beatles (Parlophone)	4	4
4	I SAW HER STANDING THERE	Beatles (Parlophone)	3	11
5	SHE LOVES YOU	Beatles (Parlophone)	5	29
6	I WANT TO HOLD YOUR HAND	Beatles (Parlophone)	6	16

When the Beatles held down the first six spots on the Sydney charts in April 1964, it became news throughout the world.

BEATLES
FOR
SALE

EMI Australia created their own "Beatles For Sale" LP jacket with photographs from Sydney Stadium. It is now an essential inclusion in all serious Beatle record collections.

Wednesday, July 1st

"The BEATLES SING FOR SHELL"

Sensational one-hour music spectacular features highlights of The Beatles' stage performances in Australia; also topline Australian and overseas singers and musicians.

TCN 9 | 7.30 pm WEDNESDAY SHELL

Radio 2UW executives Frank Jeffcoat and Ellen deVoss handle some of the 8000 letters which poured into the station (during a mail strike!) for a Beatle competion in May 1964 which asked "How would you describe the Beatles?" The station chose seven adjectives and the only entrant to submit an entry using all the words was Liverpool-born Mr. E.R. Martley, a chiropodist.

BEATLES FAN CLUB

Angela Letchford, President.
BEATLES FAN CLUB,
77 Ku-ring-gai Avenue, Turramurra, Sydney.

Hi there! Well, what a busy week it has been opening up your many requests for Beatles' tickets for their show.

But now I have to tell you that our allotment has all been sold. This should not have happened so soon, but when we rang the Stadium to ask when we could pick up our 3,000 ringside tickets, were were informed that they had been **Sold** elsewhere. So sorry, Beatles Fan Club members. Please accept our sincere apologies.

Please do not write in requesting any more tickets—if we are able to get any more I will let you know as soon as possible via this column.

Some of our members will be journeying all the way from Temora on a chartered plane to see the Show, and our Newcastle members will be chartering buses to come down on "those special days."

The airport will be closed down on June 11 and June 18 for the Beatles arrival—do hope you will all come and help give them the best and biggest welcome ever. By the way, the Beatles won't be stopping at any one hotel for more than one night.

"Can't Buy Me Love" is being released TODAY. The Beatles have held No. 1 position on the English charts with this number for some weeks now, although last week it was taken over by one of their own compositions, sung by the two University students, Peter and Gordon, titled "World Without Love". This is Peter and Gordon's first song. Some of you may already know that Gordon is Jane Asher's brother, and that Paul McCartney has been dating Jane!

Lots of you have written and asked me for the recipe for Jam Butties:—

Take 2 or 3 slices of bread, butter each piece, then spread a thick layer of jam on each (any sort of jam that you like best). Place on top of each other and cut into fingers.

Must be off now, so until next week,

Beatfully Yours,
Angela Letchford.

NEW CLUBS

Australian Cash Box had the pleasure of receiving a visit by officials of three new fan clubs which have been formed in Sydney recently.

Firstly, we had a chat with Rick Papineau, President of the D-Men Fan Club who told us the club was really swinging—with exciting news about the D-Men to be released shortly.

The address for intending members:

The D-MEN NATIONAL FAN CLUB,
2/38 Warners Ave., North Bondi.
President: Richard C. Papineau.
Membership: 5/- per year.

Secondly, came Faye McCallum, of the Searchers' Fan Club, with the news that as a special gift to intending members, every 50th new member will receive a Free Record.

The address:

THE SEARCHERS FAN CLUB OF AUSTRALIA,
45 Noble Avenue, Greenacre.
Secretary: Faye McCallum.
Membership: 6/- per year.

Finally, Ken Cameron, President of the Brian Poole and the Tremeloes Fan Club, told us that his club was filming Brian and the Boy's segment of the recent Liverpool Show and sending the film to the Brian Poole Fan Club in Britain.

The address for those wishing to join:

BRIAN POOLE AND THE TREMELOES FAN CLUB
OF AUSTRALIA,
2/38 Warners Ave., North Bondi.
Membership: 7/- per year.

When Rolf Harris was asked to contribute a little Aussie flavour to the
1963 Beatles Christmas concerts, he prepared this souvenir for fan
club distribution in the UK.

JOHN   GEORGE   PAUL   RINGO

By Debbie, our teenage cook

A BEATLE PARTY—yeah, yeah

● Be the first in your crowd to stage a Beatle Party — and here are all the fun-food recipes to help you, with directions on how to make the fabulous Beatle Balloons shown above.

● Beatle Boys — easy to make biscuits, and let your heart go with the colors to make them as gay as possible

● Ringo Starrs, Beatle Jelly Cakes, Chocolate Music Bar Cakes, Beatle Lollipops — some of the fun foods to make your party swing

● Beatle Mop heads are small cakes with chocolate hair

For George, John, Ringo and Paul, it's —

VOX
AMPLIFICATION

You'd expect the Beatles to be using the ultimate in modern sound equipment and of course they do — as top artists the world over they use VOX amplification . . . .

VOX — PRECISION IN SOUND

See the famous VOX amplifiers, reverb units, echo units, the magnificent range of VOX solid body electric guitars and bass guitars, strings and accessories at your favourite local music store, or at Nicholson's Pty. Ltd., sole Australian distributors of fabulous VOX sound equipment.

Nicholson's PTY LTD.
416 GEORGE STREET, SYDNEY 28 1641

YOU GET THE BEST AT NICHOLSON'S

IE WHOLE WORLD'S TALKING
BEATLES—
IE WHOLE WORLD'S TALKING

BOOTS
BY
BENDOR

89'6

Available at 99 out of 100 Stores throughout South Australia

. . . There's no let-up in the **Beatles** furore. Their new singles and albums are all shooting over the million sales mark here.

Everybody's

with *Disc*

16
July 8, 196

SECRETS OF THE BEATLES TOUR

FIVE - PAGE COLOR SPECIAL

YOU'LL HEAR MOST FROM THE BEATLES ON 2UW

BY SPECIAL ARRANGEMENT

"NATIONAL BEATLES NETWORK"

Featuring Malcolm Searle and Jon Royce, bringing you behind-the-scenes interviews, candid comments . . news items . .

THIS IS WHAT WILL HAPPEN

FOR BEATLES' COVERAGE AT ITS BEST stay on **2UW**

BY COURTESY OF KWIT LIQUID DETERGENT

The busy streets were so congested with shopping housewives, street traders, beggars and all the other Hong Kong dwellers that John, Paul and George hardly ventured out.

It would have been too dangerous if they had been recognised. The city is notorious for its excited mobs rapidly getting out of control and the boys might have been torn to pieces. Only Mal went out to try a rickshaw ride.

FAMILY PARTY FOR BEATLES

MELBOURNE, Tues. — The Beatles did not walk out of the party given by the Lord Mayor of Melbourne, Councillor Curtis to-day. In fact they had such a ball they went to the Mayoress' parlor where they relaxed with the Curtis family—Cr. Curtis and Mrs. Curtis and their five children. They played the piano, had a look at the mayoral robes and drank coffee. Their manager said they had not had such an informal moment since the tour began.

Australia was a fantastic success story all the way round. Paul spent a lot of time chatting about horse-racing to the Aussies, who are inveterate gamblers. After all, he'd just finished negotiations to buy the horse Drake's Drum for his father—and he wanted to pick up all the tips he could.

CUSTOMS NEVER BELIEVE THEM

The boys always have a little tussle at London Airport with the Customs men when they return from their world tours. No one will believe that they haven't got a very big hoard of presents stored inside their guitars.

Quote from Ringo on their return from Australia: "I don't think any of us bought a thing. We were given quite a few presents but they were mostly boomerangs and things like that."

George did buy a new Pentax camera in Hong Kong. Cost him £30 in duty at London Airport!

BEST-CARED-FOR PATIENT

The University College Hospital, one of the biggest in London, gave extra-special treatment to Ringo, when he went down with a bad case of tonsilitis early in June. To judge by the number of doctors and nurses who 'HAD' to visit him, you'd have thought he was just about the sickest bloke in the place. Comment from Ringo: "Everybody was just great to me. But, don't tell John, Paul and George or they'll want to be ill too."

THE boys rehearse with Jimmy Nicol. Tell him when to speed up and when to slow down. Our photographer Leslie Bryce says: "I didn't realise how difficult it was to be a Beatle until you see a new man among them." He's right. The Beatles have a special way of saying things, of talking to police, people, politicians. Jimmy, understandably, found it hard to fit in. But he was obviously very excited, very proud.

Petition For Ringo

Four female fans, none of whom wished to be named, last night brought to "The Advertiser" a 120-signature petition to bring Ringo Starr to Adelaide for a few hours during the group's Australian tour.

"Howling mob of childre

The archaeologist pointed out, "Things haven't changed much in the last couple of thousand years.

"Around about 2,000 B.C. the scarab beetle was regarded by ancient Egyptians as symbolic of resurrection and immortality.

Ringo rallies

Really sound

THE number of different "sounds incorporated" in TCN 9's videotape last night of the Beatles' Melbourne concert made the programme so much the better.

The cameras swept the stage and the crowd, giving a comprehensive coverage of the concert—from the gyrations of Johnny Devlin to the more sophisticated and exciting sound of Sounds Incorporated.

Maybe the telecast did not send shivers of tension and anticipation up and down one's spine as did the live show.

But the absence of these sensations was more than recompensed by a chance actually to hear and see those phenomenal performers—the Beatles.

Thus the telecast was a perfect complement to the performances we saw the Sydney Stadium

Beatle Day On Camera

"The Beatles Come to Town," a half-hour programme to mark the arrival of the famous Liverpool quartet, will be shown by ADS7 at 6 p.m. today.

ADS7 compere Bob Moors, who flew to Sydney to meet the Beatles yesterday, will be seen on the plane.

MESSAGE FROM PAUL

I'd like to send my very sincere thanks to everyone who remembered my birthday last month. I asked Johnny Dean, Anne Collingham and Bettina Rose before we left, to save all your cards and presents for me till I got back from Australia, when I'd be able to go through them. Hope you like the new record.

CANBERRA, Tuesday. — Beatle hair cuts have been outlawed in three Canberra High schools.

TV WEEK

In countdown BEATLES and TV WEEK tells it all in the **BIG BEATLES SPECIAL**

NO CHANCES JOHNNY!

TV CRISIS!

WEDDING BELLS

EXCLUSIVE!

TV WEEK BEATLES SPECIAL ON SALE NOW

YOUNG SCREAM

INDO EXPECTS NO CLASH WITH AUST.

THEY'RE IN IT!

ON the other hand colleague LEO BASSER thinks that with all this rain around it is most timely for the arrival in Sydney of four MOP-tops

Mayfair OF ELIZABETH AN

ALL TRANSISTOR
Plays and records anywhere!

Reduced to only

34 gns.

7/6 WEEKLY

'BEATLES' MONTH SPECIAL!
'BEATLES' TAPE INCLUDED IN THE PRICE

"I bet Ringo didn't have to holler 'NURSE' for half an hour before he got some attention."

FESTIVAL HALL
AZTEC & STADIUMS Presents
The BEATLES
MONDAY 15th JUNE
6 p.m.
TERRACE
Sec. 9 F 68

the Biggest and Best
Beatle Coverage
in COLOR

AZTEC SERVICES PTY. LTD.
(KENN BRODZIAK, Managing Director)
and
STADIUMS PTY. LTD.
(RICHARD LEAN, General Manager)
present
THE BEATLES
JOHN LENNON • GEORGE HARRISON
PAUL McCARTNEY • RINGO STARR
and
SOUNDS INCORPORATED
with
● ALAN FIELD
● JOHNNY DEVLIN
● JOHNNY CHESTER
● THE PHANTOMS

SYDNEY GORDON Farmers MIRANDA

KIDS! GET YOUR GENUINE ENGLISH
BEATLES GEAR AT FARMER'S
Beatle Bar!

BEATLE AUTOGRAPH BOOK
Red, white and blue vinyl with cover photo of the 4. 8/11

BEATLE DESK CALENDAR
Movable month, day & date set in strong plastic case. 7/6

BEATLE POWDER COMPACT
Gold-plated with lid photo of the group; deep bowled. 22/6

BEATLE PLASTIC BEAKERS
Insulated plastic for cold and hot drinks, photo insert. 8/11

2UE
Beatles! We love you!
Your records top the list in all our programmes—morning, afternoon, evening and all weekend.

BEATLE JEWELLERY IN 3 PRICE GROUPS
Gilt keychains, oblong or oval pendants with group photo, each 4/11 Gilt bracelets with five photos, or group photo in Beatle brooch 9/11 Guitar brooch with colour photo of your favourite also photo pendants 5/11

in this week's
Teenagers' WEEKLY
Australian edition only
See The Beatles against Australian backgrounds, with Australian fans!

The Australian
WOMEN'S WEEKLY

for John, Paul, George and Ringo it's—

VOX AMPLIFICATION

You'd expect the Beatles to be using
the ultimate in modern sound equipment,
and of course they do —
as top artists the world over, they use

VOX Amplification . . .

See the famous VOX amplifiers, reverb units, echo units, and the
magnificent range of VOX solid body electric guitars and bass
guitars, strings and accessories at your favourite
local music store, or at Nicholson's, sole Australian
distributors of VOX equipment.

Nicholson's
416 GEORGE STREET, SYDNEY ● TELEPHONE 25 1
"YOU GET THE BEST AT NICHOLSON'S"

BEATLES PARTY "LOCKOUT"

BOB's TRAVELLING WITH THE BEATLES!

Hear Bob and the Beatles, every day on 2SM

Bob left Sydney on May 17 and flew to London to join the four
famous frenzied Merseyville Moptops for their big European
and Australian tours. And, for the last few weeks, Bob has
been Beatling through England with John and George and
Paul and Ringo.

Yes, Bob will be travelling with the Beatles through Europe
and the East—and 2SM will be broadcasting a stream of
fantastic Beatle interviews recorded by Bob.

Yes, by arrangement with Aztec Services, Stadiums Limited
and Nems Enterprises, 2SM has secured exclusive rights to
broadcast the Beatles' smash Australian Show to you.

At the end of the tour, Bob will then Beatle back to Sydney
with the boys and travel with them on their Australian Tour.
You'll hear the first of these exclusive, way-out tapes
TOMORROW! And every day from here on in till the exclusive
2SM broadcast of the Beatles' performance in Australia.

EXCITEMENT IS 2SM

SPONSORED IN AUSTRALIA BY
TODAY'S DETERGENT—RINSE-CLEAN **Surf**

Cigarettes were flown
from Sydney for the
Beatles' special Fokker
plane to take them to Melbourne tomorrow.

The boys who brought
the Liverpool sound re-
quested cigarettes named
Edinburgh.

AS Those Four Young Men flew out of our
lives yesterday morning, one of the big
city stores simultaneously posted a significant
reduction: Beatle dolls cut from. 39/6 to
19/11. The party, it seems, is over.

BEATLES AUSTRALIAN DISCOGRAPHY

ALBUMS   *1963—1982*

-/10/63   PMCO1202   PLEASE PLEASE ME
                     (same as UK) Also PCSO 3042
19/3/64   PMCO1206   WITH THE BEATLES
                     (same as UK except diff. cover) Also PCSO3045
3/9/64   PMCO1230   A HARD DAY'S NIGHT
                     (same as UK) Also PCSO3058
11/2/65   PMCO1240   BEATLES FOR SALE
                     (same as UK except diff. cover) Also PCSO3062
30/9/65   PMCO1255   HELP
                     (same as UK) Also PCSO3071
17/2/66   PMCO1267   RUBBER SOUL
                     (same as UK) Also PCSO3075
—/8/66   PMCO7533   THE BEATLES GREATEST HITS VOL. ONE
                     Please Please Me/From Me To You/She Loves
                     You/I'll Get You/I Wanna Hold Your Hand/
                     Love Me Do/I Saw Her Standing There/Twist
                     And Shout/Roll Over Beethoven/All My Loving/
                     Hold Me Tight/Can't Buy Me Love/You Can't
                     Do That/Long Tall Sally
                     (Cover similar to US *Beatles VI*) Also PCSO7533
29/9/66   PMCO7009   REVOLVER
                     (same as UK) Also PCSO7009
16/2/67   PMCO7534   THE BEATLES GREATEST HITS VOL. TWO
                     A Hard Day's Night/Boys/I Should Have Known
                     Better/I Feel Fine/She's A Woman/Till There
                     Was You/R&R Music/Anna/Ticket To Ride/8
                     Days A Week/Help/Yesterday/We Can Work It
                     Out/Day Tripper
                     (Cover similar to US *Beatles '65*) Also PCSO7534
28/7/67   PMCO7027   SGT. PEPPER'S LONELY HEARTS CLUB
                     BAND
                     (same as UK, except later reissue in cheap single
                     fold cover) Also PCSO7027
16/5/68   PMCO7016   A COLLECTION OF BEATLES' OLDIES
                     (same as UK) Also PCSO7016
4/12/68   PMCO   THE BEATLES ("White Album")
          7067/8   (same as UK, except photos missing from insert
                     poster) Also PCSO7067/8 Apple label
23/1/69   PMCO7070   YELLOW SUBMARINE SOUNDTRACK
                     (same as UK) Also PCSO7070 Apple label
17/10/69 PCSO7088   ABBEY ROAD
                     (same as UK) Apple label
—/—/70   S-4574   MAGICAL MYSTERY TOUR
                     (same as UK except diff. cover) World Record
                     Club label
—/3/70   635056   THE BEATLES IN HAMBURG
                     (same as German issue, flag cover) Karussell
                     label (Phonogram)
23/4/70   PCSO7560   HEY JUDE
                     (same as UK) Apple label
1/6/70   PCSO7026   LET IT BE
                     (same as UK) Also PXS 1 with book. Apple label
—/11/70   SRA   THE BEATLES IN HAMBURG
          250-550   (reissue of Karussell LP with new cover of ship
                     in harbour) Summit label
2/2/72   TVSS8   THE ESSENTIAL BEATLES
                     Love Me Do/Boys/Long Tall Sally/Honey Don't/
                     PS I Love You/Baby You're A Rich Man/All My
                     Loving/Yesterday/Penny Lane/Magical Mystery
                     Tour/Norwegian Wood/With A Little Help/All
                     You Need Is Love/Something/Ob-La-Di-Ob-La-
                     Da/Let It Be
                     (originated in Australia for TV marketing) Apple
                     label
—/2/73   PCSS   THE BEATLES AUSTRALIAN 10TH ANNI-
          7533-4   VERSARY
                     (double set of PCSO7533 & 7534 with new
                     cover)
5/7/73   PCSO   THE BEATLES 1962-1966
          7171/2   (same as UK) Apple label

5/7/73   PCSO   THE BEATLES 1967-1970
          7181/2   (same as UK) Apple label
15/6/76   PCSP719   ROCK'N'ROLL MUSIC
                     (same as UK)
1/11/76   2679 040   THE BEATLES TAPES
                     (same as UK) Polydor label
29/11/76 PAS10011   THE BEST OF GEORGE HARRISON
                     (same as UK, side one by Beatles)
5/5/77   PCSO7577   THE BEATLES AT THE HOLLYWOOD BOWL
                     (same as UK) no specific label — EMI if any
9/5/77   L45733/4   LIVE AT THE STAR CLUB IN HAMBURG
                     (same as UK) Interfusion label (Festival)
21/11/77 PCSC7580   LOVE SONGS
                     (same as UK but no book)
29/11/78 PSLP261   RARITIES
                     (same as UK, bonus disc with "The Beatles
                     Collection" 12 LP boxed set) EMI label
—/4/79   PSLP261   THE BEATLES' COLLECTION
                     (existing catalogue albums placed in Australian
                     manufactured flip-top box) Parl./Apple labels
16/7/79   PCSO3077   MAGICAL MYSTERY TOUR
                     (same as US, except no booklet with gatefold
                     sleeve)
14/4/80   EMC2711   A SALUTE TO BRITISH ROCK
                     (contains "Get Back") EMI label
17/10/80 2475 662   ROCK LEGENDS — THE BEATLES
                     (Reissue of 635056 with diff. cover — similar to
                     UK Contour)
3/4/81   PLAY1005   THE BEATLES' BALLADS
                     (same as UK)
6/4/81   ENDO15   ROCK'N'ROLL HEAVEN
                     (Contains "Ain't She Sweet") Endeavour label
19/5/81   PCSO7581   RARITIES
                     (same as US. Competely different LP to PSLP
                     7581. This commercially available as individual
                     entity.)
27/7/81   VMP1092/3 MADE IN THE UK: HITS OF THE 60'S
                     (contains "Love Me Do") EMI label
27/7/81   PCSO7584   A HARD DAY'S NIGHT S'TRK
                     (same as US United Artists original issue, with
                     some tracks by George Martin Orchestra. Very
                     bad mock stereo.)

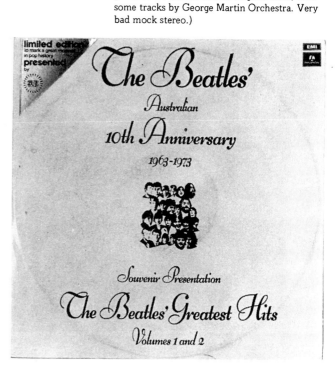

EMI Australia received special permission to issue this limited edition repackaging of "Greatest Hits Vol. 1 & 2" (themselves Australian-originated) in conjunction with a chain of Australian radio stations in 1973.

10/8/81   AXIS6439   ROCK'N'ROLL MUSIC VOL.ONE
(same as UK MFP issue) Axis label
10/8/81   AXIS6440   ROCK'N'ROLL MUSIC VOL.TWO
(same as UK MFP issue) Axis label
–/1/82   RVLP1002   THE BEATLES TALK DOWN UNDER
(interviews derived from the June 1964 Australasian tour. Cover contains tour photographs)
Raven label

NOTE: All on Parlophone label unless otherwise indicated.

A unique Apple label television promoted compilation album.

EXTENDED PLAYS

28/9/63   GEPO8882   TWIST & SHOUT (8)
Twist & Shout/Taste Of Honey/Do You Want
To Know A Secret/There's A Place
6/2/64   GEPO8880   THE BEATLES' HITS † (32)
From Me To You/That You Girl/Please Me
*/Love Me Do
19/3/64   GEPO8883   THE BEATLES (No. 1) †
I Saw Her Standing There/Misery/Anna/Chains
9/4/64   GEPO8891   ALL MY LOVING (1)
All My Loving/Ask Me Why/Money/PS I Love
You
? /6/64   EPH21967   THE BEATLES WITH TONY SHERIDAN
Aint She Sweet/Cry For A Shadow/My Bonnie/
Sweet Georgia Brown
18/6/64   GEPO 70013   REQUESTS † (2)
Long Tall Sally*/I Call Your Name/Please Mr.
Postman/Boys*
20/8/64   GEPO 70014   MORE REQUESTS † (9)
Slow Down/Matchbox*/Till There Was You/I
Wanna Be Your Man
19/11/64   GEPO 70015   FURTHER REQUESTS †
She Loves You/I Want To Hold Your Hand/Roll
Over Beethoven/Can't Buy Me Love
10/12/64   GEPO8920   A HARD DAY'S NIGHT (28)
(Extracts from the film)
I Should Have Known Better/If I Fell/Tell Me
Why/And I Love Her*
4/2/65   GEPO 70016   WITH THE BEATLES †
Devil In Her Heart/Not A Second Time/It Won't
Be Long/Don't Bother Me
4/3/65   GEPO8924   A HARD DAY'S NIGHT
(Extracts from the album)
Any Time At All/I'll Cry Instead/Things We Said
Today/When I Get Home
24/6/65   GEPO 70019   BEATLES FOR SALE †
No Reply/I'm A Loser/Words Of Love/8 Days A
Week
2/9/65   GEPO 70020   BEATLES FOR SALE (No. 2) †
I'll Follow The Sun/Baby's In Black/Kansas City
– Hey Hey Hey/I Don't Want To Spoil The
Party
5/5/66   GEPO 70026   YESTERDAY †
Yesterday/It's Only Love/You Like Me Too
Much/Dizzy Miss Lizzy
3/11/66   GEPO8952   NOWHERE MAN
Nowhere Man/Drive My Car/Michelle/You
Won't See Me
16/11/67   GEPO 70043   HELP †
Help/She's A Woman/Ticket To Ride/I Feel
Fine
8/2/68   GEPO 70044   NORWEGIAN WOOD †
Paperback Writer/We Can Work It Out/Day
Tripper/Norwegian Wood
14/3/68   MMT1   MAGICAL MYSTERY TOUR (2)
Magical Mystery Tour/I Am The Walrus/Your
Mother Should Know/The Fool On The Hill/
Blue Jay Way/Flying
4/7/68   GEPO 70045   PENNY LANE †
Penny Lane/Elanor Rigby/Strawberry Fields
Forever/Yellow Submarine

† EP jacket originated in Australia
‡ EP originated entirely in Australia

SINGLES

Date	Cat.	Title	Position on chart
21/2/63	A8080	Please Please Me/Ask Me Why	–
9/5/63	A8083	From Me To You/Thank You Girl	6
29/8/63	A8093	She Loves You/I'll Get You	3
12/12/63	A8103	I Want To Hold Your Hand/This Boy	1
16/1/64	A8105	Love Me Do/I Saw Her Standing There (d)	1
/2/64	52275	Cry For A Shadow/Why (P)	11
5/3/64	A8107	Roll Over Beethoven/Hold Me Tight (d)	2
30/4/64	A8113	Can't Buy Me Love/You Can't Do That	1
/5/64	24673	My Bonnie/The Saints (P)	–
/5/64	52317	Aint She Sweet/If You Love Me Baby (P)	23
25/6/64	A8117	Komm Gib Mir Deine Hand/Sie Liebt Dich	–
10/7/64	A8123	A Hard Day's Night/Things We Said Today	1
20/8/64	A8125	I Should Have Known Better/If I Fell (d)	1
27/11/64	A8133	I Feel Fine/She's A Woman (d)	1
11/3/65	A8143	Rock And Roll Music/Honey Don't (d)	1
15/4/65	A8153	Ticket To Ride/Yes It Is (d)	1
23/7/65	A8163	Help/I'm Down	1
14/10/65	A8173	Yesterday/Act Naturally (d)	3
9/12/65	A8183	We Can Work It Out/Day Tripper (d)	1
24/3/66	A8193	Nowhere Man/Norwegian Wood (This Bird Has Flown) (d)	1
16/6/66	A8203	Paperback Writer/Rain (d)	5
25/8/66	A8213	Yellow Submarine/Elanor Rigby (d)	1
16/3/67	A8243	Penny Lane/Strawberry Fields Forever (d) (picture sleeve)	1
13/7/67	A8263	All You Need Is Love/Baby You're A Rich Man (d)	1
7/12/67	A8273	Hello Goodbye/I Am The Walrus (d)	1
29/3/68	A8293	Lady Madonna/The Inner Light	1
20/9/68	A8493	Hey Jude/Revolution (d) (A)	1
20/2/69	A8693	Ob-La-Di, Ob-La-Da/While My Guitar Gently Weeps (d) (A)	1
9/5/69	A8763	Get Back/Don't Let Me Down (d) (A)	1
19/6/69	A8793	The Ballad of John And Yoko/Old Brown Shoe (A)	1
17/10/69	A8943	Something/Come Together (d) (A)	1
13/3/70	A9083	Let It Be/You Know My Name (Look Up The Number) (A) (picture sleeve)	1
11/6/70	A9163	The Long And Winding Road/For You Blue	3
17/5/76	A11115	Yesterday/I Should Have Known Better	–
5/7/76	A11182	Got To Get You Into My Life/Helter Skelter	–
28/8/78	A12000	Sgt. Pepper's . . . –With A Little Help/A Day In The Life	–
19/4/82	A689	The Beatles Movie Medley/I'm Happy Just To Dance With You	21

NOTE: Discography prepared by Bruce Hamlin (P.O. Box 6, Dee Why 2099 Australia), Australia's supreme Beatle vinyl collector – who has no idea at all why the serial numbers of 25 of 33 Parlophone Beatle singles end with the number three.

All singles on Parlophone, except (P) Polydor and (A) Apple. (d) denotes double A side charter. No national chart figures available for Australia so Sydney placings used, courtesy of Top 40 Research. EP chart positions refer to singles chart, with * denoting the hit track.

10: DEPARTURE AND AFTERMATH

Tired, homesick and still angry over the Brisbane airport pelting, the Beatles were in no mood to parade themselves before the 1500 fans who had gathered at Mascot on July 1 to bid their farewells. In a last minute switch of plans they disembarked at 9.35 a.m. with the other passengers at the domestic section rather than waiting for the aircraft to taxi around to the overseas terminal. A closed car sped them past the bitterly disappointed kids to a VIP lounge in the international departure area. Several girls leapt the barriers and chased the moving vehicle. One particularly agile girl in bare feet and bermuda shorts sidestepped one policeman after another on a seventy-five yard dash that was abruptly ended by Police Rescue Squad member Bill Fahey who tumbled to the tarmac with the vainly struggling fan. Another girl who had fainted was carried laughing and crying to an ambulance.

The international terminal was in turmoil for fifteen minutes as police successfully removed 100 fans who had infiltrated the terminal to pound their grubby little fists upon the door and walls of the VIP room.

Inside, the mood bore little resemblance to the flippant, irreverant, effervescent atmosphere of the early meetings with the press. John collapsed on a chair sipping milk and coffee, and would grant no more than a few indifferent grunts to questioners. Even Paul had lost his boyish charm, most notable when he dished out some cutting, almost brutal sarcasm to a smugly immature reporter from a university news-paper. "If you got a chance would you like to do a University course?" "No thanks," he stabbed back, "but if *you* get the chance, don't refuse."

Oddly enough, it was George, a virtual recluse throughout the tour, who filled most of the reporters' notebooks. Perhaps because he was the only one who had got himself a good night's sleep. "I hope that everyone who came to our shows enjoyed it enough because it was a hell of a long way for us to come," he candidly offered. After taking a deserved swipe at the primitive airport facilities at Kingsford Smith Airport ("It's a bit crummy and prefabricated for an international airport.") he moved on to the Brisbane pelters. "As we thought, they were typical eggheads. There were only about six of them and they were right schmucks. In the end they admitted that they were very childish."

Surprised when told that Ringo would be turning twenty-four the

Back on home soil, the Beatles and Derek Taylor (right) acknowledge the small welcoming crowd at Heathrow Airport.

Police work isn't without its share of cheap thrills.

following Tuesday, he detailed the group's likely gift, "We're gonna shake his hand, give him a gold watch and tell him it was nice. You retire when you're twenty-four don't you?"

Badgered for a comment on the tour, John spat out, "It's been good." Asked his thoughts on the upcoming US tour he snapped, "I'm not thinking about it because I'm too tired." Are you looking forward to seeing your family? "Yes I am, very much," he said almost eagerly. What was the most asked question on the tour? "How does our city compare to other cities you've been to. That seems to mean a lot to people."

Bob Rogers has an interesting insight into the farewell, regarding John. "In Sydney he had met a young girl about seventeen of Chinese descent. She was not beautiful by any standards but John showed a marked preference for her over the hordes of far prettier girls who were crowded in the wings. I had rejoined them for the farewell after missing the Christchurch and Brisbane shows, so John asked me if I would go out into the terminal, find her and bring her to him, which I did. The lady is now quite well known in the Australian fashion business but has never, to the best of my knowledge, admitted the relationship."

Paul was advised that the Animals' *House of the Rising Sun* had shot to number one in England and was, of course, asked if this was the new group to oust the Beatles. "Probably," he said wearily, "but last week it was Dave Clark and the week before it was Brian Poole. I've given up answering that question. Maybe. If it is, it's just hard lines and if it isn't, then aren't we lucky!"

Ringo was in a complaining mood, starting off with the refuse hurlers. "It's only because we couldn't fight back," he said, explaining the group's strong anger. "We couldn't do anything. It's like being tied to a tree with people throwing hammers at you. And they all hide behind the fans, they're just soft."

Certain sections of the print media were next in the firing line. "We've had a few knockers that just print rubbish without any foundation. I don't care if a reporter comes to a show and we die a death and he writes that we died a death but when people write rubbish, that's knocking to me."

After speaking a few *Hard Day's Night* promos for a radio station fortunate enough to have an advance copy of the album, Ringo was

The fifth and final Sydney airport vigil . . . only the strong survived.

asked if there was anything particular he wanted for his birthday. "No nothin'," he stated emphatically, "nothin' I could say on the radio anyway." His nomination for the most-asked question? "What do you think of Australia or why won't you come out and see our fair city?" How about "When's it all going to end?" "Oh that's a big one all over the world. We still don't know, we keep going, I think we've still got a few months yet."

First stopover for the Qantas V-Jet was Singapore, where some 600 Chinese and British teenagers were massed for a noisy welcome. Word had been sent ahead that the Beatles would remain on the plane but when they realised that so many fans were hoping to see them, Paul and Ringo agreed to travel to the VIP lounge in an official car, leaving John sleeping and George reading. However, news reached them to the effect that fifty of the more determined kids had clambered over steel barricades, burst through padlocked doors and fought with airport policemen, so the gesture was reduced to a brief interview on the plane. There were virtually no disturbances in Frankfurt, Germany. (Brodziak's last-minute request that they fly home via Perth — and a couple more concerts, of course — had been vetoed by Epstein before he left Australia.)

At Heathrow on Friday afternoon only a hundred fans were on hand to welcome them home, one of whom told a reporter, "We knew nothing about it until the last moment. Anyway it's a school day, isn't it?" Members of the fan club presented the disembarking Beatles with bouquets of flowers and while John snuck off with Cynthia, George told a sparse gathering of reporters, "That last mass demonstration was when we returned from the United States. I think the attitude then was 'good old English lads going like a bomb in America,' but nobody really cares about Australia or New Zealand." Neither, it would eventuate, did the Beatles. For all their emotional responses to the biggest and most demonstrative crowds that their careers would ever encounter, they never revealed or recounted any incidents once back in the northern hemisphere. It was as if they decided amongst themselves that it never really happened, or that it would upset their British and American fans to compare them unfavourably to some distant bunch of dumb ockers.

Brian Epstein, already back in the Old Dart, was a little more generous. He told *New Musical Express*, "Neither the Beatles nor I will ever forget those tumultous Australian welcomes," and compared scenes outside the Southern Cross Hotel to the foreground of Buckingham Palace on the night of the Queen's Coronation in 1953. He described his arrival in Sydney with Ringo as a "thrilling and memorable managerial moment," adding, "one of the most gratifying moments of the tour for me was when I saw 13,000 people in Sydney Stadium applaud and stamp for more at the conclusion of the set by Sounds Incorporated. This group of boys arrived with practically no publicity and went like a bomb everywhere." Never one to miss a trick was Brian.

As the Beatles arrived back in England, the Australian press was carrying reports on the resignation of Brian Somerville, the Beatle Press Agent. He was quoted as saying: "There is nothing I or any press relations officer can do for them now. They are at the top and the fun lies in building people up." He insisted that there was no ill feeling involved with the split.

Four days later, on July 6, the much-refreshed foursome attended the premiere of *A Hard Day's Night* at the London Pavilion Cinema, along with Princess Margaret and her hubby. Piccadilly Circus was closed to traffic to prevent loss of life among the thousands of lookers-on in the street. On July 10 they returned triumphantly to Liverpool for a second film premiere, greeted by a reported 100,000 who lined the route to the Odeon Theatre. Three hundred fans were injured with thirty-five taken off to hospital. Live performances were recommenced two days later at the Hippodrome in Brighton. Supporting the Beatles were the Fourmost and Jimmy Nicol's group the Shub Dubs. Little is known about the reunion.

After taping the "Big Night Out" TV show in Blackpool and performing at a London Palladium charity show called "The Night of 100 Stars," they flew to Sweden for a three day tour. On August 19 they kicked off a second American visit at San Francisco's Cow Palace, moving on through Las Vegas, Seattle, Vancouver, Los Angeles, Denver, Cincinatti, New York, Atlantic City, Philadelphia, Indianapolis, Milwaukee, Chicago, Detroit, Toronto, Montreal, Jacksonville, Boston, Baltimore, Pittsburg, Cleveland, New Orleans, Kansas City, Dallas and New York once more. A portion of the frenzy is attributed to news reports of the Australian response, which had been fed steadily into America throughout June.

Back in Australia, the media was as occupied with the Beatles as they had been during the tour. Kenn Brodziak emerged from a meeting with the taxation department officials, still smiling, to announce a tour gross (including TV and radio rights) of £254,000. "It's up to the tax people to decide who gets how much," he said, "but I can tell you that it has not only been our most successful venture but certainly the most successful theatrical undertaking in Australian showbusiness history. Although we have no firm plans or contracts, I think it is most possible the boys will come back to Australia within two years."

In mid September Jimmy Nicol rang Bob Francis in Adelaide, after having received a shipment of (a reported) 5000 letters from South Australian fans. He had just returned from a season at Blackpool replacing an ill Dave Clark in the Dave Clark 5, and was so moved by the outpouring of sentiment from the lower continent that he pledged to return to Australia to live permanently. "I will possibly come sometime next year," he told Francis. He never moved from his home in Barnes, the next year or any one after, and it is doubtful if his pocket of Adelaide devotees maintained their interest past a few months.

Radio tried to keep the Beatle bandwagon going as long as possible. "Good Guys" John Mahon and Mike Walsh bought Paul's bed sheet from the Sheraton and gave it away in tiny squares to winners of an on-air competition. When they found that the demand exceeded the supply, they went out and bought another two bedsheets.

But one "Good Guy" had had more than his fair share of Beatlemania and wanted out. "I think that 2SM realised that even though they'd got me to sign on for another two years in return for the Beatle assignment, there was little sense in forcing me to stay when I wanted desperately to get away from the young teenage market," explains Bob Rogers. "One particular incident occurred that really made my mind up for me. Nowadays it's quite common but it wasn't then.

"I was on air one night after the tour and the caretaker came up to say he'd found a fifteen-year-old girl hiding under the stairs crying. Mike Walsh, who was on after me, got very excited and wanted to put her on air, but I resisted and asked that she be brought up.

"I found that she had run away from home because her parents

Four days after arriving back in England from their Far East Tour, the Beatles attend the premiere of the first film at London's Pavilion Theatre on Picadilly Circus.

Mr. Kenn Brodziak OBE brought a staggering array of talent to Australia but has resigned himself to the fact that interviewers rarely want to ask him about any tour other than the Beatles'.

were planning to take her to Broken Hill on a holiday. You see, every day she was sitting through session after session of *A Hard Day's Night* and even though she had seen it something like fourteen times she wanted to spend the entire school holidays adding to her tally. She said her parents were very strict and couldn't understand what she was doing, so I got her to agree to let me call them and then my wife and I sat down and tried to work out the situation. They told us that since she had become obsessed with the Beatles her school marks had dropped dramatically and it was nearly impossible to speak to her.

"Having been a party to the whole Beatles madness in Australia, this incident and others like it began to needle my conscience, particularly as I had two teenage daughters myself. I wanted a clean break and, by agreeing not to work evenings for two years in Sydney, I was allowed to go over to 2UE."

Almost ironically, it was Rogers who, if you discount John

Disappointed at a swift pass-by in a closed car by the Beatles, some agile fans make a beeline for the Qantas jet carrying the four back to England.

John obliges reporters with not much more than a few indifferent grunts.

Lennon's unexpanded 1971 comment to *Rolling Stone,* was the first person associated with the Australian tour to publicly admit that debauchery did indeed consume many a boozed and pilled evening. He broke silence upon the death of John Lennon, in an interview with Delamore McNicoll of the Sydney *Sunday Telegraph.* "Some of the stories can never be told because of the people involved," he said, "but be assured that women from all levels of society were lemming-like in their headlong determination to bed a Beatle. Never before had we seen women behave the way they did during that month. Females of almost any age were prepared to fight through any security screen or face any humiliation for the privilege of being bedded." In the wake of his revelation came others to corroborate it.

Ticket sales for *A Hard Day's Night* opened at the Embassy Theatre in Castlereagh St., Sydney, on July 25, 1964. Lines began forming the afternoon of the preceeding day and 2000 were in the queue when the box office opened. At one point the surging crowd smashed a plate glass window and two girls were treated at Sydney Hospital for lacerations. Fifteen-year-old Marilyn Potent of Regent's Park was pushed through the window and gashed her leg in three places. With blood streaming down her jeans she refused to leave the line until she had bought two tickets.

On August 1, 2SM presented a preview screening for one thousand listeners, at least fifty of whom were camped in the Embassy doorway at 3 a.m. By the time the early morning session was underway, the cinema resembled the Stadium in June. First up was a newsreel documentary on the tour, which drew the loudest response for its coverage of Ringo's solo arrival. Girls wept, moaned and screamed unrestrainedly throughout the film, which culminated with a barrel draw by the "Good Guys." There were three prizes — the TAA umbrellas used by Paul, John and George during the June 11 Sydney arrival debacle. Elizabeth Brown, 14, of Hurstville and Christine Reid, 16, of Dee Why all but broke down and cried when their tickets were drawn.

All the tour principals have their own individual (and sometimes contradictory) recollections and judgements of those extraordinary days in June. All agree that it in some way had a bearing on their

Paul, giving one Sydney lass something to bore people to death with at parties for the rest of her life.

professional, and in some cases personal, lives.

Lloyd Ravenscroft so impressed the Beatles with his efficiency and competency that he was handed an envelope on the charter flight down from Brisbane containing a signed thank you note and around £200 in cash. In 1981 he is the catering manager at the Sydney Opera House. "Paul and John were the brains of the outfit, as I saw it, but they were all exceptionally co-operative. When I said 'let's move' they didn't ever ask me why, they moved."

Dick Lean still controls Stadiums Ltd., in association with his son. Most commonly associated with the boxing fraternity, he moved on from the Beatles tour to escorting Scottish club performers Kenneth McKellar, Moira Anderson and Jimmy Shand, the moment the Qantas jet was airborne. "There'll be nothing like it again," he insists.

Kenn Brodziak, who said as Beatles box offices opened, "It's all too easy, there's no challenge. I don't think a man should be able to make money so easily," officially retired in 1980 at age 66, after carving his own legend as Australia's greatest entrepreneur. Now an Officer of the British Empire he recalls, "They were impersonal, they were not temperamental. They realised that their life on tour was confined to hotel rooms. They took it in turns to wave to the crowds, they pleased the fans, they were obliging.

"I never really saw much of them as a foursome and I probably talked to George more than the others. He remarked at one point that I hadn't been at a press conference and I was impressed that he'd missed me. I mentioned Cilla Black once and it turned out that they adored her and so they opened right up. But that was the only time I got really close to them. It was nice to be informed that Paul McCartney tried to contact me when he returned in 1976. Unfortunately I was overseas at the time.

"I did actually meet them again. It was in London in July 1966 and they had just returned from the Philipines, where they'd been treated quite terribly. I asked them if they'd like to come back to Australia and they said the only reason they'd do it would be to drop bombs on Manila on the way over. The incident had really soured them on touring. Brian Epstein took me aside and said, 'Ken, don't push it. After this year I doubt that the Beatles will ever work on stage again.' " (This prediction was right. The group played their last live concert at San Francisco's Candlestick Park on August 29, 1966.)

The ubiquitous Derek Taylor, of whom Lloyd Ravenscroft once said, "He certainly liked his grog, and his women," had one too many arguments with Brian Epstein and went his own way before the year ended. After becoming a successful publicist on the American west coast in 1965, he went on to write books, manage the UK operations of WEA Records, produce Harry Nilsson's gorgeous *A Little Touch of Schmilsson in the Night* album and become the world's very best liner note writer. An outrageous storyteller, it is possible that his vividly described incident on the tarmac at Sydney (as found in the introduction to this book) never actually occurred.

Bob Rogers went on to become a superstar of Australian radio, while remaining friendly and approachable — an uncommon combination. His impressions are, of course, manifold. "I think Beatlemania was magnificent," he summarises. "It certainly was a turning point in my life, bringing me face to face with so many incidents, experiences and emotions. I got on better with John because, as the others often joked, we were both 'old married men.' He was a brilliant man, serious about the tour but determined to enjoy every minute of it. Paul was much more pragmatic; he knew how to use his charm and appeal to get whatever he wanted, though he was often unsure about exactly what it was he did want. George was deeply introspective and hard to know. Ringo, like Jimmy Nicol, was a simple fellow who seemed to me to be never quite able to catch onto what was happening."

Malcolm Cook, now a theatrical entrepreneur, says, "It was an eye opener to me. I realised that the public could never dream of the price that has to be paid for fame on that level. The two strongest personalities were definitely Paul and John. Paul was the most sociable of all but Lennon had an extra quality. One day he said to me as I was running about taking care of something, 'I've seen your face around a lot, it's a friendly face.' They had it all together in a way I've never seen since."

Ron Blackmore, an artist/tour manager of inestimable experience and now the operator of one of the two major concert staging companies in Australia, quite visibly cringes when he thinks of the area of the tour with which he dealt. "Nobody should have to perform under those conditions. They never complained because they knew

there was no alternative. The Beatles came through Australia when there was no label of drugs or sex attached to rock stars and really, the could and did get away with everything. If they wanted to put someon on a baggage trolley at an airport and wheel it down the corridors, everyone called it good clean fun. But when the Who did it two years later they were called larrikins."

Mad Mel, who disappeared from Australia shortly after the tour, ran into Paul in Portland, Oregon on August 22, 1965, and introduced the Beatles to the Beach Boys. There is no doubting his favourite: "They *were* larger than life. Paul was just a magic guy, super intelligent amazing charisma and not a nasty bone in his body."

Bruce Stewart now works at Melbourne radio station 3DB with Stan Rofe. "I went right through the tour as Dick Lean's right hand

Fans rush the ticket box of Sydney's Embassy Theatre in Castlereagh Street, as the first tickets for "A Hard Day's Night" go on sale on July 25.

Fans triumphantly hold aloft film tickets — the eventual reward for waits of up to eighteen hours.

To ensure the best seats for the August 1 2SM early morning preview of "A Hard Day's Night," these Beatlemaniacs arrived at the Embassy Theatre at 3 a.m. on July 31.

man and when it was over he gave me a hundred and fifty quid, partly in appreciation of my original suggestion. They were awesome, in those black capes. I loved every minute of it."

Johnny Devlin endured as a popular Australian entertainer and is still a strong club draw today. The recipient of his own share of adulation in a notable rock'n'roll career, his recollections remain clear. "I preferred Paul and George, they were outgoing and friendly. John obviously had a chip on his shoulder, I never saw him smile once in three weeks. When there were huge crowd reactions I felt that Paul and George were knocked out but John almost expected it." Devlin's first post-tour single was *Won't You Be My Baby* which he co-wrote (the melody) with Paul backstage at Sydney Stadium and took all the credit at McCartney's specific request.

Johnny Chester, still charting hits as a highly respected contemporary country music performer, understands how John gave people the impression of being surly. "He didn't see very well and couldn't wear his optical sunglasses indoors. He got this strange look in his eyes

because he was squinting to see. It wasn't necessarily contempt, though he did become incredibly annoyed when people tried to manipulate him. I remember best his backstage jokes which usually drew a crowd and always seemed to be about cripples or the Pope (two subjects that were still fairly taboo in 1964). John went out of his way to include me in things and would usually notice when I wasn't at a party."

Dave Lincoln is, like most musicians, still a musician. "It was good fun, in a cold sweat sort of way," he jokes. "They were brilliant as people and I think we all learned a lot from them. John was always witty and entertaining but could lose his temper and become a very different person."

Kevin Ritchie worked with EMI Records in Australia for almost thirty years and is now one of the country's big league international concert promoters. Almost blushing when he admits, "I saw the occasional little girl dragged off into a hotel room by the arm," he keeps many of his memories close to his chest. "I think back to that amazing spectacle of the four soaking wet Beatles on the truck at

Elizabeth Brown, 14 of Hurstville, finding it hard to contain her emotions as she accepts one of the Beatles' Sydney airport umbrellas prior to the preview film screening.

Unabashed Beatle clones The Flies. Ronnie Burns on right.

Sydney airport and I just can't imagine any act today doing that for their fans — they'd tell you to go take a jump. I found them to be terribly bewildered. John once confided in me, 'Look I don't know what this is all about. It's all happened so rapidly, we just hang in and make the best of it.' He wasn't the only one caught unawares; when the first records came out I was scared to take it to the big DJs like Rogers and Lappin in case they said 'not more of that crap' and tossed it in the bin.''

For Ritchie, memories of the tour were to be brought back into sharp focus in December 1980. Travelling on a plane to Melbourne with Elton John, whom he was touring, he noted a message from manager John Reid that Elton remain on board until he had reached him with some very urgent news.

"Reid came on board and walked straight to Elton with a grave face. Then I saw Elton put his face in his hands and Reid turned to us and said, 'John Lennon has been assassinated.' It was absolutely tragic, nobody could talk about it. We cancelled the press conference and went straight to the hotel and of course the international media was on every phone line because Elton was Sean's godfather and one of Lennon's closest friends. He said to me, 'I don't know what to do, should I cancel the tour?' But when he rang Yoko she asked him to continue working.

"On the day of the ten minute silence, Elton arranged a special church service at St. Patrick's Cathedral. He sang the twenty-third psalm and read the lesson. He specifically instructed that the press not be informed in case his gesture was seen as a stagey sort of thing. I don't think the public got to hear about it at all."

Most of the other principals are still highly visible. Mike Walsh is now the king of daytime television; Jim Oram is the Sydney *Mirror's* senior journalist and the author of an extraordinary and highly acclaimed book on Pope John Paul II; Cliff Baxter is a senior executive of the giant Brash's record store chain in Victoria; Ernie Sigley became a "Tonight Show" compere and is now handling a quiz show; Dick Hughes writes a fine jazz column for the Sydney *Mirror;* Bob Francis is the station manager of 5AD and still a powerful force in Adelaide radio; Deputy Assistant Police Commissioner Mr. George Twentyman remains in Christchurch, successfully applying the tricks he picked up handling Beatle hordes to similar numbers of (far more dangerous) anti-Springbok protestors, again using liberal doses of common sense; Little Pattie went on to cut some stunning pop records and endear herself to the great Australian mass with a unique sweet charm. (Today her records are released in America under the name of Pattie Keith); Jannette Carroll is a school teacher; Angela Letchford married a part-time rock promoter; Suzette Belle married Gavin Webb of the Masters Apprentices; Jack Argent still runs Leeds Music; Harry Miller is deceased; Jack Neary has retired; Brian DeCourcy, manages more artists than there are hours in the day; newsboy Garvin Rutherford now runs

2SM; John Mahon is a television personality; Stan Rofe compered the Rolling Stones concerts and gave more support to Australian music than any ten of his peers; Kerry Yates is the Sydney *Mirror's* fashion editor; Tony McArthur reacquainted himself with John Lennon in 1969, scoring an exclusive interview concerning the *Abbey Road* album; Alan Field stayed on in Australia to compere "The Go! Show" for the 0-10 TV network then disappeared back into the English midlands when replaced by Bobby and Laurie; Sounds Incorporated returned to Australia in the company of Cilla Black, Freddie & The Dreamers and Mark Wynter in March 1965 for another of Brodziak and Lean's "Big Show" tours; Mal Evans was accidentally shot dead by police in New York in 1975; and Neil Aspinall produced the *Let It Be* film and became a director of Apple.

Ringo returned to University College Hospital in early December to have his troublesome tonsils removed, refusing to allow the severed organ to be raffled off to fans. Later that month, giant crates containing the Australian birthday presents were off-loaded at Southampton docks. Sydney Stadium has long since been torn down to make way for the Eastern Suburbs Railway (and Sydney struggles on without a large capacity concert venue), and the promised second tour never did happen.

Paul came back with Wings in 1976 for an extraordinarily successful concert tour which provided many of the more interesting sequences in the "Wings Over the World" TV special. George petulantly dismissed Australia with a scant few lines in his book *I Me Mine*, including these exaggerated and erroneous words: "We drove round and round the airport under a tropical storm on an open truck so that the crowds could see us, waving to them, and after we reached the city they wouldn't let us into the big hotel and so we went into the one opposite, a motor hotel . . . And this rubbish was all happening while cloaks we had made in Hong Kong the day before were melting — the cloth, the lining, the stitching, everything vanishing. Then after the drive round and round in the rain each of us was put in a Mini with our name on it. Thanks. The promoter had done a deal I believe. Brian told him he would nail him. We were very much into not letting people use us for advertising."

So just what effect did those weeks of fantastical, unprecedented contagious insanity have upon Australia and its inhabitants? To start with Australian Public Opinion Polls announced a fifty per cent increase in the number of Australians who considered Beatle music to be a good influence. Sixty-four per cent of men and seventy per cent of women interviewed said they could readily recognise Beatle music.

Certainly Australia's young musicians could recognise Beatle music. The tour had successfully dragged Australian rock over the threshold from greasy rock'n'roll or instrumental surf to R&B-rooted beat rock with vocals. The Phantoms themselves were a prime example; an immediate post-tour single, their first non-instrumental called *I Want You*, was quite Beatlesque and the unit evolved a year later into the

The Beatles had been out of the country a month but these film preview attenders had not exactly fallen over themselves to adopt a Liverpool moptop hairstyle. Old traditions die hard in Australia.

dynamic MPD Ltd., one of Australia's most exciting scream sensations of the beat era. Groups such as the Flies copied the Beatle image right down to the boots and haircuts, while young Adelaide group the Twilights (also featuring a later superstar, in the form of Glenn Shorrock) had an initial set comprised almost entirely of Fab Four material.

The most dramatic effect wrought by the Beatles' visit was not over music but over the entire fabric of Australian society. In a sense it liberated young people who had not previously dreamed of openly disobeying their parents, police, civil authorities or indeed any adult.

By playing truant, by pushing over airport barriers, by thumping on glass windows, by standing outside a hotel in the rain, thousands of Australian adolescents had asserted their own feelings for perhaps the first time.

This release, which felt so breathtakingly daring and tasted so exhilaratingly fresh, was to mark the behaviour patterns of a decade and grow rapidly into an actual lifestyle that would eventually bore. But before appetites were sated and inevitably jaded, the liberation was glorious; the freedom that the Beatles ignited and their progeny exploded . . . all those years ago.

Flagging in the 'Liverpudlians' . . .

There's a new flag on the Adelaide skyline today! It's the flag of Liverpool and it's flagging in THE BEATLES! It flies from the top of our Rundle Street store just to put on record that we're proud to welcome the four boys from Liverpool. With an ambitious slogan like "the store that's growing with South Australia" we have to live up to it! Bringing the world's most popular light entertainment to our young people is one way of doing it. This visit has some worthwhile side effects, too. It will bring a touch of home to many of our new English families . . . it will make further goodwill between England and Australia . . . and it will swell the funds of St. John Ambulance Brigade and Adelaide Children's Hospital, who will be sharing any profits. Get the picture? We're tickled pink to have made THE BEATLES' visit possible! Welcome Beatles! And we hope you enjoy your visit as much as we're going to enjoy having you.

JOHN MARTIN'S
of South Australia

ABC-TV

Bringing you "The Beatles"..

"Will Mr Harrison take a personal call from Mr Johnson of Washington?"

George put his hand over the mouth-piece and says, "Eh, it's a call from a Mr Johnson of Washington."

"Must be President Johnson," John grins.

George nods. "Yeah, put him on," he tells the operator.

As the line is plugged through, George says: "How are yer?"

But then he falters. It is a girl.

"Who is this . . . Mrs Johnson?" says George blushing. Then he roars with laughter as the voice replies.

"No, I'm Janet. I thought I would ring you and tell you I still love you. Do you remember me?"

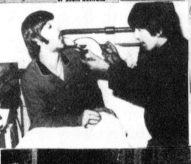

'Quite simply, the child is an extreme case of Beatlemania'

Beatle Cloaks

John, Paul and George took a big fancy to the cloaks worn by many of the Dutch people. They bought two and had them copied by Chinese tailors in Hong Kong.

Could be the start of a big new fashion.

Record Mirror

No. 160
Every Thursday 6d. Registered at the G.P.O. as a newspaper

Week ending April 4, 1964

The Beatles were told a £5000 a week contract was waiting for them in Singapore if they wanted to come back.

BEATLES FOR AUSTRALIA

IN Australia, even the kangaroos are hopping higher than ever before — in excitement at the visit of the Beatles. The foursome now leave earlier than expected and opening their tour there in Adelaide on June 12. Reports an Australian columnist: "There's never been so much interest in a visiting attraction."

And the boys occupy the top six places in "Down Under" Top Ten: "I Saw Her Standing There," "Love Me Do," "Roll Over Beethoven," "All My Loving" EP, "She Loves You" and "I Want To Hold Your Hand." As is still happing in the States, local radio stations are presenting Beatle discs almost non-stop.

Final line-up of the touring package for Australia is not fixed, but it is confirmed that Sounds Incorporated, new signing by Brian Epstein, will make the trip.

SHE LOVES THEM—YEAH, YEAH, YEAH!

ON THE LEFT, the face of a real gone Beatle fan at last night's Stadium concert. On the right, the faces of idols Paul McCartney and John Lennon, wooing with trite phrases and a twangy rhythm.

MANY EMPTY SEATS AT BEATLE CONCERT

The Beatles, idols of the teenage world, last night played to a quarter-empty house in their first appearances in Sydney.

SYDNEY

CAR DEPARTS FOR KING'S CROSS

PUBLIC VIEWING AREA

PRESS
WIRE FENCE
GATE
BARRIERS
BLAST FENCE
ROUTE FROM PLANE
TV VANS
BLAST FENCE
WIRE FENCE
GATE
STREET
THIRD

OVERSEAS TERMINAL
PUBLIC ENTRANCE
SHIERS AVENUE

The airport layout for the Beatles' arrival.

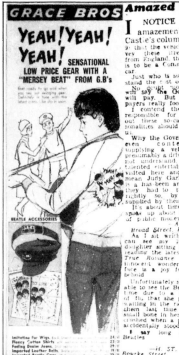

Amazed

I NOTICE with amazement in Ray Castle's column (June 9) that the vehicle to convey these irresponsibles from England, the Beatles, is to be a Commonwealth car.

Just who is supposed to stand the cost of this?

No doubt most people will say the Government will pay. But we taxpayers really foot the bill.

I contend the persons responsible for bringing out these so-called personalities should pay, not us.

Why the Government is even contemplating supplying a vehicle and presumably a driver, I cannot understand as more talented entertainers have visited here and I don't mean Judy Garland, who is a has-been anyway, yet they had to travel, and rightly so, by hire-car supplied by their agents.

It's about time someone spoke up about the waste of public money.

— C. FRY, Broad Street, Bass Hill

As I sit writing this I can see my 18-year-old daughter sitting curled up reading the latest issue of True Romance and the innocent wonder on her face is a joy for me to behold.

Unfortunately she wasn't able to see the Beatles this time due to a bad dose of flu that she picked up waiting in the rain to see them last time. Also a small bomb in her foot got crushed when a police car accidentally stood on her.

I say long live the Beatles.

— H. ST. CLAIRE, Bourke Street, Leichhardt.

AT the time of writing, the Beatles are all the talk of Sydney town and the exclusive piece of news that I have to offer you concerns Paul Macartney's birthday party. Two of Paul's special guests were Little Pattie and Noeleen Batley and they both had a ball into the early hours of the morning. The girls described the Beatles as "four nice guys"; to remember the occasion, they were given a hunk of birthday cake each. Noeleen said the cake was great, but she didn't like the idea of a newspaper reporter armed with a camera coming out to her place at 7 o'clock on the morning after the night before wanting to take pictures of her having a slice of the cake for breakfast!

MELBOURNE, Apr. 13 — Melbourne's Beatle fans had waited all week-end for it. And it was all over in 30 hectic minutes.

Preferential bookings for the three June concerts by the Beatles opened at 7 a.m. today.

Nearly 1,000 fans camped outside Myer's store in Lonsdale street and the Melbourne Sports Depot in Elizabeth street.

Some of them had been there since lunchtime on Saturday.

There were 8,000 tickets on sale at 37/- each.

Half an hour after the doors opened at Myers, all the fans there had all been served, and there were still 4,000 tickets left.

The fans could not only have saved themselves one or two sleepless nights but they could have been spared the first mad stampede as the doors opened.

The floor manager and six policemen were swept aside in the wave of squealing yeah-yeah-yeahing Beatle fans.

It was only by linking arms and heaving against the tide that the police got them into some sort of line.

THE BEATLES may not set foot on Sydney soil when they arrive in Australia on June 11 en route to their first concerts in Adelaide. They may hold a Press conference in the plane, or they may hold a conference as their plane circles Sydney.

No Beatles in Djakarta

The Minister for Culture, Mr. Prijono, has banned the Beatle hairstyle and forbidden children calling their parents Mommy and Daddy.

Mr. Prijono's instruction called on children and parents to preserve the national identity.

SHE LOVES YOU!

It seems there's no limit to the influence of that mop-haired quartet, the Beatles.

• A young couple who are marrying in June could only get tickets for the Beatles' Sydney show a few days after the wedding.

So, rather than miss them they've postponed their honeymoon.

• The foolish 16-year-old girl from Castlemaine who left school six months ago, especially to save money for a trip to Melbourne so that she could spend all her time there in a 48-hour vigil outside the Southern Cross —

DAWN BRADWELL
16, clerk, Merrylands.

If the Beatles get a reception the Government can be assured of the future concert from top—

• The police lost property office stayed open an hour later today to cope with the aftermath of Beatlemania —

14 odd shoes
Three watches
Four vacuum flasks
Three transistor radios
Beatle books and clothing
Three umbrellas
25 purses filled

WHILE we were celebrating in Sydney a radio station was also holding a birthday party for Paul

Snatching a quiet moment, Paul recorded with me a special message for these fans on the other side of the world

RADIO station 2CH announced on Friday it would ban the Beatles from the station for a week.

None of their records will be played, and any requests for them in their request programme will be passed over, and Elvis Presley records played instead.

George Harrison, the hook-nosed Beatle went bowling with his road manager and a security guard yesterday.

He scored 154 out of a possible 300 points.

"Very good for an average player" a spokesman for the Rushcutter Bowl said later.

The game was held in the early hours of yesterday after the hall had been closed to the public.

Harrison left his Sydney hotel and returned without being noticed.

A SURPRISE has been planned for the Beatles during their stay in Australia.

EMI, their record company, has no less than seven gold records to present to the boys as a tribute to their record breaking performances on our charts.

JOHN CASEY
15, typesetter, Belmore.

The sight of all that hair upset me too much to take a close interest in them.

COMMON CLAY, so those are the Beatles — frankly, we were never more disappointed.

Two arms each, two legs and one head, topped by a clump of long hair. Pink, rather plump English faces, and so desperately polite to everybody at their very correct King's Cross party late yesterday. And, except when they lapsed into Beatle-talk to oblige radio men, speaking such nice English.

As they signed an endless chain of autograph books they answered questions, sometimes with wit.

"You must sign this one," an excitable lady told Paul McCartney. "It's from Alice Springs." "Alice?" scrawling a signature. "Not Alice again?"

They May Be Back In Two Years

MELBOURNE, Monday — The Beatles would possibly tour Australia again in two years' time their manager, Mr Brian Epstein, said today.

Of Melbourne's welcome to the Beatles yesterday he said:

"It was the greatest reaction I have ever seen to them anywhere.

"We were all thrilled proud, and grateful as well for the way it was handled and controlled."

A reception at the Southern Cross Hotel today commemorated the release this week of the Beatles' one millionth record in Australia.

21 Ask: What Are They?

AUCKLAND, Monday (A.A.P.) — Not just one boy, but 21 admitted today in Auckland they had never heard of the Beatles.

They are members of the Vienna Boys' Choir. Told about the Beatles, one choirboy asked: "But have they heard of us?"

THERE are four persons to be barred from the Beatles' Melbourne hotel show presented at fabulous expense by Channel 9 on Wednesday:

1 Johnny Devlin should go on a diet before he wriggles into tight leather suit again.

2 Sounds Incorporated's drummer must not be let loose on the skins an hour till he's learned how to hit the darned things.

3 Johnny Chester should see a doctor about his tone deafness and buy a new hair lacquer.

4 The Beatles will soon be out of business if they don't give the customers a bit more for their money.

I AM happy to say, with reasonable certainty, that I shall be out of the country when the Beatles arrive in June. Happy because I am becoming sickened by the way we are being rehearsed for the drearily predictable mass seizure associated with The Arrival.

It is time someone spoke up for adults like me — and I suspect we are legion, as they say — who think the Beatles and their imitators is unholy, inartistic and, as music or entertainment, strictly null and void.

I do not question the right of teenagers to adore, worship or even beatify the Beatles.

But is there anything so silly as the vacuous grinning imitations by adults of teenage and teen enthusiasms.

What is happening to adult pride and dignity?

The kids have been catapulted into the pop era which must, no doubt, run its course to be superseded in time, one hopes, by something of greater merit.

Meanwhile the least we adults can do is not to run along behind picking up the hysteria and the jargon like dutiful terriers eager to please.

BEATLES IN SYDNEY

When the Beatles first hit Sydney their welcome was washed out in the worst flood weather for years.

But the thousands of fans who were baulked then can look forward cheerfully to their return three-day visit.

The Weather Bureau says: "There is a better than 50 per cent chance of fine weather for the Beatles."

Hectic SINGAPORE GETS MANIA

Meanwhile, about 600 screaming teenagers gave the Beatles a noisy welcome when they arrived in Singapore from Sydney on their way home to England.

The Liverpool group, however, did not leave the plane during their one-hour stopover.

In an interview on board their Qantas jet plane, Paul McCartney said they were "dead tired" and had not slept for the past 14 hours.

ONE of the most alarming symptoms of this frightening disease of 'Beatlemania' is the loss of a sense of 'self-preservation' in its sufferers.

On the day of the Beatles' Sydney arrival last week, employers and teachers only had to read the papers or listen to news broadcasts for a "roll-call" on many of their missing numbers.

It must have been hysteria which persuaded many teenagers "wagging" it from school or work to give their names and, even in several cases, the names of schools where they should have been — and weren't.

Or could it be something even worse than "Beatlemania" — an attitude of contempt for authority?

In any case I'd like to know what went on in schools this week in the lull between Beatle visits. Did "square" teachers take reprisals?

Or, cowered by teenage tyranny, and in an effort to show they're "with it," did they turn a blind eye to the unscheduled holiday?

It's a discipline which unhappily, may well be needed if events in the Pacific continue on their present course.

Thinking of this we can only rejoice that our children have enjoyed at least some of the lighthearted "irresponsibility" of peace time.

GREETINGS poured into the Sheraton Hotel from all corners of the globe on Thursday for Paul McCartney on his twenty-second birthday.

On behalf of the Good Guys and listeners of 2SM presented Paul with an enormous toy kangaroo almost five feet high with the world's largest birthday card signed by thousands of Australian well-wishers.

Paul is now wondering how he can fit this huge present into his suitcase.

Socialites say.... send me a Beatle

By MARSHA PRYSUSKA

"**S**OMETIMES," said the woman who must be envied by thousands, "I wish I had a bottle of anti-Beatlemania. It would come in handy."

". . . and please don't wash your hands after you've shaken hands with THEM," an 11-year-old girl pleaded with Mrs. Eleanor Knox.

Mrs. Knox is used to such requests. They've been coming thick and fast since word got out that she's handling the Beatles' publicity

When the telephone rings in her office in Collins St., Melbourne, she never knows whether the person on the other end will threaten to commit suicide if he she doesn't get tickets for the Beatles' show, or humbly ask for just one hair, be it Paul's, John's, George's or Ringo's

Or a cigarette butt (she doesn't know whether any of the Beatles smoke), or you-name-it, the fans have thought of it.

And if you think all the Beatles fans are young people you are mistaken.

"**Prominent business people** have been ringing up too," Mrs. Knox said. "Parties? If the Beatles accepted the invitations they've had to date, they'll be here for two years instead of three days."

24 jars of jam

Melbourne's socialites, are now bidding for single Beatles for their parties, having realised that they'll never get the famous four together

The Lord Mayor's office suggested a "visit to the Town

★ ★ ★

IN Sydney, **Patricia Rolfe** went, tongue in cheek, to the Press conference:

I ASKED Paul a pretty searching question about the tendency of their songs to precipitate the ear into a false modal frame that temporarily turns the fifth of the scale into the tonic, but he apparently didn't understand, or, as the youngies would say, "dig". He went on talking to a heavy-breathing blonde from one of the 'Under 21' sections about the secret of his sex appeal.

I've discovered not only Joycean rhythms and Lewis Carroll echoes but Dostoyevskian overtones and Brechtian undertones in John Lennon's "In His Own Write". Given enough time I'll find nuances of the NSW Government Railways Timetable in it.

But one devastating touch came from John Lennon. A newsman said "Why don't you ask us some questions?" "Yeah. If you have only three newspapers in Melbourne, how come you get 50 or 60 at a Press conference?"

A city hairdresser reported that a girl gave him a photograph of the Beatles and asked him to build her a hairdo around it—and he did so.

A pre-kindergarten wanted us to "smuggle the boys in" because the children love them so much.

Five young men offered their services. They were prepared to do anything, from driving the Beatles' car to polishing their shoes.

"**And then, of course,**" Mrs. Knox said, "**there are the business interests which hope to gain something by being associated with Liverpool's most famous four sons.**"

For instance:

The proprietress of a hairdressing salon who asked whether she could buy the Beatles' hair;

The PRO for a bowling alley who wanted to give the

Hall." Mrs. Knox wouldn't say whether or not this would be a civic reception.

And also:

The University Students' Representative Council wanted to confer an honorary Doctorate on the Beatles (laughter).

Following a report that the four dote on jam sandwiches 24 jars of home-made jam landed on Mrs Knox's doorstep.

Then I ask myself "Why is it that Sir Alec Douglas-Home — or alternatively Mr Harold Wilson, or possibly Mr Joe Grimond — can rely on the Beatles to win the British general election for them, while this country hasn't yet produced a guitar-player who could win the Parramatta by-election for Menzies?

I moved across to John Lennon and asked him how he thought the British elections would go. "I don't follow politics," Lennon said. This seemed a fairly interesting reaction, as the election depends on him.

BAN BEATLES

THE BEATLES should be banned from all centres of decent entertainment simply because of their "music."

I definitely like most modern music, but I just fail to grasp the reason why young people swoon over them. The Beatles seem to have the idea that life is a dream — the sooner they wake up to reality the better.

D. B. Hocking, Pius XII Seminary, Brisbane.

Beatles the use of the alley after their concert.

"When we said no, he told us we could hold our Press reception there," Mrs. Knox said.

"**I don't suppose there's a nightclub or hotel in Melbourne,**" she added, "**that hasn't told us how glad they'd be to have the Beatles drop in.**"

Incidentally, reservations for the Beatles are being held at all leading Melbourne hotels and two motels.

"That way, if there's any trouble at all," Mrs. Knox explained, "the boys can move at a moment's notice"

While plans for the Beatles' arrival are kept secret, Mrs. Knox said that they would definitely "be seen" at Essendon airport.

"They have a horror of being touched," she said, "so we'll have to arrange some way by which they can be seen from afar."

FOOTNOTE Although Mrs. Knox has photographs of the artists she has handled in the past two years, Shelley Berman, Sophie Tucker, Helen Shapiro, Eartha Kitt, she has no picture of the Beatles on her office wall

"How long do you think it would stay there?" she asked "Everyone in this office is crazy about them"

TO ALL PARENTS Here is the frankest analysis of Beatlemania—by Dr Joyce Brothers, a leading U.S. psychologist who met The Beatles in New York recently. This is what she told American parents . . .

THE Press was waiting . . . the Beatles were boozing . . . and Brian Epstein was talking.

And when Brian Epstein talks you just listen. This is the man who retails pop music to the millions and makes millions doing it.

After one short morning in Sydney Mr Epstein moved rapidly from room 810 of the Sheraton Hotel to take up residence across the way in the Chevron-Hilton

"The boss kicked me out said the Brain-behind-the-Beatles

At this time Mr Epstein was looking down from his penthouse suite on the 13th floor.

Brian Epstein is a complete contrast to the Beatles. He does not joke . . . treats life very seriously . . . drinks neat scotch and worries

But the one thing Brian Epstein does not worry about is the Beatles

"I was sick, very sick, the way pop singers used to carry on before the Beatles arrived They were so nice Frightened to damage their public image.

"You know what I mean —buying houses for their mums and all that rubbish. The Beatles are ordinary blokes. If they want to go on holiday with their dolls they can

All I say is good, because I know they need a holiday

These are just four normal blokes who have the same habits of any one their age.

They will not invest any money in Australia. Compared with what we normally get this trip is just a working holiday. What we earn here we are taking back with us.

People say I lay down the law and keep them shut away got to be brought out for publicity reasons. If I did that they would go on strike.

"**They can go to or have all the wild parties they like. I have only one rule—that they are on stage on time.**

"I try not to get them frightened about the money they earn and I don't think they are

"Not so much frightened but amazed. To me money is a wonderful thing. I was well off before I had heard of the Beatles

"Now I'm rich. So are they —and we are all having a nice time, thank-you-very-much.

Big Freds

MISS L. CHRISTY, Mosman: Millions and millions of brickbats to TV Times for dedicating the magazine to those Big Freds called the beatles. Why can't you give us some pin-ups of other groups, such as the Beach Boys? Jimmy Little has released two records which have become hits and are five times better than all the Beatle hits put together.

An open letter to Beatle George

IT'S JUST A COINCIDENCE

COINCIDENTAL ITEM: Aztec Services put tickets for the Beatles' Sydney concerts on sale on the same day as Pan Pacific Promotions put out their tickets for the Mersey Sound shows. There was much muttering.

Last week the Pan Pacific people announced that Judy Garland's Sydney first night would be May 13 On that same night Aztec Services' *Stop The World—I Want To Get Off* opens at the Theatre Royal.

DEAR GEORGE, On behalf of all your fans in Canberra, I would like to thank you and your three colleagues for the endless enjoyment you all give us, through your records and TV interviews.

Now, I am not a small blonde, but rather a plump brunette, so maybe you won't like me asking this—but why oh! why, don't you come to Canberra? You have hundreds of fans down here, and after all, it is the capital city of Australia.

I know you don't like to be away from England for long stretches at a time, but surely a few more days wouldn't hurt? Please ask your manager and road-director if this little extra trip could be made.

Tell Paul I will argue religion with him until I am blue in the face, if that's what he likes; I'll talk to John about his book and I'll even buy it; I'll give Ringo a million rings; and I'll even find a small blonde for you—anything to get you down to Canberra for a concert.

Yours hopefully,
SISSY GALLAGHER

Beatles' Visit To Sydney

Sir,—One can understand the sarcasm of your correspondent Dudley Goldman, in his letter about the Beatles ("S.M.H.," June 11), but the real purpose of their visit seems to have escaped him. Their mission is to teach us musical appreciation as demonstrated in Liverpool taverns and caverns, and is a sincere endeavour to raise our cultural standards to Lancashire level. The labourer is worthy of his hire, so the Beatles and the promoters of their tour will be justly rewarded.

As far as our teenagers are concerned it is far better that their earnings and pocket money be subscribed to so worthy a cause rather than be frittered away on such frivolous and trivial things as books, or bank accounts.

BEN CAPLAN.
Vaucluse.

DESPITE knock-backs from a couple of top Kings Cross pubs (as reported here yesterday) the Beatles aren't worried about accommodation, according to their local sponsor KENN BRODZIAK. "We plan to split them up in different hotels and move them around," Brodziak told me yesterday. "I'm sure many hotels will be pleased to accommodate one or other of the boys for a night or so. We want to protect them—but we don't want to keep them in cotton wool."

RADIO Free Europe is going to beam Beatle music into the Communist countries. What effect do you think it will have!

PATRICIA TURNER, 17
Kirrawee, teacher

I don't think it will take on—and I can't imagine what Mr. Kruschev will think of it. Within a couple of hours today Sydney Airport will see a galaxy of show business stars pass through.

First the Beatles will leave for New Zealand. Then Artur Rubinstein pops in on his way from Brisbane to Melbourne. Shortly afterward Kenneth McKellar and his company of Scottish entertainers arrive for their Australian tour.

Atten-shun' Beatle fans!

Thousands of young Australians could be better employed in National Service than "chasing these blinking Beatles all over the place," the Australian Country Party (N.S.W.) annual conference was told yesterday.

THE conference adopted a motion that the Federal Government be asked to resume compulsory National Service — but with a modernised training system.

Mr. John Stokie, of Coramba, said he was a cattle dealer who travelled Australia. He said: "Things are really bad in this country."

"The morale in this country is low. I say, give the young people something to do instead of chasing the Beatles and things."

Opposing the motion M K. Mapperson, of Tamba Springs, said National Service training would cost too much.

It would be better than spend money training a small army than to give a bigger army little training they would soon forget.

Mr. Mapperson said: "Anyway, the best way to learn hand-to-hand fighting is to go to see the Beatles."

The motion was carried by a substantial majority

STOCKHOLM, Tuesday.—More than 1000 enthusiastic fans welcomed the Beatles today and then chased their car as it left the airport.

Stockholm beauty queen Kerstin Dahlloef presented each of the singers with a bouquet of flowers before they were whisked away.

We Beatles

Sir—During the war talking to a quiet man with streamers, paper roses Sydney bar. He didn't and wrapped gifts for Paul's mop hair or an electric guitar birthday.

just the Victoria Cross, which had been pinned on his breast that morning at Government House.

He was having a solitary glass of beer because he knew nobody in Sydney, and Sydney couldn't have cared less about modest Jim Gordon, one of Australia's most gallant soldiers. Sydney didn't even recognise the ribbon on his breast.

We're a weird mob. Yeah, Yeah, Yeah, we are!

BEN JOHNSON.
Wahroonga

THE SUN
BEATLES' RIVALS HERE!

FOOTPATHS of this city have long been effective vehicles for conveying profound messages, from the simple reminder of 'Eternity' to the soul-wrenching demand for 'More female migrants for lonely bachelors.' But this last week a more earthy voice has spoken out with a bold, forthright statement stencilled all over town in dead of night: "Beatles bug me!"

● The 90-year-old fan from Hobart who flew to Melbourne with her 55-year-old son, claiming she wanted to kiss all the Beatles. She didn't get the opportunity.

● Girls in Adelaide singing "We Love You, Coppers" to police who held the crowd in check while still giving the fans a clear view.

WE LOVE THE BEATLES BECAUSE...

They're insex

ADELAIDE, Sun. — The prime attraction of the Beatles was sexual, a psychologist said today.

Miss Mary Smith, psychologist to the Adelaide Children's Hospital said, when the Beatles had left for Melbourne today after two frenzied days of screaming by their fans:

"There are many factors in the appeal the Beatles have for teenagers.

"They have a personal warmth and a simple direct approach to young people through their music.

"But the prime attraction is sexual.

"With their tight pants and long hair, the Beatles really look asexual — they could be either boys or girls in tights and they have an attraction to both sexes.

"I think there are few women of any age who could resist a face like Paul McCartney's.

"His baby face appeals to the mother instinct.

"But those girls who called out for Paul if he were to retaliate a great many of them would run for their lives."

BEATLE FILM ON BANDSTAND

An exclusive film clip from the Beatles' film, "A Hard Day's Night," is the highlight of tonight's Bandstand programme on TCN 9 at 6.30.

Sandy Scott, French nightclub singer Janine Arnault, the Cicadas and Margaret McKenna are also on the programme.

At 2UW we are covering every aspect of the Beatles' tour of Australia.

Among the records I'm playing at 2UW is "Husky" by Jimmy Nicol and the Shubdubs. This group has just broken up but Jimmy is forming another and the vocalist on "Husky" Johnny Good will be in the line-up.

Jimmy Nicol was stand-in Beatle when Ringo was husky.

Sir,—I heartily endorse Mr Goldman's views on the lack of concern for the Beatles ("S.M.H.," June 11), and suggest that our ill-mannered City Fathers mend their ways and pay tribute to the Beatles by renaming part of our airport Beatle-Port to commemorate the landing of the great four, pardon, GREAT FOUR, on Thursday morning. It might keep the seagulls away,

(Mrs) B. M. MILIC.
North Bondi.

JOHN BENDON
16, joiner, Lindfield.

The Beatles give teenagers more good clean fun than the Government ever has.

SANDRA BASSETT
19, teacher, Belmore.

I think the Beatles have a good act but some of the young teenagers acted badly at times.

Ringo's collapse was swiftly followed by word that he would miss the European and not the Australian tour.

There was further shock news that the Federal Government might increase personal income tax by five per cent next financial year.

WEEK OF SHOCKS

THE resignation of Sir William Spooner from the Cabinet this week was Number 1 shock, closely followed by the news that Ringo might not be able to tour with the Beatles.

Accommodation for The Beatles

Sir,—News that Sydney's leading hotels have refused to accommodate the Beatles for their forthcoming visit provides a wonderful opportunity to advertise Sydney Harbour. Pinchgut Island would, I suggest, prove ideal for their accommodation. Its stout stone walls could withstand any number of determined commando assaults by Beatle fans. Trips 'round the Beatles" would prove very remunerative and stimulating to harbour traffic.

N. K. E. ALEXANDER.
Cremorne.

Yellings

I LIVE in Macleay Street, Potts Point.

On Thursday morning at 7.30 when I came out there was a crowd of teenagers (mostly girls) waiting in the rain for the Beatles in front of a Kings Cross hotel. They were calm and quiet enough.

At 6 p.m. when I came back home, they were still there, but completely transformed.

They were turned into little obsessed beings in jeans: soaked to their bones, their pendulous hair stuck together, clumsily stamping like bears, and screaming, screaming, screaming, without any articular reason, or success.

Their idols were cosily inside out of the rain, too busy smiling for cameramen and answering questions ("Do you like Australian beer?") to care about it.

I did not notice any significant expression in those girls' faces; nor any firm conviction in those yellings.

So why?

Who said: "All is forgivable, except stupidity"?

—FABRIZIO MASSIMO.
Potts Point.

Mel goes up in the world

IT'S been a frantic week for Mel. Not only have his beloved Beatles actually arrived in actual 3D living colour . . .
BUT HE'S GOT A RISE.

Up went the basic wage by £1 and up went Mel's salary by 6d.

But his responsibilities have jumped, too. Now he must also clean the Sharea-din hotel.

ABC guest of honor talk

People often ask us how different receptions compare, you know, for say, America, Britain and Australia — to mention but three — and which were our biggest receptions.

Australia pipped it by — I don't know — by the amount of older people as well that were at airports and standing around the street, which made the Australian reception the biggest we've ever had; whereas the American was wild — that reception — but there wasn't the amount of older people there.

In Australia, we seemed to have a wide range of fans from all ages which is rather good. You usually don't have older people knowing anything about you until after about four visits or something like that.

Very flattered

In Britain, parents didn't know what we were until we — for about a year before they clicked, and we're very flattered when we see people of 80 and 90 and 60 — all ages — standing on the roadside waving.

The most exciting thing that's ever happened to us in the way of crowds and appearances was the arrival at Adelaide, because we hadn't expected that. You hear rumors, you know, everywhere you go. When you're on the plane, they radio in and they say, "There's going to be 29,000 at this place!" — and 80,000 nothing, because people can't sort of assess how many people are there at all.

But we've got a better idea, and you get off and there's 5,000 people which is good.

But it's a sort of disappointment after people have said there's going to be this and that.

But in Adelaide it was true, and they kept saying it on the plane — or wherever it was — I think it was the plane — yes, it was — and we said, "Yes, yes, I'm sure there are a lot of people", and "You've never seen anything like it" and "We believe it", you know (because they always say it).

Never forget it

And when we got off, it was true, and then we couldn't believe it — especially the drive down that road Anzac Highway, yes. I'll never forget that, will I? But then I wasn't really bothered about the road itself — the people were the good bit.

I think it was Melbourne and Adelaide were the most English-looking towns. Of course, the buildings are sort of flatter, you know, more sort of built for the sun. I think than us at home, but they did remind us vaguely of some parts of England which is quite pleasant, isn't it? You could almost be home.

"How do you think Australian rock groups would go in England?" Paul McCartney: "By plane or boat, I suppose."

WHO IS ELVIS?

WILL someone please tell me who Elvis Presley is?

I've got an idea that he was hanging around about ten years ago, but I thought he had been pensioned off.

If he hasn't, it's about time he was. I mean like he wasn't a bad guy apparently, but surely he doesn't think he can shape up to our Beatles. They're really fantabulous.

Let that poor old man go, please.

John Stacey, Burwood Road, Sydney.

The REV. GORDON POWELL, minister of St. Stephen's Presbyterian Church, Sydney, and formerly of Melbourne and Adelaide, agrees that Beatlemania is just a mood of the moment, but believes that prosperity has made today's teenagers different from their predecessors.

"Modern teenagers seem to have lost their foundations," he said. "They follow whatever happens to be in vogue. Someone starts something new, it becomes a craze and soon teenagers the world over are full of it.

"I've great faith in Australian children. They are a fine, decent lot. But there is always the extremist, the one who wants to show how big he is, the one who does a strip at a mixed gathering."

YOUNG UPSTARTS

HOW Elvis must be chuckling to himself. Who are these young upstarts?

The King just lets them yodel on their way 'cause he knows and knows that they'll be forgotten in about six months.

P. Hansen, Brisbane.

MELBOURNE'S Southern Cross Hotel, where the Beatles will stay during the Victorian section of their tour, has created special concoctions for the occasion.

Head barman Mr. Bruno Semeia invented the LONG BEETLE FIZZ cocktail. He has given the recipe to TV Times:

1½oz Vodka
½oz Calvados
½oz Blue Curacao
½oz pure lemon juice
½oz sugar syrup
¼ of one egg white.

Shake with ice, and strain into a 14oz glass; add fresh ice cubes and fill with soda water. Decorate with maraschino cherry and two pineapple leaves. Place small marzipan beetle on top, and serve.

TV TIMES: "Any message for Australian viewers?"

PAUL: "Viewers? Oh, yes (cheerfully) this is the TV TIMES. Of course. Hullo. Australian viewers. This is an English viewer speaking. Can't wait to get out to Australia. I love your country from what I read in the brochures. I want to see the Great Barrier Reef. I did that in geography."

JOHN: "And the elephants."

PAUL: "They don't have elephants in Australia. Well, John won't be coming then. And the sun. I want to do all the things people do in the sun — swimming and surfing and smoking. . ."

TV TIMES: "It's winter in June, y'know."

PAUL: "It's never winter in Australia — I've read the brochures."

GEORGE: "Tell 'em to keep the sun out till we get there and we'll see 'em all there."

The boys whipped off to change for the afternoon film—

AUSTRALIAN bossed BEATLES SHOW

Australian director Robert Fleming tells the Beatles exactly what he wants of them as they start filming for Ready, Steady, Go!

ADELAIDE
A Postscript

When *The Beatles Down Under* was published in Australia early in 1982, it marked the conclusion of an exhaustive, year-long search for photographs, artifacts and information. Through television and radio appeals I had managed to persuade a great many Australians to part with their memories and memorabilia concerning the tour.

Of course it was inevitable that some usable material would reach me after the publishing deadline. In most cases there was nothing of real importance but I was greatly excited by a large packet of photographs supplied by the John Martin's department stores in Adelaide.

These shots provided expanded coverage of what history books now acknowledge to be the largest outpouring of Beatle devotion ever witnessed by the group itself. Adelaide was the location of the Beatles' first Australasian concerts and, with Hong Kong, the only city in the Southern Hemisphere where Jimmy Nicol performed in place of Ringo Starr.

This deluxe American edition has given me the opportunity to present 27 of those Adelaide photographs as a special appendix to the original book. I believe they add significantly to the comprehensivity of the work.

Since original publication in Australia, *The Beatles Down Under* has enjoyed considerable international attention. Tour press officer Derek Taylor has conveyed his delight with the documentation, and highlighted a couple of small inaccuracies which have been appropriately altered for this edition. The two Beatles whom I have met over the past two years have offered conflicting reactions. Ringo claimed that a number of the original press reports which I quoted were guilty of undue sensationalism, but indicated that he generally enjoyed the book. George simply didn't like it, claiming that it should have been titled "The Beatles Put-Down Under." But then, as you may glean from the book, George didn't appear to like the Australian tour very much either.

Three years on, *The Beatles Down Under* still stands as the only detailed study of the Beatles on tour and of Beatlemania outside the United States and Britain. Certainly it is controversial but it is also a vital "missing link" of sorts in the unravelling of the most extraordinary social phenomena of this century.

Glenn A. Baker
Sydney, Australia
January, 1985

Say Aaaah

Adelaide police were among the most tolerant and good-humoured in the world.

Awaiting the arrival motorcade on Anzac Highway.

South Australia's Parliament House (at rear) was all but closed for business when Beatle fans found that the steps gave them a vantage point for the Fab Four's hotel.

Although Ringo was never to set foot in Adelaide, his fans chose not to forget him.

Not even the Queen could have brought the city to a complete halt in the manner of the Beatles.

Clear vision was secondary to Beatle worship.

Adelaide stores sold as many plastic Beatle wigs as they could import.

Mothers, grandmothers, grandfathers, teens, toddlers and babes-in-arms, out in force to give the Beatles the most memorable welcome of their entire career.

A politician couldn't have treated his constituency better.

The endless round of identical questions.

Mad magazine was required reading in the Adelaide ticket queues.

Outside the South Australia Hotel.

Madame Tussaud's couldn't have posed them better!

Beatlemania it may have been, but nary a fan left her seat at Centennial Hall.

A post-concert memorabilia display by John Martin's department store was located thoughtfully in Ladies Lingerie.

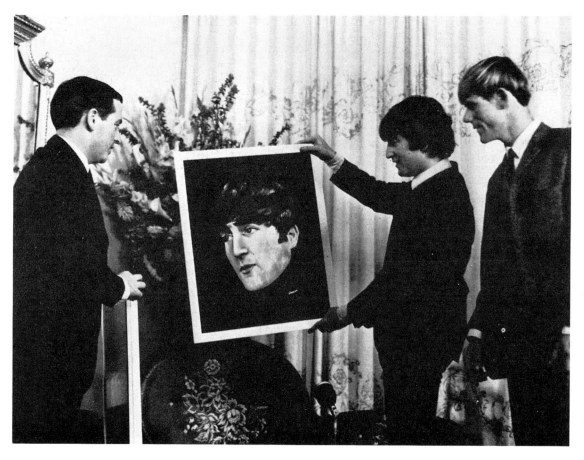

John accepts a portrait from Adelaide artist Peter Findlay.

It seems newspaper editors think the same in every city.

George remembers that he left the gas on in London.

DJ Bob Francis discussing *In His Own Write* with John Lennon.

Who knows what they would have done for a ladder!

George being uncommonly accomodating.

The very first concert on Australian soil.

Born to be great!

Souvenir hunting, like all good tourists.

John sets a journalist straight on Liverpool geography.

Paul was Adelaide's favourite Beatle, in the streets . . . . .

. . . . . and behind closed doors.

With the Adelaide concerts undertaken, Jimmy Nicol was a matter of days away from a reunion with his son Howard in London.

Adelaide's devotion endured until the Fab Four's final moments on South Australian soil.

INDEX

Magnum Music

Available from all good record and video stores or by mail order

Compact Discs

THE BEATLES "Quote/Unquote" CDTB 506
Double compact disc featuring fascinating interviews
from the mid-1960's.
Mail Order Price : £19.99

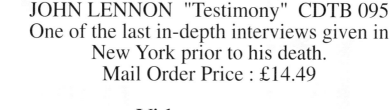

JOHN LENNON "Testimony" CDTB 095
One of the last in-depth interviews given in
New York prior to his death.
Mail Order Price : £14.49

Videocassettes

THE BEATLES "Down Under" MMGVE 008
Previously unseen footage of the 1964 Australian
and New Zealand tour.
Mail Order Price : £9.99

THE BEATLES "On The Road" MMGV 019
Classic archive footage of the band on the road in
the U.K, U.S and Japan plus press conferences
and interviews.
Mail Order Price : £14.49

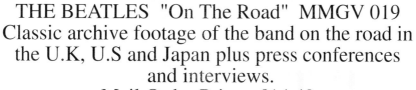

MIKE McCARTNEY "Alternative Liverpool" MMGV 033
Featuring all the well known people and places in the city.
Mail Order Price : £14.49

Poster

THE BEATLES "Stroud, 1962" P003
Re-print of the original poster for this 1962 appearance.
(Size: 625mm x 450mm; Colours: Red, Black, Beige.)
Mail order price : £9.99

MAGNUM direct
MAGNUM MUSIC GROUP

Magnum Direct,
Magnum House,
High Street, Lane End,
Buckinghamshire,
HP14 3JG.
United Kingdom

Prices include postage and packaging.
Overseas customers add £3.00 per order.